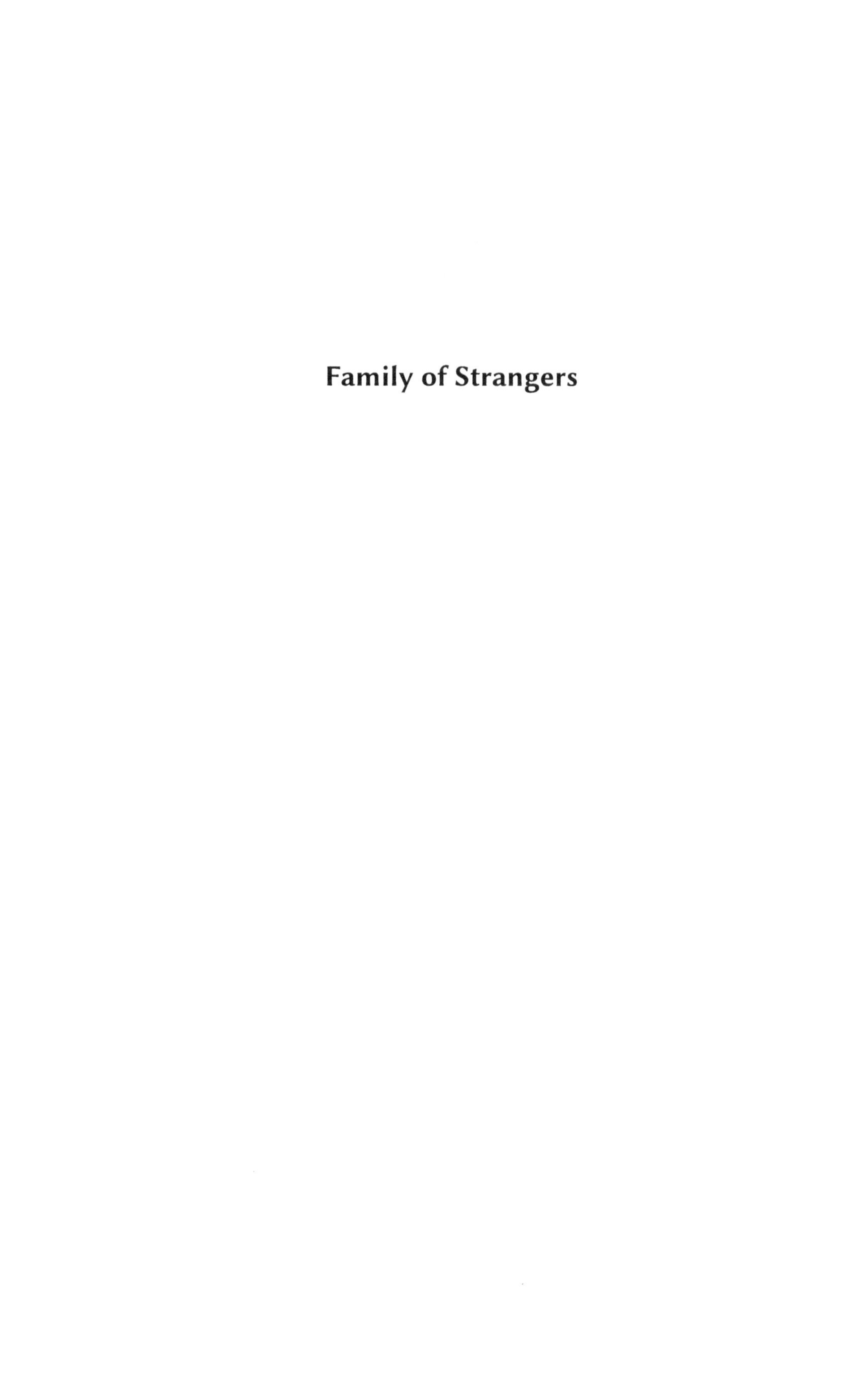

Family of Strangers

Family of Strangers

Barbara Willis

Published 2021 by Next Chapter
Cover art by http://www.thecovercollection.com/
Back cover texture by David M. Schrader, used under license from Shutterstock.com
Edited by D.S. Williams
Large Print Edition

For Elisabeth, Meredith and Adam who delight and inspire me.

For Steve, who gave me the time to fulfil a dream.

Contents

Prologue

Remember by Christina Rossetti (1830 - 1894)

Remember me when I am gone away,
Gone far away into the silent land,
When you can no more hold me by the hand,
Nor I half turn to go yet turning stay.
Remember me when no more day by day
You tell me of our future that you'd planned:
Only remember me; you understand
It will be late to counsel then or pray.
Yet if you should forget me for a while
And afterwards remember, do not grieve:
For if the darkness and corruption leave
A vestige of the thoughts that I once had,
Better by far you should forget and smile
Than that you should remember and be sad.

Found and Lost

She found me a short while later, sitting on a bench as far from the gate as I could get. Hands folded in my lap and my mind far away, the first I knew of her presence was when her hand gently covered mine. Although it was an unexpected touch from a stranger, my instincts didn't cause me to jump or recoil and I looked up into her face. 'May I join you?' she enquired gently, although she didn't wait for me to answer.

Looking back now, I realise that I'd felt safety in the way she held my hand beneath hers.

Up until that act of warm companionship, I'd felt more frightened than I had ever imagined possible. My hand had relaxed beneath hers; just one part of me that felt some release from fear.

This diminutive lady holding my hand made me think of a child holding the string of a balloon, feeling it bouncing and bobbing in the wind, where release would see it escape high into the endless sky. Then it would drift and bob through clouds and breeze, until it grew too small for the limits of the eye and would never be seen again. I thought I could be the balloon and reality was this old lady's grip, from which I could easily slip away. I didn't want her to let go.

My day already felt so unreal that a tea invite from a little old lady I'd only just met seemed almost normal in comparison. It had started off just like any of a hundred other days before, with not a hint of what would soon be revealed.

I used to work in a shop, a small and friendly place. In the twenty-four months I worked there I'd grown fond of all Mr Grayson's regular customers knowing their likes and dislikes and, for a few, their peculiarities. Mr Grayson and his wife are very kind and I've always been happy in their company. My job was like a comfortable pair of slippers or an old jumper; it was reassuring and familiar. Over time it moulded to fit me, and me to it I suppose, the same way that the town I live in seems to have done.

Fielding is a small, uncomplicated place; the main street runs straight through the centre like the unyielding trunk of a tall tree – there are the usual parks, houses, schools and shops which run through the centre, providing its core and centre of activity. A church stands at the very edge of the town with a farm to its left. There are fields curling around to the right and the church's face is turned to the town it serves. It sits slightly raised on a natural incline befitting its status, its foundations laid two hundred years ago and its doors perpetually open.

I wasn't raised in Fielding but spent my childhood in the arms of its close and smaller neighbour, Rushton. Rather than following the widespread tradition of leaving home only when marriage enveloped me, I moved to Fielding on my own in May 1937 having found my job and a lovely couple to lodge with. My new independence fitted, as they say, like a glove.

I know I took my straightforward and happy life for granted, rather than realising how fortunate I'd always been to live in security and contentment.

The day I found myself sitting in the park was during a strange time of nationwide doubt and insecurity. So many people were voicing their opinions about if and when our country and its men might once again have to step forward and face the horrors of war. Although too young to have experienced the Great War – I was born in the year it ended – the ripples and repercussions are still felt often and stories, anger and sadness are effortlessly stirred. It's an old wound and although from outward signs it appears largely healed, it remains so fragile that even the slightest trauma can cause the sticky blood of recollection to flow freely once again.

I prayed many times that we wouldn't be thrown into such terror once more. The most common opinion at the time was that conflict was certain, but we could find reassurance in the fact that all would be over by Christmas. I certainly hoped the forecast would prove true, although some voices were heard muttering that we'd all said that before. I'd not known the paralysing fear of waving goodbye to a loved one until, uniform clad, they disappeared from sight for months or forever. In my innocence, despite the rumbling throb of unease always just audible throughout our daily lives, I had been free of care or worry. Such fear was, for the moment, unknown to me.

Saturdays were, and still are, my favourite day of the week although my habits have changed a little now. My old routine was to hop on the bus, as soon as work finished at one, and travel the eight miles to Rushton to spend the afternoon with my closest friend, Annie. This often included a trip to the library to restock, with us comparing notes and recommending new reading matter to each other. I don't have so much time for reading now and the library only welcomes me now and then, as you would a distant but much loved friend.

Many of my old Saturdays were completed by sharing one of Aunt Kathleen's lovely family meals. I'm smiling now as Aunt Kathleen and Uncle Bob are always telling me I must visit more often, even though I never fail to pop in whenever I'm back in Rushton. As is a customary sign of respect, I grew up calling Annie's parents Aunt and Uncle; I still do, even now.

Despite all the changes that the world absorbs, we always seemed cocooned in our two friendly towns. As my own little world felt warm and safe the occasional signs of bigger worldly changes – such as the lack of availability of certain things in the shops, or rumours of evacuations, or the drafting of young men – almost didn't feel real. Back then I carried on with life mostly unchanged. There was, of course, the occasional conversation with people visiting the shop about what may or may not happen in the months to come; sometimes I heard similar talk among those passing their time in the street. But things happened to other people, not me, and life in our closely linked towns carried on undisturbed and unchanged.

Beginning and End

On the Saturday in April when I thought life ended, I stepped onto the bus bound for Rushton and sat in my usual seat two rows behind the regular driver of the route. Eight miles later, I let a quick goodbye float over my shoulder as I hopped down the bus steps and headed for the library. Annie wasn't outside, so I ventured in to look for her. We never had a set plan of where to meet; sometimes it was outside, at other times we found each other inside among the deliciously long corridors of books which waited to reveal their stories to us.

As Annie wasn't yet there I wandered up and down, occasionally taking a book down from a shelf to decide if it would be going home with me. If books were living things, I wondered if they would hold their breath with anticipation when lifted from the shelf to be considered.

Maybe they would then sigh dejectedly through their silent pages if replaced. I whispered 'sorry' as I replaced a book and smiled to myself as I walked along the aisle. I'd have to tell Annie; it would make her laugh.

The minutes passed. Annie wasn't there. An hour passed. Annie wasn't there.

I'd collected a few books as I strolled between the shelves, two for me and one that I thought Annie might enjoy, but I couldn't wait in line to sign them out. I left them on a lone chair at the end of one of the literary rows, something I would normally frown upon if I saw another patron do the same, and hurriedly left. Something inside me was disturbed, unsettled, but I couldn't find the source of it, the reason remained just out of reach. Annie was *never* late; maybe my disquiet came from a concern that she was unwell.

I was at her house in ten minutes, when it would usually have taken twenty.

'Hi!' I called breathlessly, pushing open the back door. 'Aunt Kathleen, Uncle Bob! Annie, are you home?' The sing-song tone of my casual greeting was ringing in my ears, a smooth veneer covering rough edges of unease which grew sharper as worry chipped away at them.

'Hello lovely,' smiled Uncle Bob, coming in after me from the garden. 'I didn't expect to see you today.' He kissed me on the cheek and went to the sink to wash the earth from his hardworking hands. I looked at the back of his dear, balding head as he stood at the deep white stone sink. Turning to face me, he picked up the towel to dry his rough hands.

'I confess that I wasn't actually planning to come by today, Uncle Bob, but I'm looking for Annie.' No time for happy and pointless small talk.

Then it came.

The moment my life changed.

'Sorry love, I don't know her. Does your Auntie Kath?' Uncle Bob was now rummaging and rattling about in a drawer. 'Ah, there you are.' He held up a ball of twine, proudly showing me what he'd discovered in the drawer's chaotic depths. 'Got a few jobs to do down at the veg plot today, so I won't stop. Tell Aunt Kath to put the kettle on in a bit, will you love? Come for dinner soon, won't you?'

Then he kissed me again and was gone.

I stood there, completely immobile, staring after Uncle Bob through the kitchen window as he disappeared down the path and out of view, waving a hand up to me without turning around. *He can't have heard me properly*, I reasoned, as I repeated his words in my head. As there was no sign of my aunt, I headed through the hall towards the front of the house then turned and jogged up the narrow stairs. I turned right at the top, towards Annie's room.

'Annie? Are you there?' Annie's bedroom door opened slowly with my tentative nudge. I stood in the doorway staring, realising a second later that my mouth had dropped open. There was no Annie, but there was also no Annie's room. The space that had been Annie's – where we'd spent many hours as we grew up, giggling and imagining, playing make believe – was gone.

The walls were bereft of Annie's few pictures. None of her personal things seemed to be there. No dressing gown thrown across the bed, nor books on the nightstand. No hairbrush on the dressing table or tatty childhood teddy bear on the chair. No notebooks with oddments of paper sticking out, or a mound of pencils and pens. The furniture remained, but nothing more. I crossed the room to the chest of drawers to find them now containing pillowcases and sheets. The wardrobe then; an old winter coat of my Aunt's, Uncle Bob's dual-use wedding and funeral suit. I felt sick and covered my mouth with my hand.

Footsteps climbed the stairs behind me. A voice.

'Hello Eva. Were you looking for me?'

I spun around when I felt my aunt's hand on my arm.

'Um, no, I was actually looking for Annie. We were supposed to be meeting at the library.' My aunt's face confirmed that Uncle Bob had heard me correctly, and he wasn't the only one having some sort of breakdown – she looked concerned for me, as though *I* was the one who was confused.

Then her words confirmed it.

'Are you alright? Come and sit down, love.' She looked so worried, but I felt no warm flood of affection or reassuring comfort at her concern. All I felt was anger. It was an emotion that I now knew

I'd never experienced the full force of before. Until this moment, I'd pinned the word anger to feelings which could be better labelled as irritation, frustration or annoyance. This was the first time I'd ever had *true* cause to be angry and the sensation was hard and unpleasant, sitting like a cold jagged rock in the depths of my stomach after scratching the back of my throat on the way down. This new emotion, until then a stranger, made my head heavy and every muscle tense. I struggled to talk through this intense new feeling and the dry abrasiveness in my throat.

'The last thing I want to do is sit down Aunt Kathleen.'The sharp tone to my voice surprised me as it left my lips because I'd never raised my voice to her in my life. 'Where's Annie? Where are all her things? What's going on?' The questions tumbled out, falling over each other and giving her no time to respond in between. I stopped to watch her. And waited. Her puzzled eyes gazed at me for a moment, as if she was working out what to say or do next.

'Darling, please sit down. Are you poorly?' She put her hand up to feel my forehead but I pulled away. There was a noise downstairs. My aunt half turned her head as if to direct her voice over her shoulder and down the stairs, still watching me all the while. 'Bob? Is that you? Eva's not well. Can you come up?' Her expression, and the way her voice was projected down the stairs while she blocked my path, reminded me of the day she'd found a little bird who'd managed to get lost and make its way down the chimney into the living room. She'd cornered it, blocking its escape to freedom, while calling over her shoulder for my Uncle Bob to come and help. Maybe he'd catch me in a pillowcase too, and set me free outside.

She turned back to me 'Come on love – stay with us for a few days so we can look after you. Are you feverish? You must have a temperature, you're delirious.' One hand rose again to cup my forehead, the other firmly held my elbow as if she expected me to collapse. I yanked my arm away.

'Really, I'm fine. It's you two who are sick, not me. Where's your daughter?' The words were spat rather than spoken.

'Eva, you're not making any sense love.'Her voice was slow and soft. 'We live on our own. Since you moved to Fielding it's just the two of us. There are no children, sweetheart, you know that.' She sighed and sank into the old wicker chair which waited faithfully on the landing to be called into service, always there but rarely used.

Uncle Bob had reached the stairs and was standing still, as if frozen in motion, halfway up. Pictures flashed through my mind from a book of Sleeping Beauty that I'd had when I was small. All the castle residents had been frozen, at the very moment the princess pricked her finger, part way through whatever task they'd been undertaking at the time; a maid cleaning, a cook stirring something on the range, a guard outside the palace gates, a little boy chasing a dog in the courtyard. Uncle Bob had joined them, immobile as a statue. He still had the ball of twine in his hand, which if not for the awful scene that was being played out, might have seemed amusing. Now, however, it seemed as if he'd just been waiting, string in hand, to climb the stairs. Now the string seemed almost threatening, as if he was approaching to truss up the madwoman standing at the top of his stairs.

Watching me, Aunt Kath called, 'Get the doctor, Bob'. She spoke the words too loudly, as if she thought Uncle Bob was further away than he was.

'I... don't... need... a... doctor,'I enunciated slowly, offering them one syllable at a time. Recovering, my aunt stood, putting her arm around my shoulder. I shrugged her away for a third time, pushing past her and knocking into Uncle Bob's arm as I hurried down the stairs. 'This is ridiculous!' I threw the words out behind me with venom. 'I'm going back to the library. She's bound to be there by now. Then Annie can tell me what this ridiculous charade is all about.'

I stopped and turned at the bottom of the stairs and was met by the twine that I'd dislodged from Uncle Bob's hand. It had bounced down the stairs after me, as if also trying to escape. It now lay unravelled and tangled at my feet. I looked back as my aunt who had joined my uncle at his halfway point, his arm winding protectively around her slumped frame. My anger was fading and morphing from rock hard rage into delicate, fragile and trembling fear.

'I don't know what on earth you're doing, but this has to stop right now.'I paused, hoping for explanation. 'Have you had a row with Annie?' Then I asked a little more softly, 'What can be so bad that you'd disown her?' I sighed and shook my head, a touch of exasperation joining the fear and confusion and mixing into a strange cocktail I didn't like the taste of.

It was so unlike my aunt and uncle to have a cross word or show anything but compassion for anyone, so I couldn't imagine what would have brought about this terrible fracture in their family. Theirs was a family unit so complete and solid that nothing had ever made it sway, let alone fall completely and brutally to pieces. Now they looked at me as though I'd gone mad and imagined the existence of my dearest friend – their only child.

My aunt's head was bowed and I couldn't see her face; my uncle, however, was watching me intently and when he spoke his words were slow and considered, as if he was writing it down and reading the words back to himself first. I could hear true sadness in his voice and I wanted to force myself back to consciousness, escape this horrible dream, and blink my disbelieving eyes open to daylight and safety.

'And *I* don't know what's got into *you*, pet, but whatever it is, you clearly don't want our help. You can see you're upsetting your Aunt, so I think you should leave. It pains me to say it, love, but until you can explain yourself…or accept some help with this—'My aunt looked up at him and put her hand on his arm as if to stop him, but he patted her fingers gently without looking at her and continued '…you should stay away.' We stared at each other for several seconds, an eternity of waiting, before I turned and left.

As I stormed down the garden path, my face flushed and hot with anger, I had faith that Annie would explain everything and then we could begin mending whatever it was that had been broken. So many thoughts tumbled through my head, but none of them were so bad that I could imagine this sort of reaction from Annie's mum and dad. They were caring and supportive, unflustered and practical. Any hill they met, no matter the size, was always climbed with optimism, faith and togetherness.

Gradually my angered footsteps slowed and I walked at a more normal pace towards the library. The cold breeze slapped the dampness onto my face. I understood the phrase 'cold sweat' now, as my face was cool and damp and I shivered as though icy fingers stretched down my back. I was thinking, or at least trying to think. But no matter how hard I tried, it was impossible to make sense of something which could make no sense.

I kept scanning the people around me, sure that Annie would bound up behind me at any second, making me jump and then laughing at my expense. I hadn't seen her on my walk back to the library and assumed she must be inside wondering where *I* was. I stepped into the cool of the familiar and safe old building, the reassuring smell of paper and books welcoming my return. Among the shelves I found my deserted pile of books still sitting forlornly on the chair waiting to be reclaimed or for each to be returned, disappointed, to its shelf-bound life by the librarian. I picked them up and sat on the chair, placing them in my lap.

I sat unmoving for so long that my back began to ache. Eventually I stretched and looked at my watch – it was three hours since the time that Annie and I had agreed to meet.

Reflection

I left the books for a second time that day and blinked as I stepped out into the late afternoon sunshine from the subdued and almost reverent atmosphere inside the library. Not knowing what to do next I stood still, looking up and down the street as people carried their lives forward; visiting shops, going to the post office, or heading home maybe, and stopping to chat to their friends on the way. My life, in cruel contrast, had been halted.

My feet began to take me without purpose or knowledge along the street; not heading anywhere in particular, but carrying on anyway. The tears left my eyes without warning, my footsteps sped up in reaction and I turned my face away from anyone I passed. I bowed my head, my aim to become invisible hurrying me along and turning me towards the little park that was hidden away behind the main shopping street.

There are two parks in the town and most people frequent the larger one which has a small boating pond and swings. This park, however, is smaller and prettier, with well-tended flower beds and green painted benches. There's a small central green with a path around the perimeter, nestling between the flower borders and meandering around the edges of the park like a stream following a time worn path through the woods.

Hurrying through the big iron gates at the park's entrance, too flamboyant really for the size of what lies within, I bumped straight into a little old lady as she was stooping to pick something up. I mumbled a rushed apology as I continued past with my head still lowered and my eyes purposely avoiding contact with hers.

I found a secluded bench at the far end of the park and there withdrew further into my thoughts, so much that I was unaware of my surroundings until a hand gently sheltered mine. She'd asked if she could join me, but as she was already sitting herself down I didn't answer.

And I suppose this might really have been where it began. Looking back, we must have remained like that for some time; my head bowed in confused reflection and this little elderly lady silently holding my hand. Although I didn't know her, strangely, I didn't mind the contact. She'd come at just the moment when I'd needed comfort. She had warm dry skin and didn't say another word for quite some time. I took in, subconsciously at first, neatly trimmed nails and small old hands carrying no adornments of any kind – no wedding ring or watch. Although I kept my gaze lowered, my peripheral vision told me this lady didn't look at me either; she just sat very still looking at the view fanning out before her, watching the few visitors to the park as they came and went.

Finally, she turned and smiled. 'It's getting chilly dear; shall we go now? I don't know about you, but I could do with a nice hot cup of tea.' She stood up slowly, collecting the old shopping basket which had been sitting at her feet like a faithful hound. It seemed laden with purchases, all neatly tucked beneath a coloured scarf so I could only guess at what she might have bought in the town.

My mind snapped back to her question, still unanswered.

'Yes, why not.' My response surprised me. I wasn't sure what I was going to do next about Annie, so a pause while I decided wouldn't do any harm. After all the day couldn't get any stranger, could it? Betty's, my favourite little tea shop, was only a few steps away so I assumed we might head there for our refreshment.

'We live in the cottage on the end of Mill Street.'

'Oh. I was thinking...' Then it dawned on me that Betty's would be closed or closing by now; time had seeped away quickly through the cracks which had zigzagged like a wicked earthquake into my day. I glanced at my watch and realised it was after five o'clock. The normal routine of this morning seemed a lifetime ago.

The lady smiled. 'It's so much nicer to sit down at home, don't you think? Besides, the park's getting a little chilly now isn't it?' She offered her hand to me, wiping away my unshared doubts with another smile. 'My name is Lola.'

I was taken aback by this strange little old lady, in the park with a basket full of shopping, asking a sad young woman to join her at her house for a cup of tea. 'Oh, sorry – Eva Thorne.' I held out my hand in response and smiled back.

Lola's House

Lola had replied with a 'Pleased to meet you, Eva.' She then explained that she had 'a couple of places to dash' but would be home in about half an hour. I couldn't imagine her *dashing* anywhere as, not only was she clearly quite elderly, but she seemed relaxed and unhurried, a state of mind that I suspect often comes with age rather than a physical need. Although my body was tired and heavy with worry, I didn't want to go home yet as that felt like submission – I hadn't lost Annie at home, I'd lost her here somewhere or somehow. And I'd already decided that I was going to join Lola for a cup of tea at her cottage at the end of Mill Street.

Lola smiled and walked away and I was alone again with my thoughts. I stayed in the park for a few more minutes before I slowly stood and strolled back through the gates and into the centre of the town. Seeing people but not seeing them, I wandered slowly past the emptying shops and retreating shoppers towards Mill Street. I checked my watch and slowed my steps even more, trying to exhaust time and not arrive at my destination before my host. With each step I searched faces and glanced down side streets, peered in to closing shops and raked through groups of people. My friend, my quarry, was lost.

When I finally saw Lola's cottage, to discover it was a red brick house seemed wrong. After bowing and bending through the overgrown trees and shrubs which embraced the little path and obscured all sight of the house, I was surprised. Although the garden gave the impression that the house it surrounded would have been deserted long ago, I still had the sensation of walking through a garden that had once been loved and tended – or maybe it was just the dense and free spirited greenery which made it seem romantic. I was somehow reassured that, despite my state of fear and desperation, my sense of the romantic seemed unharmed. The fact that I was musing on such irrelevant things gave me hope that the sick and almost immobilising fear bubbling inside me might not be permanent.

My subconscious had told me to expect a thatched cottage, with stone mullion windows and the traditional roses arching delicately around a sheltered little wooden door. Instead I saw a rather ordinary red brick house. It had a pale blue door at its centre with paint that was peeling a little, leaving dry, curled up shards which revealed the previous colour choice of primrose yellow. There were windows each side of the door and two more above those. I think I drew many pictures of such a home when I was growing up; the traditional dolls' house design with a door and four windows, all symmetrically placed.

The garden was so overgrown and untended that I started to doubt this was the right place. If Lola lived here she certainly wasn't a gardener; I wondered if the interior of the house would be the same as the garden – unloved and neglected. I looked back up the path I'd trod, hesitating.

My doubts returned. What on earth was I doing here? Maybe Annie's apparent disappearance had unsteadied *my* mind too, and not just my aunt and uncle's. Why on earth was I visiting a strange little old lady rather than sorting out the family mess I'd discovered only this afternoon?

Despite my misgivings, something made me turn back towards the house and carry on towards the door.

As I approached I thought I heard music playing –just a piano. I pushed the half-thought from my mind as I knocked on the door.

'Hello. Come in, come in,' Lola smiled as the door opened wide and she stood aside, motioning to the hallway with a sweep of her arm.

Lola was several inches shorter than me and her whole body softly rounded, from her cheeks to her fingers to her legs. Her hair, a silver grey, was loosely pulled back from her face, held in place just above her neck with a complex, or maybe just completely random, hairpin arrangement. I suspected it would be quite long if left to fall untethered. Now free of the large raincoat, she wore a navy dress dotted with tiny pink flowers. Over this was a navy cardigan, all the buttons done up but straining a little, and a well-worn pair of slippers. And was it my imagination, or were the two slippers of slightly different colour and design?

'Let me get you a cup of tea, can I? Come on through to the kitchen. It's so nice to have a visitor – we don't have very many'. I noted the word *we* and imagined a host of cats mewing and curling around our ankles, fitting housemates for an eccentric old lady.

The piano music began again and I turned away from my host, distracted by the sound. Someone close by must be listening to the wireless. The music whispering its melody into my ears was haunting, beautiful. I jumped when Lola's fingers gently touched my arm.

'That's Gabe.' She turned away, her hand moving to my shoulder and willing me forward. 'Come on; let's sit down in the kitchen.' With that she drew me further into the house with her gentle touch. I wasn't sure who she was talking about but I didn't ask and the moment was gone.

As we left the hall and walked through the sitting room (though where you would sit I wasn't quite sure) to the back of the house, I scanned the area in astonishment. There was barely an inch of space anywhere which wasn't covered in household items. I'd never seen anything like it. On every surface, each piece of furniture and each shelf, there were pots, papers, shoes, ornaments, vases, books and goodness knows what else. There were pieces of fabric, stationery, bags, cushions and picture frames (all of which were devoid of photographs or pictures). I saw jars, pens, boxes, baskets...the list was never-ending.

I felt like I'd stepped inside an overstocked rag and bone yard. Nothing was ordered. Nothing seemed to have found just a *temporary* roost in these places; it all looked chaotically permanent. If Lola noted my surprise she didn't show it and continued leading me into the kitchen. Maybe she would have needed to be aware of the strangeness of the surroundings to pick up on my surprise at them. She casually hoisted up a folded heap of clothes from a kitchen chair and added it to its neighbour's pile. 'Sit down, sit down' she beckoned, gently pushing me into the allotted seat.

Lola busied herself filling the kettle and lighting the stove. While the water was heating she collected cups and saucers – all odd, not a set. Before long, we were leaning over our mismatched cups of tea and might even have looked a little like old friends just catching up with friendly gossip.

'Now then.' Lola smiled, but said no more than that. She merely watched me as I stirred my tea distractedly (and pointlessly, as I don't take sugar). I sighed and stared into my cup, watching the swirling liquid gradually lose its momentum, replaying events in my mind before I replayed the events for Lola. I didn't even realise how easy it was to tell her about my day, and all that had happened before meeting her in the park, until I'd already confided all. I didn't hesitate to relay every piece to her, including not only the facts as I interpreted them, but my feelings too. She didn't say a word, just listened and nodded once or twice, smiling encouragingly at each pause.

When I finished recounting the day's events she put her hands flat on the table and pushed herself up to stand. She moved towards a chair by the sitting room door and I watched as she picked out a neatly folded handkerchief from a pile of similar items teetering on its seat. I hadn't realised until then that there were tears on my face. She was soon back at the table, handing me the small square. Smiling weakly I opened the folded piece of soft white cotton and wiped my eyes, breathing in the freshly-laundered scent which, strangely, made my emotions even stronger and my eyes more tearful. There's nothing quite like kindness to perforate your brave resolve when emotions are already delicate.

Lola returned to her seat. Looking down to straighten an ornate milky blue stone brooch on her cardigan, she exhaled quietly and slowly.

'I think... 'She looked up at me then shook her head as if to correct herself. 'No, I don't think – I know.' Taking a deep breath, she continued. 'Eva dear, there are some things you need to know.'She laced her fingers together on top of the table. 'I didn't realise it earlier when we met, I just thought you needed a friend.' She frowned momentarily and then smiled again. 'But I must have been drawn to you. I do believe that some things happen for a reason and this is one of those times. We were meant to meet, Eva.'

She wasn't making any sense and the thought crossed my mind again that she may indeed be quite dotty; just a dear little old lady, eccentric and harmless.

Lola continued. 'You're confused, upset and frightened; if you need to cry, you should cry of course, but you mustn't do it for long. You need to find Annie. Your tears can't resolve anything.' Then she added wistfully, 'If only they did.'

It was me who frowned now as I tried to decipher the meaning or message behind her words. She was very kindly and tactfully telling me I couldn't remain in this distressed state, but I had absolutely no idea what to do once I did eventually pull myself together. Lola clearly didn't fully understand the nature of what had happened – or appeared to have happened. I certainly couldn't explain it to her with any more clarity, as I didn't understand it myself. 'I'm sorry Lola, but I don't know where to start. You've been very kind, but I'm at a loss. I haven't a clue what's going on with my aunt and uncle. I don't know why Annie's gone, or where. I don't know who to ask or where to look.'

I shook my head and blinked a few times, wondering if this action might wake me from this terrible dream. However, my state of consciousness didn't change, so instead, I watched Lola's eyes for a clue. They were a watery blue-green and, although aged, I'd noticed earlier that there was a sparkle somewhere deep inside them. It was a shiny penny at the bottom of a pond. I imagined that the sparkle I saw there was akin to a door slightly ajar, leading from a room of muted tones and colours and just providing the tiniest tantalising glimpse of the room beyond; a room with glistening rainbow colours and flashes of light, promises of excitement and joy and maybe even mischief.

However, her eyes now seemed distant and had dulled a little, and I couldn't see the sparkling penny anymore. 'Lola. What do you mean we were meant to meet?' I prompted ever so gently, almost afraid to disturb her. She could have just meant that we were meant to be friends, as simple as that. Something was niggling at me, however, whispering that it wasn't that simple; that maybe Lola knew more and that she could somehow help.

'I'm sorry dear.'She seemed to shake herself slightly, almost as though she'd stopped breathing and suddenly started again. 'Fate. I mean fate, if there is such a thing. You needed someone – you were there and I was there. If fate threw us in each other's paths, then fate has done its bit and the rest is up to us. There's a lot you need to know, but it makes for a long, long story.' She smiled kindly and sighed. 'I'm rather tired, Eva. I wonder if we might talk more tomorrow?' She reached across and took my hand. 'I'm certain Annie's alright. She'll be confused like you, but I'm quite sure she'll be fine. With a good friend like you searching for her, she has nothing to worry about.'

Her reassuring words didn't reorder my confusion into something I understood, but they did confirm that my suspicions were justified. If this little old lady thought she might have some answers to my questions, then it was worth hearing them. After all, I had no other ideas of where to start so, at the moment, Lola was all the help I had. She hadn't passed judgement or said I was mistaken or going mad – she'd listened and amazingly, even shockingly, hadn't been surprised by a single word I'd said, which in turn had surprised *me*. At that point, however wrong, I didn't think things could get any more peculiar no matter how eccentric she was. She seemed certain of her words and, strangely, I was comforted.

I had to take an inventory of what I knew, hoping this might highlight some choices. What other options did I have here? My mind wandered back to the thoughts I'd run through in the park before Lola found me - a doctor to see Kathleen and Bob? No, clearly a family falling out, nothing medical. Family friends then, people who knew Kathleen, Bob and Annie? No, this was personal to them, not to be discussed publicly with friends or acquaintances. Annie was the one who could tell me everything, then we'd put it right together, just as we'd faced the music together all our lives; the broken teapot of Aunt Kathleen's, the secret kitten we'd hidden in the bedroom for three whole weeks, the ruination of Aunt Kathleen's best tablecloth which had served as a tent in the garden, the covert trip to the pictures when we were supposed to be fruit picking...

All the options for help that I'd come up with, I had to dismiss. The only path I could follow was to find Annie and seek the answers directly from her. Then we'd sit down with Kathleen and Bob and sort everything out. I had an inkling that the mysterious but motherly Lola might know where to start looking.

'I'm sorry Lola, I can see you're tired.' I was frustrated that this incredible mess wasn't going to be sorted out straight away, but I didn't like to press her as she suddenly looked very small and frail. As much as I wanted her to talk to me, I wouldn't be responsible for distressing her. What if I upset her by pressing my questions on her? I didn't know her age or circumstances but I was drawn to her, as she said she'd been to me, and I could not force my situation upon her no matter how desperate I felt.

'Yes, dear, I am rather. I usually have a little nap about now, before dinner. Do you mind if we speak again tomorrow? I can introduce you to Gabe, I'm sure he'd like to meet you. Maybe you could come to afternoon tea?'

'Tea would be lovely, thank you.' I didn't much care to meet this Gabe, but if it smoothed the way to seeing Lola again and draw out some answers, that was fine.

'Well then, that's settled. Here at four o'clock. And try not to worry dear, Annie will wait for you for another day.'

And Annie was waiting. She'd waited for her parents, she'd waited for recognition in the town and she'd waited for someone to come looking for her; to find her curled up like a baby in the shed on the unused allotment plot. But no-one came. She waited in the shadows outside the library. Then the doctor who'd known her all her life bumped into her. When he apologised without recognition and tipped his hat as he passed, Annie ran. She didn't know where she was going, but she ran. She ran away from the doctor, her parents and all the strangers in the town. She tried to run from her anonymity, but it clung to her every step like a shadow. Her story blurred and she knew nothing of the town she ran in or the places she passed.

'Thank you, I'll see you tomorrow.' I stood up and Lola started to do the same. 'No, don't get up. I'll see myself out.' And it was my turn to cover *her* hand as it lay on the table. Smiling, she sat back down and the age which was suddenly evident in her eyes was now visible in her features and body too, although I briefly caught a little glimpse again of a distant rainbow sparkle.

Despite my resolve not to press anything upon her, the words left my lips quietly and meekly before I could stop them. 'Will you help me?' I don't know why they escaped, or what I was really asking for, but a gentle yes came in reply.

As I moved away, I thought I heard a quietly mumbled 'Oh dear,' but I couldn't be sure.

I glanced at my watch, a twenty first birthday gift last year from Annie and her parents, and it was almost seven.

As I walked from the kitchen through the sitting room and into the hall, I realised the music had been playing every minute I was there. It had been gently floating through the hall and sitting room, past the peculiar stacks and bundles, heaps and hoards, and into the kitchen the whole time. I'd heard it but I hadn't been listening. Pausing in the hall before I opened the door to leave, I *did* listen. And I wondered who Gabe was.

Waiting

I strolled slowly towards the bus stop and home, repeating all the day's events over and over and over in my head. I turned them from one side to the other, rolling them around, twisting them to and fro, and examining them carefully.

I didn't bump into anyone I knew as I walked through the town and was grateful for the solitude. As my thoughts fell over each other and bumped their unsteady way through my mind, one of them suddenly shone like a beacon. Annie would come to me! She'd be at Mrs Burgess's waiting for me. Idiot! Why hadn't I gone straight home?

I caught the last bus, thank goodness, and despite willing the driver to go faster with every ounce of telepathy I could muster it was after half past seven when I opened home's welcoming door. Mrs Burgess popped her head around the kitchen door and asked if I was hungry – she was more like a friendly aunt than a landlady. She didn't like being labelled 'landlady', telling me that this was a home and I was a house guest who helped out with the bills. My bright anticipation and burgeoning relief turned to dark desolation when there was no mention of anyone waiting for me or having dropped by. I responded to Mrs Burgess's enquiry by saying I might get myself something to eat a little later on, but I knew that I wouldn't as hunger wasn't something I could imagine feeling for some time, my appetite seemingly lost along with Annie.

Before I left the room, I asked, 'Mrs Burgess, did Annie drop by or maybe telephone?'

'No dear, not today,' was the casual response, my landlady not knowing the force with which her innocuous words hit me even though I'd known what they would be.

As I wearily climbed the stairs, I wondered how I would get to sleep or pass the time tomorrow until I saw Lola again. It seemed wrong not to be doing something for Annie in the hours which would pass until then, but I surrendered to the realisation that there was nothing to be done until afternoon tea at four.

I crossed the landing, glad to be home. Then I cracked my elbow really hard on the door-frame to my room, my concentration anywhere but where I was walking, and the pain shot up my arm cruelly. Instead of rubbing it better and silently reprimanding myself for not watching where I was going, the unexpected jolt gave me permission to cry in the form of physical pain and I did as it offered. I closed my bedroom door, sat down on the floor just inside and cried my confusion out.

When I couldn't cry anymore and my eyes were stinging, my sadness waned for a few moments and I felt stupid instead. I stood up and was embarrassed even though there was no one there to see me. Maybe a bath would help. Many swear by a 'nice restoring cup of tea' as a cure-all – I've always preferred a bath. I knew I was spoiled at the Burgess's; we had a nice bathroom. The old outdoor 'facility' stood unused and solitary in the back yard, the door long since closed and forgotten. I dreaded to think of what spiders and other multi-legged creatures might be resident out there and was so glad we had the comparative luxury of the bathroom on offer, and the chance to close the door on the world.

After checking with Mrs Burgess that it was okay to have a bath (she always said yes, but it was correct procedure to check first), I walked across the landing with towel in hand and stepped down the two steps into the bathroom. This room had been a later addition to the property, built on top of the kitchen which previously had protruded in a lonesome fashion from the 'back room' – the front (and best) room was seldom used and the back room served for eating and living and was warm and inviting, with the fire always either roaring or just 'ticking over', waiting to be stoked back into life by returning residents.

I often wondered, as I stepped down into the bathroom, whether the fact that it was slightly lower down was planned or whether this was a miscalculation on the part of the builder. The room was usually cold, only warming a few degrees with the steam, so there was no time to dawdle. Despite the temperature, the bathroom never failed to invite me; always well stocked with clean towels, it boasted the palest pink walls, black and white chequerboard lino and a tiny pot of old silk flowers on the windowsill.

I ran the bath, allowing myself a more luxurious depth of water than I ever did on a normal day – this wasn't a normal day. I wanted to wallow and that would only be achieved if I could immerse myself indulgently up to my chin. Once the bath was filled I undressed and stepped in to the decadently deep water. Sinking down until all but my head was immersed, I closed my eyes as the steaming heat of the water gradually made every part of my body tingle as it warmed me through. I could feel each limb relax as I was warmed to my core. I sighed as my back curved into the shape of the bath and my neck muscles released. I *did* feel better – I felt physically free from being tense and stiff with worry and fear. Mentally there was little release but, without the added strain of supporting the physical weight of my woes, I could divert all my energy to working through things inside my head instead.

When something unpleasant happens and I dwell on it, even something as simple as a rude comment that makes me feel uneasy, I look forward to forgetting it. We only have the capacity of recall for so many events and things that will show themselves as trivial with the passage of time are eventually forgotten. However, I knew that I would never forget today. It would never become an insignificant memory, no matter how quickly or easily I could help Annie, Kathleen and Bob heal their rift.

The water was almost cold when I finally stood up, shivering a little. I wrapped my towel around me, shrugged my dressing gown on over the top, pulled the plug and gathered my clothes. Watching the swirling water being sucked down through the plughole my thoughts found their own direction again. My body trembled, as if to remind me of its need for continued warmth, and I shuffled quickly to my room. I changed straight into my nightclothes and hopped into bed. I pulled the cold covers up to my chin, hoping to recreate the sense of relaxation the heat of the water had brought as my body slowly warmed the covers around me.

No warming covers enveloped the young woman with chestnut hair and huge brown eyes and she shivered. She was about to spend a third night cold, alone and afraid.

The morning came as reliably as always and I was surprised that I'd slept so soundly, a state possibly aided by the physically relaxing warmth of the bath. My wild thoughts had eventually been forced to capitulate; sleep had won, thankfully. A gentle sunlight was glowing through the thin bedroom curtains. They were the first and last source of light in my room each morning and evening. They offered no restful darkness when drawn, unless night was already embracing the earth, merely providing a means to privacy.

My room was at the back of the house and the window overlooked the small backyard. This was contained by a high brick wall over which, from my room, I could see some of the farmyard beyond although much of it was obscured by a large hay barn. This was solid on three sides, with my side being open; hanging from the rafters was a length of rope and, when the hay was piled high enough, the farmer's children were able to swing from the rope and leap into the hay giggling and screaming with delight. I stared at the empty barn, visualising this scene of childhood frolics and was surprised that my thoughts had wandered to this carefree place with such a force trying to drag them towards scarier places. Maybe they were trying to escape. I couldn't blame them.

After breakfast with Mrs Burgess, who then busied herself preparing Sunday lunch, I retreated to my room again. I lay on the bed staring at a little crack in the ceiling and forced myself to recapture yesterday moment by moment, piece by awful, jagged, painful piece.

Some time passed and I could hear Mr and Mrs Burgess getting ready to leave for church, Mr Burgess begrudgingly as he wondered out loud how long the 'blessed sermon' would be today. I joined them most weekends and today should be no different. At least this routine could remain unchanged. After putting on my Sunday best, we strolled the relatively short distance up the road and past a row of nestling cottages to the church on the edge of our small town.

The familiar smell of the old church greeted me as I followed my companions inside. We headed towards our habitual seats in the fifth pew from the front, while the organist played his ecclesiastical backdrop to the muted mutterings of the congregation. I was caught unaware then by the memory that this music had snapped into my mind, like a child proudly thrusting a picture in front of my eyes without warning. The gentle traces of the church music were replaced, expelled, by the lilting sounds of the music I'd heard at Lola's. All through the service the feeling of that music remained with me, hovering somewhere in my mind as a theme tune to all my thoughts. The service passed with me present in body and going through the religious motions, but I couldn't tell you which hymns we sang, what readings we heard or the subject of that week's carefully chosen sermon; my mind was somewhere else and it was somewhere there was beautiful music.

Gabe

Impatiently, and still in my Sunday best, I caught an earlier bus than necessary to Rushton. Being a limited Sunday service I had fewer choices and decided that being a little early shouldn't matter too much.

After church and lunch, I'd retreated to my room and tried to occupy myself – I started to read but ended up repeating the same paragraph over and over as I couldn't concentrate on it, I pointlessly arranged and re-arranged the things on my dressing table, I lay on my bed, I cleaned my teeth, brushed my hair. When, at last, I could restrain myself no longer, I left. I was satisfied that I wasn't going to be ridiculously early, as long as I didn't rush. Once in Rushton I willed my feet not to hurry as I left the empty shopping streets behind me and headed for the little red brick house, checking my watch so many more times than necessary.

Lola answered the door and, with a musical accompaniment, we once again made our way to the kitchen. My chair from yesterday was still unencumbered and Lola tapped it with her hand as she passed it. 'Sit down. Sit down.' I did as I was told. 'I've been looking forward to seeing you again Eva, but I have to confess to a little change of plan. I can't stop for tea right now as I've got some errands around the town, but I'll make a fresh pot and let Gabe know you're here.'She was making it sound as if my afternoon tea appointment was with him and not her. She stopped suddenly, looking towards the sitting room door. 'Ah, no need.' She smiled as she turned back to me, and I realised the music had stopped.

'But…' I was stunned, and more than a little annoyed. She'd mentioned meeting this Gabe, but I was expecting tea with Lola and just a passing introduction. I was expecting her to tell me what she thought was happening with my dear Annie. I was expecting a resolution, for I'd optimistically convinced myself that she knew the answers; that she knew where Annie was hiding and why. She seemed to know so much yesterday and had been keen to help me. She'd been gentle and caring, warm and kind. I was expecting answers and expecting them today.

Yet now, she was deserting me and leaving me with someone else, a new stranger. What did she have to do now that was so important anyway? Why couldn't she stick by her promise of friendship and stay with me, talk to me and help me? Didn't she realise I needed someone? I needed someone to help me.

Although I'd been mildly intrigued by this person Lola had mentioned yesterday, wondering if it might be her husband or brother and whether they would appear unconventional like her, today I'd swept those thoughts away. I didn't need to know who shared her home, or who played the music.

I just wanted to reunite Annie with her parents.

I considered whether Lola might be a friend of the family who I hadn't met, however unlikely, or that she knew Annie in some other capacity that I wasn't aware of. Maybe she'd comforted Annie recently, in the same way she'd comforted me. Had she, by pure coincidence, stumbled across Annie before meeting me and added up the sum of our connection? Had she pulled that rug of reassurance from under Annie's feet, like she was now doing to me? Invite me, send me home, invite me back, disappear into town.

Now I was left confused once more and, worryingly, the deep hard core of anger that had been born yesterday at my aunt's house was waking up, stirring and stretching sickeningly inside me. I hated the feeling and worried that this might be a sensation that could become familiar – I tried to will it away, ashamed that this anger might now be focused towards a sweet little old lady who, actually, had shown me nothing but kindness so far - hadn't she? Had she?

I heard a door open and close somewhere in the house and my new ball of anger quickly shattered into little fragments. The familiarity of these broken pieces told me they were fear, only this time it was fear for me. Lola busied herself filling the kettle, setting it on the stove, dropping tea leaves into a little silver coloured tea strainer in the shape of a tiny teapot. Then she removed her apron and carefully hung it from a peg on the back door while I watched her every move, willing her to stay, to look after me, to be my friend. 'I'll be off now,'she smiled, 'but we'll meet again very soon, maybe even later today.' I stood up.

'I think I'll go too, Lola. I would love to speak to you about Annie, for you to tell me about Annie. Maybe we can do this tomorrow?'

'No, please stay dear; Gabe will look after you. I hope I might even be back before you leave. I really just have a few little things I need to take care of. Just bits and bobs. And the truth is,'she paused, 'I wanted to talk all this through with Gabe too, see what he said, how to help. And then I thought, '*Lola, why don't you just let Gabe speak to Eva*'. I do get a bit confused, get myself lost in other stories and find it hard to find the path again. Gabe will look after you and he'll explain much better than me. I'm a little doddery sometimes!' She paused again, and then she chuckled. 'Really, old age does sneak up on one, or should that be *creak* up on one?'

I hesitated, unable to share her joke in my confusion and disappointment, and then sat down again. This was mad. Old lady? Strange man? Stay? Go?

I watched her as she prepared to leave and my mind swung backwards and forwards.

I knew why I'd never noticed her in the town before – she looked very similar to so many other ladies of her age, or apparent age. But she felt different to me now. Despite her imminent desertion, I knew she was the person I'd have chosen if I could have picked out my own grandmother. As it was, to me, my grandparents were all just faded grey and white photographs with curled up corners – long gone before I was able to remember them, or maybe even before I joined the world.

I was nudged back to my present dilemma by Lola briefly touching my shoulder with her warm hand as she passed, a gesture I appreciated even if tinged with irritation at her abandonment. I took a slow breath. My brief fear and annoyance, surprisingly, seeped away; if she had places to be then that was fine and, for some reason I couldn't work out, I trusted her. We'd catch up again.

It really hurt that I'd been expecting today to be the day I'd sort out the mess that surrounded me; it was like a thick treacle, seemingly seeping into every pore and muscle, weighing me down and confusing my brain. I sighed, feeling tired and worn. I didn't have enough fingers to count the range of emotions I'd experienced over the last twenty-four hours or so. How many more sensations could there possibly be?

Only a moment later, a man appeared in the doorway. Without hesitation, he crossed to Lola and tenderly kissed her on the forehead. He took her raincoat from the back of a chair and held it out while she slid her arms into it. She touched my arm again then smiled to the young man, their relaxed closeness immediately apparent. They didn't speak to each other, but it seemed that they didn't need to. Then Lola left, with her handbag over one arm and a patchwork shopping bag over the other. As she left for her unknown chores the man who must be Gabe turned to the whistling kettle. I wondered what things Lola had to do so urgently as I stared at the back of his head. He'd only been in sight for a few moments, but I'd already decided on an approach of suspicion.

He lifted the kettle from the flame, placing it next to the teapot, switched off the gas and turned back to me. 'I'm Gabe Adams.' He smiled amiably and offered me his hand, which I shook. It was warm and strong.

'Eva Thorne.'

'I'm sorry Lola's rushed off and left you, but I don't expect she'll be gone very long.'His smile was friendly, but maybe a little guarded, shy even, and while he filled the teapot I continued to watch him warily. He was tall and, admittedly, a nice-looking man, perhaps in his mid-twenties; so I was guessing at a grandson or even a great nephew. 'I'm the lodger,' he smiled, as though he was party to my age calculations and meagre attempt at working out Lola's family tree. I didn't know what to say, so I just smiled in response. 'I'm sorry about Annie.'It sounded as though he was offering me his condolences and that worried me again, sending me towards new and even more frightening thoughts. Maybe he realised how his words sounded and he added,

'Lola told me what happened yesterday. I hope you don't mind.'

He seemed hesitant. I realised that when I'd been unceremoniously left in his company, I'd subconsciously expected to dislike him. It obviously couldn't be anything he'd said or done, as we'd only just met; it was because I perceived him as standing between me and my mission, as though he'd forced Lola out. Had my own manner or expression betrayed me? Did he sense my hostility? His shy and slightly apologetic manner both surprised and softened me. Maybe he felt as awkward as I did, being forced into each other's company like this. Maybe Lola's endorsement of his character should have been enough to reassure me.

'Uh, no, no, that's fine. I was a little upset yesterday and Lola was very kind to me.'I played down yesterday's emotions and wondered if he thought I was mad, given the story Lola must have recounted to him. It shouldn't matter what he thought, but my mind was pondering this before being admonished by consciousness. 'She said there were some things I needed to know. I think she might know my friend Annie, and where she is?' I hoped the questioning inflection in my voice might hint at my hope that he could answer my questions in Lola's absence.

His response was certain. 'No, she doesn't know Annie.'

Now my confidence ricocheted again; maybe I had indeed stumbled on an eccentric little old lady, whose heart may be well meaning but nothing more. What had she thought she knew? Or had she simply seen a matchmaking opportunity between me and her young lodger, or whoever he was? It was cruel to invite me, raise my expectations then leave. My tattered hopes slid further into despair.

I wondered if he could see the concern in my face, as some panic started to set in. Maybe the new-found feelings of hope and safety, which Lola had gently offered, were misplaced. I was alone in a cottage a good walk from the town with a man I didn't know. He didn't strike me as a murderer, but the situation went against all common sense no matter how unbalanced my mind was. He seemed to become aware of my growing unease as he deliberately moved further away.

'Tea?' he asked.

Best to say yes, be polite until I decided what to do next. 'Yes, please.' The tea was soon in front of me, yet he didn't sit down at the table but returned to perch against the cupboard a good three yards away. There was an awkward silence as I sipped from the dainty china cup on mismatched saucer, burning my tongue. The sharp burning made tears threaten my eyes and I tried to absorb the moisture back into them.

'Do you live in Rushton?'

'Okay, small talk is good. 'No, in Fielding, but I grew up in Rushton.'

'Do you work?'

What did he think I did, beg on the streets? 'Yes, at Fielding Home and Grocery.'

He nodded. 'Oh yes, Mr Grayson isn't it?'

'Yes.'I wondered how long it would be before we ran out of things to say and decided to remind him of the reason for my visit. Sometimes it was better just to get straight to the point and I was tired of waiting so I jumped straight in. This must be it. 'Do you know Annie?' This must have been why Lola had introduced us. 'Is Annie in some kind of trouble?'

My splintered mind sparked off in a multitude of new directions that hadn't occurred to me before; feral thoughts like fireworks were lighting up all around me as I tried to catch sight and make sense of each and every one. Was this man involved? Was he responsible? What had he done? My anger snowball set off at speed, rolling down the emotional hill inside me, getting bigger and bigger in the few seconds before he answered.

'No, I'm sorry, I don't know Annie either.'

All my impatience, all my wild thoughts, were halted. My solid snowball hit a rock and burst apart into harmless flakes of disappointment, tiny but a thousand-fold and I was buried beneath. I'd actually been sure he must know Annie, hence the reason he'd been summoned in Lola's place, so his negative response made me slump in the chair. It was involuntary; I was a marionette whose puppeteer had suddenly let go of the strings. I was deflated, but oddly relieved at his lack of involvement at the same time. My head was spinning.

'Oh, I thought...' But I couldn't tell him what I thought, as I wasn't sure myself and the tears began to roll down my cheeks. I was cross with myself for not realising they were coming.

His apparent care to keep a reassuring distance from me seemed forgotten as he was soon at my side, sliding a big white handkerchief into my hand.

'Thank you,'I sniffed pathetically. A few days before, I wasn't someone who cried this easily and I was embarrassed at doing so in front of this man. 'Sorry.' My second tearful encounter with a stranger in as many days and these people were in danger of running out of clean handkerchiefs.

'You've nothing to be sorry about, Eva,' came his tender and quiet response. I hadn't been prepared for tears and I hadn't been prepared for my reaction to hearing my name on his lips. Another emotion was added to my growing list.

He didn't move away but spoke the words again very softly, while clearing the chair next to mine, relocating a pile of papers to the table then turning the chair to face me and sitting down. I inhaled sharply with surprise as he grabbed the seat of my chair and turned it towards his with a scrape, so we sat facing each other, our knees only inches apart. And there we were, me quietly trying to compose myself behind the large white linen square and him with his elbows on his knees and his hands linked together between them.

'Lola and I will help you.'

Not knowing what else to do in response, I smiled weakly.

'Eva, there's an awful lot to explain. Can you keep your mind open while I try?'

Worried, confused and relieved all at the same time, I nodded.

'You've stumbled into a situation that's going to be hard for you to believe, but not impossible. Lola didn't know how to start, what to say or how to tell you. This situation is a little different, admittedly, but each time it hurts her more. It hurts her to give hope and take it away at the same time. I know that sounds strange, but if you can give me the chance to explain you'll understand what I mean.'I watched his eyes, willing the truth to come. They stared back at me, unblinking. 'Eva, there was no Annie.'

The chair scraped the floor as I stood, keen to leave. I had to get out quickly; I couldn't look at him.

My promise to listen forgotten, I turned away sharply, but his hand darted to mine and gripped it before I had chance to move away. Panic rose instantaneously, a new emotional leader, pushing sadness and fear aside.

'No. Please.' He spoke in a soft, fluid voice. 'Don't be frightened,' he soothed 'Please, don't be frightened.' He tugged at my hand gently. 'Please sit down.'

With gentle green eyes he looked at me so earnestly that I couldn't imagine he'd ever harm a soul. Or construct and regale me with such a story if he didn't believe in it wholeheartedly himself. The moments stretched between us as I looked into his face, his eyes beseeching. He didn't speak again but watched me as I fought between instinct and intellect. Instinct won. Finding honesty somewhere in the eyes that pleaded with me, I slowly sat back down.

'Thank you.' He smiled as he started to talk, still holding my hand and searching my eyes for reaction or reassurance.

Revelations and Earthquakes

Sitting there in Lola's kitchen, all my belief in how the world worked might have crashed to the floor, had I let myself truly believe what I was being told. I couldn't have felt more wobbly if there'd been an earthquake that had physically shaken the ground beneath me. I couldn't speak as I listened, struck dumb by the words he was saying. Despite my incredulity at his explanation, I did know that something in my family had been disturbed and disturbed way past what was normal. His words shouldn't be true, but my experience with Kathleen and Bob was murmuring that they might. My aunt and uncle's behaviour was so absurd that no sensible explanation fitted. This man, this seemingly gentle man whom I'd met only moments before, was imparting ridiculous, far-fetched things. And although I fought against it, trying to deny myself access to the path that led to belief, I started to feel some truth in his words as I took the first step.

I was jerked rudely back to the present and my strange environment by the front door opening. I'd forgotten all about Lola – it had taken all my mental strength to absorb Gabe's words and there'd been no room left in my head for anything else. I wasn't sure how long she'd been gone. All sense of time had been lost, listening to this man's words as they'd wound around my heart and my head like a weed, suffocating me, depriving me not of air but of something else; was it understanding? Sense? Safety? All of these?

'Gabe? Eva?' Lola's voice called from the hall, sounding as if she'd called those names in unison a hundred times. Gabe rose and moved to stand at the door leading to the sitting room. For all my fear of Lola's departure, I now suffered a surprising twinge of disappointment at her return.

'We're still in the kitchen Lola.'Gabe turned back to me to softly say, 'I'll just be a minute,' and I watched him go, still speechless after his revelations; things he clearly believed, true or not. I heard him speaking very quietly with Lola and assumed they must be talking about me. It was only then that I glanced at my watch and realised that the last bus for Fielding would be leaving soon. At that moment, Gabe returned to the kitchen with Lola. Composing myself, for the moment at least, I stood on unstable legs.

'I really should be heading off. The bus leaves in about twenty minutes. Thank you for the tea.' I hesitated, my voice and body shaky, not knowing what to say or do now. Should I be running away, as quick as my trembling legs would go, escaping these people before they wound their tales so tightly around me that I couldn't move?

Lola was the first to respond. 'I'm sorry I left you earlier Eva. But I knew Gabe would be able to make more sense than me.'

Her tone was sincere and apologetic, but I almost laughed at her remark – how could any of this make sense, no matter who spoke the words? Anyway, she could have stayed with me while he imparted his words of confusion couldn't she?

Lola's words continued. 'With all of this in your head, I'm not sure you should be on your own. We can make space if you'd like to stay here tonight. We can talk more. You'll have a thousand questions.'

I was shocked, stunned, by her offer to me; a stranger until twenty-four hours ago. She appeared to have no idea how peculiar it should seem for her to be offering me a bed for the night. From the corner of my eye, as Lola made her offer, I caught a sudden illuminated flash of anxiety in Gabe's face; instinct told me it was concern at her offer rather than concern for me with my newly acquired knowledge. He'd looked at her in a way that I felt sure was alarm, but she'd not met his eyes; maybe because she knew that they bore into her offer like fire through paper.

The thought of not venturing out into the cool evening appealed on a purely physical level. The idea of untangling this tonight, teasing out any fibres of truth from the jumbled mass of fiction that blocked the path before me, also tugged at me. But not for a second did I seriously consider Lola's offer. Me? This house? These strangers with their wild ideas? Go home. *Get out now*, were the words I heard above all the other chaotic voices in my head.

Gabe's fearful expression was making me uncomfortable, so I quickly thanked Lola for her kind offer but said my farewells and started to leave. Lola offered Gabe's services to walk me back into town and the bus stop, but I declined as gracefully as I could in my hurry and left. They'd not given me a physical reason to be fearful of them, just a mental discomfort which tugged at me after the strange things I'd been told, but I was pleased to be alone again. As I strode away from the house, I thought about how Gabe seemed almost afraid at Lola's offers. Maybe giving their well-meaning answers was one thing, but offering me anything more was something entirely different.

I took some deep breaths as I walked, trying to steady my heart's anxious and insistent drumming on my ribcage and slow down my eager footsteps. 'Calm down, calm down,'I repeated as a mantra. 'It's all a dream, just calm down. Breathe slowly.'

I was relieved to step onto the bus and take my seat, out of the now cold evening air. At least *this* was familiar and unchanged. I leaned my head against the juddering glass of the window and closed my eyes, willing myself to wake up in my bed and find that this had all been the awful nightmare I thought it must be and prayed it was.

Earlier that day, the young woman with the big brown eyes had also caught a bus. Her bus went in the opposite direction and, as she fastened and unfastened the clasp on her bag over and over again, she watched the landscape flood past the window and she silently wept.

As I opened home's front door, I could hear Mrs Burgess humming along to 'Moonlight Serenade' on the wireless. I said an early goodnight, climbed the stairs with heavy feet, and collapsed onto my bed. I lay where I fell for a long time, at first listening as the music rolled up the stairs to my room – I closed my eyes and concentrated on each instrument, trying to separate the musicians in my head, playing games to guide my anxious mind to places other than those it had been forced to this afternoon.

There were some strange people around – maybe Lola and Gabe were two of them. Annie had just fallen out with her mum and dad. It was obviously something so big in their eyes that they all sadly perceived the damage as irreparable, but I knew that nothing could be so bad we couldn't fix it. Their hearts wouldn't let this separation continue for long. Should I go back to see Aunt Kathleen and Uncle Bob? Maybe I should call the police after all, if Annie didn't turn up soon.

The curtains weren't drawn and I opened my eyes and lay staring out at the darkening sky for some time before changing groggily into my nightclothes and resuming my position looking heavenwards. Other melodies from the wireless downstairs made their way to my room and left again, and all the while I watched the sky. The stars appeared and a few clouds breezed delicately past them, unaware of all that occurred so many thousands of miles below. No matter what happened, each day started and ended, the night sky darkened and the sun rose. Rain would fall and sun would shine. During my dreamy musing and wandering thoughts, I fell asleep as the cold covers on the bed gradually warmed with the heat of my body.

Somewhere between sleep and wakefulness I heard tapping. No, it was a knocking. So insistent and nearby was the sound that I was forced to sit up, disorientated, trying to locate the source. I fumbled in the darkness for the switch on the bedside lamp. When the lamp finally glowed, I picked up my watch to check the time. Half past one? I looked closer. Yes, half past one. Still dark. As my senses awoke I realised that the knocking was on my bedroom door. And there was a voice.

'Eva?' A gentle and familiar voice called my name. I hurriedly put on my dressing gown and then moved quickly to open the door, still tying the belt.

'Mrs Burgess. What's wrong?' My gaze moved behind her to the dark landing, to a tall man in a dark suit and a lady next to him, then back to my landlady. 'What is it?'

'Eva...these people...' started Mrs Burgess; she half turned to gesture to the pair standing behind her, as if needing to illustrate who she was talking about. The unknown lady stepped forward from the shadow. She wore a dark cape which reached just past her waist, a plain white skirt stark and crisp below it. A nurse? My mind was full and empty at the same time.

'Eva? We're here to help you, to look after you,'the woman said, smiling benevolently. 'Mr and Mrs Carter have asked us to help.' I was confused. 'If you'll come with us, we can take care of you.' She took another step forward, past my worried and now tearful looking landlady, and hovered just outside my door.

'Is this really necessary?' Mrs Burgess asked the woman, placing her hand firmly on her forearm. 'I'm sure there's been a mistake, there'll be a sensible explanation.' The nurse turned to her and lowered her voice conspiratorially as she patted Mrs Burgess's hand reassuringly. Although almost a whisper, in the silence of the night her words were quite clear.

'In cases like this, Mrs Burgess, we really must intervene. We never know whether they may be a danger to themselves. When the mind is unbalanced, one never knows how serious things might become. It's best that we take Miss Thorne with us tonight, to ensure her safety.'She turned back to me and spoke louder, returning to normal volume, clearly under the impression that I couldn't hear her unless she did. 'Would you like to get dressed dear? Then we can take you somewhere you'll feel safe.'

I struggled to believe what I was hearing. My aunt and uncle had sent people to take me away? To somewhere 'safe'. They thought I was a danger to myself? Unbalanced. What do I do now, can I run? Shut the bedroom door maybe, jump out of the window, climb down the drainpipe? I had visions of sterile white rooms, locked doors and squeaky shoes on polished corridors. What to do? What to do? Time to think, I needed time to think.

'Uh, yes, let me get dressed.' *Give yourself some time Eva.* I closed the door on the trio gathered outside it and turned the key as quietly as I could, although I know they would have heard. I could think while I dressed. I'd need to be dressed for an escape anyway. Two birds, one stone. My mind raced backward and forward as I quickly gathered my clothes. Once dressed I sat down on my bed, then I lay down, then I closed my eyes.

New Day

I woke up with a start, my neck stiff from sleeping awkwardly, and realised that I'd not even undressed last night, falling asleep fully clothed and shod. Then I recalled a dream – I felt it more than remembered it, so vivid were the images. I knew the emotions of it and sensed the fear of it.

I looked at the door as if I could tell by looking at it what lay on the other side. I looked at my watch. Twenty to eight. A deep sigh escaped my lips as I relaxed back onto the bed.

Relief.

The dream had been so real and frightening that the emotions I'd felt still lingered in my chest and my head. I knew it would stay with me all day, hovering just out of sight but leaving me with the shredded remnants of those awful moments; thinking that I'd been labelled unstable, deranged, dangerous.

But it was just a dream – the knock on the door, the business-like nurse, my troubled landlady, the sinister presence of the man standing behind. A sense of relief blew across me in one big, happy breeze. Just a dream. Thank goodness. Just a dream. But I feared it was the only part of this waking nightmare that was.

Okay, enough. My mood was decisive, I was facing a fresh day and a fresh start. A quick hop in and out of the bath to wake me and wash any remaining indecision away, some fresh clothes – then off to Annie's. She'd be home by now and no doubt waiting to explain everything, if she wasn't already on her way to see *me.* She would know, without any doubt at all, that I would be there for her unquestioningly, unconditionally. We were so close, like sisters.

Annie and her parents had been part of my life all my life. Annie and I, with birthdays only a few weeks apart, shared everything. It felt as though we were actually closer than sisters as we so rarely fell out. We thought the same, felt the same, liked the same things, and I couldn't imagine life without her. We'd be alright, I'd sort it all out myself. The little red brick house pressed itself into my vision, along with its occupants and a surprising splinter of regret that I wouldn't come to know them better.

I stopped at Fielding Home and Grocery and explained that I had some unexpected family issues to take care of. Never having taken a sudden day away from work, my bosses were concerned and understanding, offering any help they could and as much time as I needed. Feeling guilty I left the shop, gritted my teeth and walked to the bus stop.

My feet hesitated on the doorstep that used to welcome me home, that I'd crossed a thousand times, rather than wandering straight in as I normally would. The back door was ajar, but I couldn't bring myself to enter. Instead I pushed the door ever so lightly. 'Aunt Kathleen? Uncle Bob?' I didn't call Annie's name. If she was here, she'd rush to meet me at any moment. There were no answering footsteps coming into the kitchen to greet me, so I called out a little louder.

I heard Uncle Bob's familiar steps before I saw him coming towards the door. Aunt Kathleen wasn't far behind. They stopped at the door and I smiled weakly. They both returned warm smiles. My aunt's features always betray her feelings with utter transparency and today I could see absolute relief. Uncle Bob's face was painted with caution, but even that couldn't harden the soft fatherly features I'd known all my life.

'Saturday,' was all I could say.

In a moment, my aunt's arms were around me and I relaxed into her hold, closing my eyes and feeling, for a second, respite and security. Years melted away and I was a little girl, finding comfort in the arms of someone who knew every answer and fixed every heartache. Maybe everything was going to be alright after all. We were soon seated in the living room, where I'd had every intention of being very blunt. For the second time in the same number of days, I knew there was no point in edging around something when the quickest route was to walk straight up to it. Having rehearsed this moment all the way to their house, when faced with my aunt and uncle's gentle faces I couldn't speak. My mouth was dry and barren, no strict words would come. In fact, no words came at all.

Instead of the lines I'd planned and practised, all I could hear inside my head were Gabe's words. Again they tangled themselves weed-like amongst the words that my aunt and uncle were saying, suffocating the sense out of their assumptions, weaving a coarse black thread of despair through the delicate pastel fabric of their concern. They were anxious, worried about me; was I working too hard? Did I have concerns about money? My aunt even intimated at the possibility of a broken love affair, of all things. I clearly must be unwell as I wasn't at work; had I seen a doctor? Was I sleeping and eating properly and looking after myself?

All the words that were spoken displayed clearly that there had indeed been no falling out with Annie, but this realisation caused both relief and the most incredible fear at the same time.

The relief was in the confirmation that I *did* know them after all; they *were* the people I knew and loved and for whom nothing in the world could cause them to disown their only child. They were themselves to me again. I could almost reach out and touch the relief that seemed to hang in the air between us.

The fear was in my sudden awareness that Gabe had been telling the truth.

Realisation

Having all my carefully constructed plans of re-uniting a family torn screaming from my grip, I struggled even more to know what to say. Thankfully I think my hesitancy helped to add credence to my hastily formed excuse, the story that was suddenly forming in my mind and on my tongue. Yes, I was under the weather, there was a nasty fever working its way around my friends, causing awful delirium in some cases, and, although clearly over the worst, I still didn't feel quite right. I was quite fuzzy and confused. A few days of bed rest and I'd be fighting fit once more, I was sure. I was sorry to worry them, but I'd be better soon.

Saturday's encouragement to stay and be tended by my aunt was repeated with fervour but I declined, not wanting to expose them to my germs any more than I already had. My mind darted to days gone by, of childhood bugs and my aunt's gentle nursing and I wished that this could all be soothed with chicken soup, a cold flannel and honey and lemon. My aunt and uncle's offer to stay in the spare room while I was recovering stung as soon as the words were spoken, causing me to flinch. Because there *was* no spare room, just Annie's room. Their words squeezed my heart. It took lots of self-control not to respond sharply, with anger or verbal rebuke, to their ingenuous words.

Uncle Bob offered to walk me to the bus, then make the journey home with me to ensure I was alright, to see me back to the Burgess's safe and sound. But I reassured them I would be fine and, very reluctantly, they let me leave with promises of visits and food parcels.

Once home I did take to my bed as I said I would; not because I was ill, but because I wanted to be. I wanted my lies to be true. I wanted this all to be the result of a fever which had confused and mocked me. I wanted to sweat this out of my head and wake up to a new and normal day. I kicked off my shoes, t curled up under the bedcovers fully clothed, drawing the sheets and blanket to my chin and closing my tear-filled eyes tightly. I willed a fever to come, then to leave and drag with it all my hallucinations and fantasies.

Denial

Startled, I checked my watch on waking a couple of hours later. I was surprised that I'd slept but felt refreshed and, even more surprisingly, optimistic. And stupid. How could I have started to fall for this? There was sure to be some rational explanation. Maybe my fairy tale fever was in fact what my aunt and uncle truly had. Maybe they actually were ill. Jumping out from under the bedcovers, I snatched up my bag and hurriedly put my shoes on. I rushed down the stairs and out into the street. I needed proof. I needed proof that everyone I knew hadn't gone completely mad.

Boarding the bus for my second visit to Rushton that day, I recited a mental list of people to visit. My visits would take the form of a casual passing by, dropping in to say hello and steering the conversation deftly around to areas that would include Annie; then I'd wait for her to be mentioned, invited into the exchange. Then I would get the doctor for Kathleen and Bob. Then they would tell me where Annie had gone. Then Annie would come home and explain everything.

I visited the small and familiar secretarial agency where Annie worked, under some pretence of job hunting for a friend, making small talk about the weather, family and mutual friends and smarting at the sight of her empty desk, devoid of any personal items. They didn't ask after Annie or mention her absence.

I bought two cakes, Annie's favourite and mine, at the bakery where Annie's neighbour worked. She admired my scarf.

I wandered past the allotments (after confirming Uncle Bob's absence) and passed a few minutes with 'Geranium John' who had the plot next to my uncle, praying he wouldn't relay my casual visit to his allotment neighbour but willing to take the risk. We chatted briefly about the weather.

I enquired at the library whether my friend had any books outstanding to return, but the librarian shook her head as she checked. She could find no mention of Annie Carter in her records.

I bought cinema tickets for Wednesday's matinee of 'Goodbye, Mr Chips' from the kiosk at the Palace, served by Alex who was a friend of mine and Annie's from school. He told me to enjoy the film.

And as for Annie? No one asked after her. No one spoke her name.

Deflated and depressed, I wandered through the town with two cinema tickets in my handbag and two cakes in a paper bag.

In contrast to all the wild thoughts that had crashed about in my head since Saturday like cold stormy waves, my mind was now absurdly calm and flat. I didn't know what to think anymore. I was cold and low, empty and emotionless. Bereft.

Once again I was wandering without thought or purpose, until I realised that I was walking along Mill Street. Maybe I did have a purpose after all, my feet clearly knowing something my head had been slow to work out. I stopped for a moment to regain my bearings, then continued on my way towards the only sanctuary I could think of.

Friendship

The front door opened and I offered Gabe the crumpled paper bag. He took it from me without a word, smiling gently and standing aside for me to enter. He closed the door quietly behind me and I followed him to the kitchen. Odd plates were taken from the cupboard, and the cakes gently tipped from the bag and placed between us as we sat opposite each other. Gabe sat with arms folded, leaning on the table and looking at the plates.

'Which one's Annie's?' he asked. I was startled, amazed by his insight; it was as though I was walking a familiar path, something he'd seen before. I pointed to the shortbread and he nodded. 'Any sign?'

'Everyone I could casually drop in on, I casually dropped in on.'

'No-one knew her did they?' It was more of a statement than a question and I shook my head. Gabe pushed the other slice of cake towards me. 'Well, at least now you know. You know for sure.'

He didn't seem offended that I'd so obviously doubted his and Lola's story, any sane person knowing I would. I discreetly took deep breaths to calm myself, hoping he wouldn't be aware of my panic.

He tapped the plate gently. 'Come on, you still need to eat.'

I couldn't respond.

'No appetite?' he asked softly. I shook my head again as Gabe stood up. 'Will you eat with us tonight then, stay for dinner? Lola loves to cook – and she's good, I promise.' He smiled as he filled two glasses from a jug of water.

Side-tracked, I found myself looking around, taking in once again the piles of papers and stacks of clothes, shelves full of jars and pots, books and boxes.

This time I saw everything with new eyes; the piles, stacks and collections, although chaotic at first glance, were somehow ordered. I hadn't noticed it before, but most things seemed to be with other matching items; a pile of freshly laundered linen, a stack of plates, a glass jug full of buttons. Although there were things everywhere, all was clean and, possibly to Lola's eye, sensibly ordered. Admittedly, some things were threadbare and worn, but as I looked round I saw a fresh and light kitchen, the floor swept and the net curtains the brightest white. I was sure that if I viewed the sitting room with my new vision, I would see the same. I could see past the never-ending collections to the strange order beneath. And the house was no longer a mess; it was a sanctuary, just as my subconscious had clearly known when my feet had carried me here.

'Go on then.'Gabe turned to me with a young boy's grin spreading tentatively across his face, wanting me to ask a question he had the answer to. I frowned, unsure what he meant. 'Ask me about Lola. Ask me why she lives like this and who she is, and ask me how I've come to be here amongst it all'.

When he put it so directly I realised that these questions had been shadows in my vision and possibly, when banished by the light of the answers, I'd be able to see other things more clearly.

They might even provide answers to other questions. However, now my questions had actually been voiced, spoken aloud by Gabe and not me, they sounded intrusive. He must have seen me soaking in my surroundings and the strange environment in which he and Lola lived.

He continued. 'It's alright to ask, honestly. You must think Lola and I make strange housemates, and are probably strange people. We tell you all sorts of odd things and confuse you and frighten you.'He surveyed the room. 'And we live in this little house together, with all this.' He smiled kindly.

'I—' was all I could manage without agreeing. He carried on, despite my hesitation, obviously needing to explain more. I wondered if he felt the need to justify our surroundings or even in some way exonerate Lola to me.

'Lola's one of a kind Eva – the very best kind there is.'He sounded proud. 'She's unusual, I know, but she's allowed that. And it only adds to her charm.'

I started to voice my defence at his assumption of my views on him and Lola, their characters and living arrangements, but he put a finger to his own lips to indicate that I should silence my protest at his disclosure. 'It's okay,'he continued. 'I see that she could be considered a little... eccentric. And I love her all the more for it. She's been lost and alone for so long and this is how she's coped. It's all part of her.' He gestured at the room with a large sweep of his arm. 'Her collecting is like a... a kind of comfort blanket. As you can see, she finds all sorts of things. If it's lost she'll bring it home.'He smiled in such an affectionate way then, thinking of Lola, that I had to smile too. My panicked heart was calming a little along with the non-Annie conversation and I listened as Gabe continued. 'You name it, we've got it. Odd shoes, socks, toys, pots, baskets, books, ornaments, ribbons and screws, strange little pieces of machinery that I haven't a clue about. Oddments of this and bits of that. We've had a few stray cats too, over the years. Even a chicken – Hortense. We didn't cook the old bird, she died a very elderly and beloved member of the family.'

My lips shed a small giggle at an image, for some reason of a chicken in a bonnet like the one worn by Whistler's mother in his famous painting, and Gabe smiled back.

'I don't know when it all started – this house has only just got *more* crowded with Lola's collections since I moved in; if that's possible. It felt jammed to the rafters when I arrived, but Lola's somehow managed to get more in. We might have to start pushing the walls out soon!' His eyes glowed with affection for his unlikely companion.

Gabe stood up, pushed his chair under the table and filled the kettle for the now obligatory cup of tea. He moved to light the stove under the well-worn and oft used kettle, taking a long time to blow out the match, and I assumed he was also hijacked by his thoughts.

'I don't really understand. She finds things? She's not a kleptomaniac?'

He turned back to me with laughing eyes. 'No,'he laughed 'She's no kleptomaniac. She quite literally finds things; well, she looks for them. You must have seen an odd shoe at the roadside and wondered how on earth someone could lose such a thing? Have you noticed a rogue glove on the pavement, or the odd button on the floor?'

I smiled again at the thought of Lola and nodded, trying to recall each instance of seeing such lost things on my travels, knowing that I had but not remembering what, when or where.

Gabe continued. 'Well, all those things, if Lola spots them, end up here. We're like a lost property department where nothing is ever claimed.' His hand and his gaze swept the room again. 'Lola very rarely comes home with an empty shopping basket. I'm not really sure how she does it, or how far she walks, but she manages to find something every single day.'

An image of the day I met Lola flashed into my vision; the first time I'd seen her stooping to pick something up, the seemingly laden shopping basket at her feet by the bench. I thought of her now, heading off to her 'chores' and wondered what might return in her scarf-swathed basket or patchwork shopping bag. Could she really find so much or were her wanderings as much about solitude as finding things? I wondered how many years it had taken to amass such an amount.

Gabe had talked of Lola but not of himself and his part in the story. It all still didn't quite add up for me with regard to his presence. Maybe she needed financial help and having a lodger provided that, although their bond seemed much closer. 'How long have you lived here?'

'Five years'. He looked down at his feet and shifted his weight from one foot to the other. When he saw me watching, he started to busy himself. He positioned himself on the opposite side of the table, clearing a third chair and piling the table higher with the things he'd evicted. He didn't sit but turned to the dresser, rummaged in a drawer and added odd cutlery to the table, then foraged in a cupboard and found a variety of plates which he placed by the stove. He turned back to the table, sitting down this time, and looked at me across the collections piled on it. He smiled a little ruefully. 'I was one of her finds.'A half chuckle escaped, but his features soon replaced this with sadness. 'If it hadn't been for Lola…' His voice trailed off and the sentence was lost. I thought I saw his eyes gain a shine, as they generally do before tears escape, but I couldn't be sure as the moment disappeared quickly and the subject was closed. 'Lola's been on her own for over eighty years now.'

My mouth dropped open involuntarily and the familiar prickle of gathering tears was now felt behind my eyes rather than seen in Gabe's.

'What happened?' My voice was so quiet I wasn't sure he'd heard. My face couldn't conceal my horror as well as I thought my voice had and I knew the shock that my features now betrayed.

'She was about eleven when she lost her family. She was never found, and never found anyone, so she was all alone until she collected me.'

I was horrified to think of the little girl, lost with no-one to care for her.

'I think I might be the grandson, or maybe even the son, she never had,' he smiled, 'and I was luckier. Lola was just a little girl when she was lost. I can't imagine what it must have been like for her eighty years ago and in all those empty years which followed.'

He'd let a little of his own story escape and I struggled to piece some of it together whilst being haunted by visions of an eleven-year-old Lola. They met, what was it, five years ago? How long had he been alone before they met, where was his family and how old had he been when he'd suffered the same fate as his housemate? Who were his family and how could he get them back? And where had he gone after losing them? Maybe the answers to these questions could help me find Annie. I couldn't stop myself pressing just a little bit.

'Where did you go when you were lost? How old were you?'

He breathed out very slowly like he was summoning up the courage to answer and I wondered if I might be the first person apart from Lola to discuss this with him, or try to. I felt bad for drifting away from Lola's story but I couldn't steer back to it, the current was too strong. 'Well I didn't have a plan.'He tapped his fingers nervously on the table and I could also hear his foot tapping quickly underneath it. 'I can't remember the names of all the places I went. I just drifted about for a couple of years until I ended up in Galton and then I met Lola; well, Lola found me actually. We've just muddled along together since then.' He stood up and moved to the kettle, which was preparing to summon up its final whistle. He turned his head to talk to me over his shoulder while his back was turned and he waited a moment for the kettle. 'Lola got me a job at Harry Stanley's market garden through Chris McCabe. Chris is a friend of Lola's and he knows Harry quite well. He put in a good word for me.'

He continued with the tale, telling me how much he enjoyed his work; taking pleasure in all the changing seasons and the variety of tasks each one brought. He wasn't sorry when the summer sun was replaced by autumn winds, as this meant there were new things to be taken care of and a shifting set of seasonal tasks to be carried out. He was able to bring home fresh fruit and vegetables and the occasional bunch of flowers for Lola and said he enjoyed his walk to and from the gardens. Sometimes he used the old bicycle he'd discovered in the garden shed – it had taken some time to make this discovery as it had, of course, been concealed by a multitude of boxes, crates and pots. When using the bicycle he sometimes cycled home at lunchtime to see Lola although, he explained, he often found her absent, just leaving a note of reassurance for him in her stead. He'd obviously cycled today, meaning I found him home, and I was grateful.

I would have guessed that Gabe had a job that took him outside much of the time as he was broad shouldered and strong with a healthy glow to his face. When he moved, it was with assured and sturdy actions.

I was watching him, looking him up and down, and was suddenly thankful that he was still turned away from me as he reached for the teapot – brown pot, blue lid. The kettle finally boiled. His hand hovered over the teapot for a moment before he stopped and turned. 'Actually, I have a little time before I need to get back to work. We've been starting earlier than usual for a few days, packing and shipping, so Harry said we both deserve a long lunch. Do you fancy a walk?' he asked, as he took the kettle from the heat and set it to one side. He didn't continue with the tea, as if he knew I'd say yes.

Memories

Gabe closed the rickety garden gate behind us and we strolled silently away from Lola's cottage. Our path took us along a little country lane parallel to the town but slowly rising with each step. After only a few minutes of walking it felt as though we were miles from anywhere. I was pleased that it was warmer than it had been the past few days; there was a fresh breeze but the sky was bright and blue and the air, although crisp, didn't feel cold. Our silence didn't bother me; in fact, it was nice not to be talking for a little while. Sadly, despite the relaxed and easy silence, there was still no slowing of the thoughts stirring round and round and round in my poor aching head.

I felt Gabe's warm hand search mine out, but he didn't turn to me or speak. His hand held mine firmly and naturally and I wanted to spin around and hug him, to thank him for being a friend. I wondered if he realised how much his kindness and humanity meant to me at that moment, how much I needed someone to hold my hand, providing much needed physical reassurance that I wasn't alone. Lola and Gabe both seemed to have a knack for knowing the right moment to, quite literally, offer a hand in friendship. I'd only known them for a couple of days, but it felt so much longer. Maybe it was because my head had turned a hundred somersaults since I'd met them and it seemed an age had passed since Annie disappeared. Or perhaps it was because they were the lifeline to which I was desperately clinging with every fibre.

We walked on for a while, and then turned left through a gate into a large sloping field. Gabe let go of my hand to offer me passage through the gate first and his hand gently touched my back as I passed. The view that met my eyes surprised and delighted me. I couldn't believe that I'd never been up here before. From this vantage point at the top of the field I could see for miles – the town spread out beyond the bottom of the field and around it all I could see were more fields, farmland and trees. It was very beautiful. I hadn't realised I'd stopped until Gabe gently caught and tugged my hand.

We moved along a short way to the top of the field, finding a worn wooden bench against the hedge, obviously well-used over the years by many people admiring the same view as we were now – a view whose only call to change was with the dawn of each new season.

'This is lovely.' I sighed as I sat down and closed my eyes, raising my face to the weak sunshine.

'It certainly is,' he agreed, and I peeked through one half-closed eye to see that he was now doing the same as me. We must have looked comical sitting there, faces upturned to the sky with half smiles dancing on our lips. 'Apparently, so Lola tells me, the top of this hill was known many years ago as the Six Siblings, although no-one's called it that for years. There were six trees here, planted by a heartbroken father after losing his six children.'

'I never knew any of that. What had happened to the children?' I was surprised by this piece of local knowledge and turned to look at him.

He must have been aware I was watching him because he turned to look at me. 'Some say it was the plague, that's how long ago town folklore says it was, but others just say they disappeared.'He hesitated, as though trying to impart the relevance of the story. 'The trees grew tall and strong but the father, so they say, lost his mind and chopped them all down in a fit of madness, or anguish. Or more likely grief.'

'That's horrible.'

He took both of my hands and smiled carefully. 'Or maybe it's just a tale. Maybe it's a lot simpler and the whisperers over the centuries have embellished it and turned it into a mystery when it needn't be.'

'It's still a sad story, true or not.'

'Yes, it is.' We both turned our faces back to the view but I closed my eyes again as he looked across the patchwork of fields towards the town.

Still with my eyes closed and my face once again turned heavenwards, I asked, 'If Annie's disappeared from everyone's memory, Gabe, please tell me why not mine?' I had asked this and other questions many times in my head. I secretly peeked sideways again.

He bowed his head, untangling his hand from mine. He was looking down at his hands now where his fingers were knotting together, tangling then untangling, tangling then untangling. I turned once again to look at him fully, eyes wide and searching.

He shrugged. 'Good question. A memory is something remembered,' he began. 'Obviously you can only remember something you knew in the first place. To everyone apart from you, to all her other friends and family, Annie never existed. That's how it is at the moment anyway, so they can't *remember*. There's nothing there at all. It's all gone.'

He didn't seem at all exasperated by my questioning and I thought I could see affection in his eyes as he watched me. A small smile began to show on his lips. 'With regard to you and why nothing's changed for you, I really don't know.' A hesitation. 'Maybe you're special?' His eyes held mine and I was the first to look away, wondering if it was the sun or his words that had warmed my cheeks.

There was a silence and I didn't know what to say. In the end, I just returned his smile then turned once again to the breathtaking view over the countryside. His words could just be a kind way of trying to find a reason why I wasn't included in this widespread lapse of memory or, maybe, he was trying to tell me something else at the same time.

I pushed the thoughts away; I could only deal with one jigsaw at a time. At the moment I was still struggling to put together all the pieces I'd so far been given of Annie's puzzle. I was convinced that many were missing and that the absent ones were those most vital to seeing the whole picture, a picture I didn't have in front of me to follow and which would only be revealed when the jigsaw was completed.

Annie had disappeared – that now seemed like the easy part – she could be found, couldn't she? But knowing that my dear Annie was missing from her own life, as well as physically from her home, tore at me and my heart felt shredded.

When Lola had left me with Gabe on the afternoon that felt more like two months ago than two days, he'd told me things that I only now believed.

He'd carefully explained that Annie was lost, but not the kind of lost where you just need a map or directions or the aid of local knowledge.

She'd disappeared from her life.

It was as though she'd never been born.

There was no record or sight of her ever having 'been'.

She was somewhere else; maybe not aware of who *she* was either.

And the only person in the whole world who remembered her was me.

Deep inside, I'd known that something very powerful had happened but this explanation was so far removed from normal life that it was quite ridiculous. I'd been hoping for a dream, to hear the morning alarm and breathe a sigh of relief. I'd wake up, smiling sleepily at the strange way the mind sometimes weaves stories in slumber. But I was already wide awake. I still felt that I wanted to shake myself – shrug off this silly dream, or practical joke, or whatever it was. Things like this were the basis for books and films. This was in the realms of the Land of Oz, which Annie and I had read of and then experienced at the cinema just weeks before, where

I'd eventually wake up but believe it had all really happened. Maybe after a while I'd be sure it wasn't real.

At the moment, though, I *was* believing. I knew Annie was lost, I believed Gabe and I trusted Lola.

However, questions were still hanging in my head. I wanted to tear them down and throw them all away like dusty old nets at a window. Although I thought I was as alert as I could possibly be, my mind felt fuzzy. Sharp edges had blurred into unclear shapes, as though I was trying really hard to look through a window so covered in ice that I couldn't see anything clearly.

I must have been silent for some time when I realised he was watching me – not just looking at me, but really watching. I had to wonder what emotions my face had betrayed while I'd been trying to make sense of the last couple of days; horror, sadness, maybe even a smile at how silly this would all be if it wasn't so real. I couldn't work out his expression – it was resting somewhere between sadness and compassion.

'I know now that what you say must be true, this strange phenomenon of disappearance; it has to be. These last two days point to nothing else. I just can't... ' As I hesitated, he turned his body towards me and took my hands again.

'I know. You don't need to say it. It's just normal to me now as I've lived with it for so long, but I do understand how you feel. I promise I do. I know how mixed up it all seems and how terrifying it is. I know how scared you are, believe me.'His expression betrayed guilt, as if he felt responsible. 'I do know. I'm so sorry.'

'You don't need to be sorry Gabe. You and Lola have been incredibly kind. I see that this is real, I honestly do. I know that, in a way I can't fathom, Annie has disappeared from her own life. She's just somewhere else at the moment. Her mum and dad haven't any recollection of their own daughter at all, no-one does, and neither should I.'I noticed his grip on my hands tighten slightly, as if to anchor me. 'I have to stop trying to work out why I still remember, because that's not the most important thing here is it? I need to leave that alone and concentrate on getting Annie home.' I was truly decisive for the first time since Saturday and it felt good.

'I agree. I don't know why you're still aware of Annie's presence. Nobody should remember her, no-one at all. When you're lost, you're lost. But to get tied up in working that one out would be to stop concentrating on the real issue. Let's just be grateful you do remember her. At least you'll be looking for *each other*, rather than Annie just working all this out on her own.'

I tried to summarise in a vain attempt to order my thoughts into a plan of action. 'So, one minute Annie's there and the next she's not.' I clicked my fingers. 'Just like that. I'm the only one who remembers her or will be looking for her.' He nodded. 'I'm sorry I keep going over it.'

'It's alright, I understand. But you must find a way to accept what's happened, and then move forward.'

'I know. I will. I mean, I do. Now I just need to find out where she is, and restore her life to her.'

'If you can accept it, that's the first step. And yes, next is to get Annie back. But, Eva, it won't be easy. Please don't think it's that simple. There's no answer to it, no pattern and no common ground. The fact that there's no common reason makes it hard, but if Lola and I can do anything to help...' His voice trailed off, his eyes dropped again and I didn't know what was going on behind them. His eyebrows moved into the slightest of frowns, so fleeting I almost didn't notice, as though he briefly wrestled with a memory of his own.

My mind was chaotic with practical questions; how, where, what next. But suddenly, as though a door had been opened, there was now another issue. There was something else to add to what I was trying to work out but, at which, I was failing dismally.

'Hang on.' My mind raced back to his earlier comment. 'People?' It was ridiculous that this hadn't registered before. If this terrible event, situation, loss – call it what you liked – had happened to Annie, Lola and Gabe, it could happen to others too. And the six siblings, if this folklore was borne from fact, so long ago. How long had this been happening? 'Have there been lots of others? Are there lots more people out there then, who are in some sort of...' I struggled to find the words, '...lost state? Lots more poor frightened souls who've just been forgotten?' Once I started I couldn't stop, the indignation just kept tumbling out, sticking its tongue out at Gabe's privacy and his pain. 'If your family were to see you, would they not recognise you? Why can't they see who you are? How can they just forget? It's mad. No, it's not, it's heartless.'

I'd just started to organise things a tiny little bit, ready to chase Annie, when a flock of other questions had shoved, pushed and fought their way in. Some weren't really questions at all, though, just a way to voice my fury at the people who forgot, at the injustice and the cruelty.

I sighed. No answers came. I could feel tears stabbing fiercely at my eyeballs and I tried very hard not to cry, although I really wanted to. Gabe was watching me again and I suspected that I caught a look of fear in his features – not *of* me, but *for* me – but I didn't know him well enough to be sure.

'It's hard and brutal. But it's the situation that's cruel, Eva, not those who forget.' He sounded saddened. 'They don't choose to, nor do they have any control.' Looking at his crestfallen face, I was immediately guilty. I was ashamed of my outburst, directing my anger unwittingly at his family about whom I knew nothing and who he must love and miss with an ache I couldn't understand.

'I'm so sorry, Gabe, I didn't mean to say that your family were... that they wouldn't...' I stumbled over my words, until Gabe put one hand to my cheek before pulling it away quickly.

'Don't worry, it's alright. I know what you were trying to say.' And all was forgiven.

I thought then of Kathleen and Bob and how they, too, had temporarily fallen under the feet of my hatred. Gabe's family could be as kind and loving as them. This wicked thing was inscrutable and indiscriminate, making strangers of the most loving families and tearing apart the most solid of homes.

Thankfully the tears that had waited in my eyes hadn't materialised and I was pleased that I could save them for when I was on my own. I did need to be on my own for a little while, just alone with no-one else to join my thoughts; no matter how kind and well-meaning they were, no matter how much I needed a hand to hold. Besides, Gabe couldn't see me cry again now despite the closeness that we seemed to have forged in such a short space of time. I didn't want to be the weak, dependent, tearful female any more today.

'I should go. Can I see you tomorrow? Where will you be?' As I uttered it I wished I hadn't. He was lost. He had so few places that he would need to go, and I was sure I'd just highlighted my ignorance to him.

'I'll be at home first thing – morning off.' He shrugged, then smiled ruefully. 'Nowhere else to go. You're not coming back for dinner?'

'No, thank you. I just need a little time – some absorption time.' I offered a weak smile.

'I understand. Tomorrow we start. Alright?' He looked to me for agreement and I nodded. 'I'll tell you all I possibly can think of that may help. We'll make plans.'

Without thinking, I kissed him quickly before I stood up. He rose after me and we left the view of the town and headed back along the lane.

'Gabe, do you think the six siblings just got lost like Annie?' I didn't add 'and Lola, and you.'

'Maybe,' was all he said.

At the end of the lane, Gabe turned towards Lola's and I started in the direction of the town.

After a few steps I turned to look back – Gabe hadn't moved but stood watching me leave.

I sat for a long time under the gnarled and battered old tree. I'd walked to the churchyard of all places. I've never found churchyards frightening, as books and folklore would have you believe. Far more frightening was this strange world that I'd stumbled upon – a place where loved ones could disappear completely and heartbreakingly, with no warning, in most cases leaving you unaware that they'd even been there in the first place. How could such a thing happen? Why would such a thing happen? And I couldn't even begin to question the mechanics of such a deviant event. If a person could just disappear from their own life, the erasure of all their material things was a small issue to come to terms with. Or maybe even, conversely, it was too big a thing to come to terms with and if I tried my head would just implode.

Sitting on the grass next to hundreds of years of history was comforting, reassuring. I hoped that all the people who rested here beneath the earth hadn't been lost; that they'd been tenderly laid here by loving family and friends.

I put together what I knew; it sounded brief and simple. Annie had disappeared and no-one but me knew she existed. It was down to me to bring her home. And I'd met Lola for the first time. And I'd also met Gabe.

Gabe who was gentle and caring.

Gabe who knew what was going on.

Gabe who was lost too. His name repeated in my head. I couldn't tear my thoughts from this man I'd met – he seemed to have secrets, or at least a past so private and painful that it was kept locked away. I didn't even know if he allowed *himself* access to it – the fleeting expressions I caught in his gentle face and behind his frequently sad eyes made me think that memories sometimes caught him unaware. I didn't know whether they were stirred by the newness of my situation or if the memories of his own past just kept visiting him, unable to let him go. I wasn't sure I ever would know. His story seemed closed, and I had to pass that door with acceptance and not try to force entry. If he wanted me there, he'd invite me in. Despite this, I didn't feel that he was hiding anything. Maybe rather than a door, it was just a chapter of a book that he'd closed; just one chapter of his story if there was another life to come. In some way I found his lack of chat about himself reassuring. I hardly knew him but his presence was warm and I was sure that he cared.

My mind was wandering and I mentally shook myself – this was silly. I had to find my friend and restore her to her family and her life. I couldn't get involved in whatever problems or history Gabe had anyway, not now - I had Annie's problems to sort out. The only thing I had time to care about was finding her – anything else could wait. These emotional ups and downs had to stop. I stood up, brushed the grass from my skirt and walked, resolute and renewed, to catch the next bus back home to Fielding.

Explanation

Sleep had taken so long to catch me that night as my mind hurtled from thought to disturbing thought that I didn't feel at all refreshed when I woke. I didn't stir gently, taking a few moments to remember the events of the last few days – they were with me already, with an immediate jolt of awareness and horror. There was no brief reprieve while my senses gathered and remembered as sometimes happens when, in the first moments of wakefulness, you forget what day it is. Everything was sadly too clear.

In a town miles away, someone else was stirring after yet another restless night. When she'd stopped running, she found herself at the bus station. She was glad to find enough money in her purse to catch the first bus leaving the town. When she stepped down at her destination, she took a deep breath. She needed somewhere to stay, some-

where to think, somewhere to call for help and so she walked until she found what she was looking for. The room was cheap and the bed clean.

I lay in bed for a few minutes, processing all that was in my head. I would have liked to curl up under the warm blankets and let the dull, cold-looking April day beyond the window continue without me for a while. Sighing, I hauled myself upright and joined the day – whatever it may bring. Judging by the past few days, anything could happen. Guilt clouded around me for a moment to remind me, that in the eye of my employers, I was dealing with family issues and was also a little unwell. I pushed the thought from my mind as I washed and dressed, telling myself it was more truth than lie.

Walking to Lola's house from my stop gave me time to refresh my senses; the air was cold and the sky a chalky grey, hinting at rain to follow. It made sense for the world to look as if it was about to cry; a sunny cheerful day wouldn't have fitted with my mood. I hugged my coat tighter to insulate me and pulled my hat further down in reaction to the sharp wind which caught me harshly as I turned the corner towards the cottage. I knew that Gabe was taking time away from work to talk, to help, even though he'd told me he had the morning off as though it was the norm. But any guilt I felt at his sacrifice was erased completely by my need for help. I hoped he would have enough time for me and for Annie.

I trod down the familiar green tunnel towards the front door. Soon I was inside by the fire, my hands encircling yet another cup of tea. When Gabe had promised to tell me all that he could that might help me I guessed that, so far, he and Lola had revealed only small pieces of what they knew.

Since meeting Lola in the park, the day that seconds, minutes and hours felt as though they'd been trapped, time had begun moving again only very slowly. Or was it me who was moving slowly? There seemed no urgency in my search for Annie; the urgency appeared only to be in my head. Had Lola and Gabe slowed me, held me back? With all that they'd unveiled, they still gave the impression of being guarded. Could they be unsure of what they were revealing? Maybe their hesitation was with the aim of being gentle, of trying not to bombard me with the true futility of the situation. Did they think that there was no hurry to find Annie, or did they know somehow that I couldn't?

'I'm having trouble with this.' I warned, offering a tiny apologetic smile. 'Annie disappeared three days ago. At least that's when *I* found out. I hadn't seen her or spoken with her for a few days before that, so who knows when she went. I'm glad that I met you Lola, and Gabe; you've been very kind, but since Saturday I've done nothing towards finding Annie. Now I know she's really gone, in the way that you say, and I need to find her.'

Gabe's eyes smiled back patiently as he sat in the chair opposite. 'Eva, I know you're frustrated by the days passing. It's just such a big thing, we wanted to be gentle, open the door to it all carefully, a bit at a time.'

'Alright, I understand that. And thank you. But I can't wait any longer. I have to do something now. If you can't help me, that's fine, honestly—'

'Eva.' Lola, who'd been carefully watching me up until then, cut in, gently stopping me midsentence. 'We will help you, in any way we can.

It's a complicated thing and, always, a painful one. Someone will get hurt. Sadly, we know that you can hide yourself from pain for only so long before it eventually seeks you out. I hope and pray that this time will be different. But we will help you. I'm so sorry you've had cause to doubt that.' Gabe, who had moved to stand next to Lola's chair, moved a little closer to her and gently squeezed her shoulder, his hand remaining there. She raised her hand to pat his without turning to him. 'I'm sorry, I'm just a sentimental, gabbling old woman. Don't take any notice of me.'She smiled. 'I'm overdue for some baking. Why don't you two sit and talk while I'm in the kitchen.'

She stood, smiling at us both, and turned towards the kitchen; but even I could tell after the few days I'd known her, that her smile was a poor mask for the concern lying beneath. A little chink of clarity sparked in my mind and I wondered if her desertion that day I'd met Gabe, and her retreat now, were her armour. I suspected she had her own way of protecting herself just a little from her pain, or the pain she feared may find one of us. I pushed the thought as far away as it would go, assuming in my innocence that the pain to which she referred would be felt if Annie couldn't be found.

Gabe sat down in the spot Lola had vacated.

'I can only tell you what Lola's told me after all her years of knowing and what I've learnt myself as time's passed. There's no instruction book or magic cure. I don't know where Annie is. As you know, these people are lost to their families and themselves. One day they're just lost, with no warning or reason. They leave no trail. They don't know who they are or where they're from.' He spoke about *these people* as if he wasn't one of them. 'Over time, they do usually remember their history but their families don't; well, they don't without considerable help – the families need something to *make* them remember. You can't imagine the range of feelings that come when the lost person discovers the extent of it all. They remember who they are with a relief that's incomparable and they go home with joy in their heart. Then they're left completely desolate, isolated again. The only difference is that this time they're alone amongst their family and friends. It's not just like being physically lost somewhere and being able to ask the way. They have no-one to ask. Help only comes if another lost person happens to recognise their situation and holds out a hand to them – like Lola did to me.'

'It must have seemed like salvation,' I offered.

'It was. Is.' He paused for a moment, and then continued. 'When a lost person goes home, the fear turns to such an enormous relief. Relief that whatever caused their amnesia is gone. Relief that life will be normal again with loved ones falling over themselves to get to them, asking where they've been, arms outstretched and tears of relief coursing down their faces. Then, when no-one knows them and all sight and recollection of them is gone, the fear is back, along with confusion and pain. Worse than anything physical, tangible; it's a pain deep inside. Why does my family not know me? Why do my friends not acknowledge me? They're the darkest moments – like an endless tunnel. When they realise that in the eyes of the world they never existed, most leave the place they know – kind of like trying to lose themselves again. Sometimes they're labelled mad or eccentric, or just the nutty old homeless guy who people turn away from and pretend they haven't seen.' He paused, watching me. 'We have to be realistic, Eva; only a few lucky ones ever find their old life restored to them.'

He stopped again. I wonder if he feared he'd frightened me or been too honest. He was waiting for my reaction. The rain started to fall as we sat there in the warmth of friendship and the fire, the sounds of baking preparation coming from the kitchen. Despite the warm glow of the cottage, the grey day outside the window was like a mirror of the bleak thoughts in my head.

'Go on' I instructed, now feeling the familiar anger in my chest that this should be possible and a determination to put things right, to find an answer for everyone.

'Are you sure?' he asked gently. 'It's such a—' I didn't let him finish.

'Go on. Please. I need to know it all.'

He sighed. 'Sometimes families and friends feel the nudge of a memory, something they can't quite put their finger on. They might think it's the remnant of a dream.'He paused, as if thinking of a way to illustrate this, then asked. 'You know when you feel you've forgotten something or left something behind somewhere or you recall a dream? So vivid it feels real, sitting in the back of your mind all day?' I nodded, remembering my dream about the nurse – so clear it really had seemed real. 'It stays with you, following you for hours, colouring every thought you have that day. Sometimes there's a faceless person in the dream, but it seems perfectly right and natural at the time. Or maybe you see someone in the street and think they look familiar, but you don't know why?' I knew I'd felt these things, a faceless or familiar person, but struggled to recall a particular instance. He continued, 'That's what the families sometimes feel. But it's not always just a dream, not always what they dismiss it as. It's actually the tiny bud of a memory that never grows. What they're feeling is the presence of that lost person, but the bud needs to bloom into a memory, a real knowledge, for their lost one to return to them. Your family could see you but you'd just be a stranger to them; even if one of them felt you looked familiar, they wouldn't know you as you. As I said, when families don't take them back, most lost people move away, sometimes far away. It's much less painful than being close by. Being forced to see familiar places that aren't part of you anymore is bad enough, but seeing friends and loved ones is like having your heart ripped out.'

The unmistakable fact that he spoke from bitter experience could be seen from his face and heard in his voice. He bowed his head momentarily, possibly to cement his composure, and my eyes fell to his neck where lightly suntanned skin met shirt collar. I wanted to move to his side to embrace him, inhale the scent of him and feel the prickle of his hair on my cheek as I kissed his neck and told *him* everything would be alright.

Instead, I gently asked, 'How many lost people might be restored to their families if only someone could remember them? How do we know, when we feel like that, when we think we're remembering a dream, that there isn't someone out there that we've lost?' He looked up at me sadly. 'Have I lost someone else Gabe, someone I don't remember? Do you think there's someone other than Annie? Or have we all got missing family? Missing friends?' I was suddenly talking fast, afraid of what could be possible, the gentleness in my voice replaced by anxiety, my lips stumbling on the words like feet on wet rocks.

I started to panic, couldn't breathe, chest tight, eyes wide, head spinning, breathing shallow, fast, shaking - had I lost someone else? Gabe was with me in an instant, kneeling before me with my hands in his and suddenly aware of how terrified I'd become. I'd worked myself up into a state of wild distress.

'Calm down Eva, please.' One hand stroked my cheek. 'It's okay. I'm here, you're alright.' He called for Lola over his shoulder.

I tried to slow my breathing and grabbed frantically at my thoughts. I took another deep breath, still trying to calm myself. *Concentrate Eva. Annie, just think of Annie.* Gabe's soothing voice joined mine in my ears. 'Eva, please. Just breathe slowly, calm down. It's alright. It'll be alright.' His slow, rhythmic words and warm hands around mine started to relax me more than my own deliberate breathing could. The panic began to subside, slipping away from me and into Gabe's waiting hands.

I looked up to see Lola in the kitchen doorway, swathed in an oversized apron and wringing her hands worriedly over and over in a tea towel. 'Gabe?' was all she asked.

'Lola, could you get some water please? She's alright, just panicked. She needs a moment to calm her thoughts.' Lola turned hastily back to the kitchen and was soon at my side offering me the glass of water, which I sipped to please her as her hand rubbed gentle circles on my back. She moved away and sat back down in the chair she'd left earlier eyeing me with concern and wringing her hands again, only this time in her embroidered cotton apron.

Gabe, still kneeling before me and holding my hands in his, answered the questions I'd panted a few moments before. 'The answers are I don't know, I don't know and I don't know.' He shook his head while not taking his eyes from mine, offering them like a lifeline for me to focus on and cling to.

'Sorry.'I breathed deeply. 'I'm okay. Sorry. Thank you.' Despite my apparent calm, I couldn't stop to order my thoughts properly, needing to know it all, everything, right now. 'You said they need help to remember, the families. So can you do something to help them?'

'Eva, can we stop? Let's just leave it for now. You're upset. It's too much.' He raised my hands towards his lips to kiss them softly. His pleading to halt the explanations was met with nodding from Lola.

'No.' My response was as confident as I could muster. 'Please, go on. I'm fine. I'm alright now, honestly. I can't wait any longer. I need to know it all.' I paused for reaction. 'All of it.'

Gabe sighed, knowing he was beaten, and acquiesced. 'Okay. You asked if it's possible to help a family to remember. Well, the answer's yes and no.' He remained kneeling as he continued. 'I'm sorry to be vague. Lola calls it a *gift* or *bequest*.' Gabe looked at Lola, who nodded again.

This is it, I thought, *this is new – this will answer everything.*

'One touch, but a mental connection not usually a physical one, can pass on a gift. Sometimes the lost have something they can pass on – something which is peculiar to them that can cause a memory to return. The person they emotionally touch takes on that trait or ability, or even desire. They might think they've suddenly found a talent, or a natural flair, or a desire for something, but it's actually a bequest; a gift from someone hoping it will be enough to remind that person of them. It might help a memory to grow or even create that new old memory in the first place. It can be the tool which enables them to return to their family, as if they never left. It doesn't always work, but if there's just the slightest chance, it's a chance worth taking isn't it?' It was a rhetorical question and he carried on. 'Of course, if it doesn't work, that's that avenue closed. There's no control over whether the gift will have any effect.'

Lola stood and touched Gabe's arm lightly as she passed him to return to her baking. He looked out of the window from his crouching position in front of me. 'Let's get some fresh air.'

He stood up and, gently pulling me to my feet, led me out into the garden. I wondered if Lola's withdrawal and Gabe's move to the garden were more in the interest of discretion than baking and fresh air.

The rain had slowed to a very fine sprinkle, but the air felt clean and invigorating after my earlier panic and the rain soaked garden smelt good; it had the wonderful post-rain scent of earth and nature. If the scent that wove its way around the garden and into the air we breathed could have had a colour it would have been the richest green.

I was sure I already knew the answer, but as we stood outside the front door I asked anyway. 'Did Lola make a bequest, give a gift?' Maybe Lola's gentle touch on passing Gabe was an offer of consent and Gabe's subsequent move outside was to spare Lola hearing the discussion to come.

'Yes.'The cold air stroked me and I shivered, instinctively moving closer to the warmth of Gabe's body. 'Apparently Lola's family always said she had green fingers. And she passed that on. If it wasn't so sad, you could almost laugh that anyone ever said that about her.' He smiled as he surveyed the garden. We walked across, or rather through, the damp grass and slowly around the perimeter.

Despite the lack of care or attention lavished on it, the garden was green and lush with lots of colour although this was mostly courtesy of the myriad of weeds that thrived there. It seemed wrong to accuse some of being weeds, interlopers to flowers and shrubs, as they provided such vivid and varied hues. The most abundant plant in Lola's garden was the grape hyacinth, one plant I did know. Small purple-blue grape-like blooms standing proud on bright green stems – true to their name, from a distance they looked just like tiny hyacinths. I knew that they grew easily and quickly, laying claim to the earth swiftly and profusely. I quite like them, proud little flowers flaunting themselves and standing their ground amongst taller and more flamboyant flora, but my aunt always tuts, 'Oh, they grow like weeds those things.'

Gabe noticed me looking at them. 'They mean something to her. I'm not sure exactly what, I don't ask. I just get the feeling that's too personal. But whenever they're flowering, she has a jug of them in her room. She comes out and cuts them very gently, just a few, and then they live in a little white jug on her nightstand.'

I smiled, then, softly, I asked, 'Gabe, Lola's gift, who did she pass it on to?'

He pursed his lips and moved around some dry earth beneath a shrub with the tip of his shoe. He sighed. 'Her brother. Her little brother. And then she didn't even have *that* left. When people are talented at something or even just find joy in it, no matter how good they are, it's an escape. It's like an old friend, or somewhere familiar to go, or something even better than that. To be able to lose yourself in something you delight in is its own gift.'There was an undertone of passion in his voice as he spoke of this wonderful escape, then it was gone and he continued. 'I think, if Lola had still had that safe familiarity, something that helped her to feel a little normal again and keep something of herself, she may have been able to move on. Maybe she'd have found a new family, or even made one of her own. As it was, she had nothing left that she held dear or recognised; nothing of her loved ones or even herself after she gave that away. It was final. The last door closed. She was sad, frightened and alone. And she was like that for years, just in an in-between place.' The rain started to pick up again with renewed fervour and, without discussion, we turned back towards the house.

'So the bequest is passed on then, it's not shared?'

He shook his head in backward acknowledgement of my statement. 'Once it's been given, it's gone. Then there's no interest or desire or ability for it left in that person. You give it away freely, in the hope that the reward it will bring will be greater than its loss.'

'Did Lola ever see her brother again?'

'I don't think so. She moved around for a few years, then ended up here. Her family home is some distance away.' He smiled, but with a now-familiar sadness in his eyes. 'She hasn't spoken of her family for years, Eva. She did tell me her story after we first met, sharing the experience and all that, showing me she understood. She said her brother always used to tease her about her flowers – a boy thing. You know boys, all scraped knees, frogs and conkers. There was quite some brotherly mocking about her garden. She had a little part of the family garden that her parents gave her. I imagine it was quite something – she drew a verbal picture of it for me. She described the colour and the blooms, the abundance and variety. She told me of the hours she would spend there and how she planted seeds in little trays, picked flowers for her mother, watched the insects and discouraged pests. She welcomed the bees and mourned the autumn.

But she couldn't tell me the names of the flowers, however hard she tried. Although she spoke with affection, it was as if she was recalling a long past family holiday or something; once enjoyed, but in the past and over. She seemed in pain as she struggled, but failed, to recall plant names or characteristics. As I watched her pain, I knew I wouldn't ask her to talk about it again.' He sighed. 'She wouldn't get anything to grow properly here and doesn't care to try, has no enthusiasm or interest in it. She did joke that it was her revenge, giving her brother her bequest rather than anyone else – giving him the very thing that he teased her so relentlessly for. But, in reality, I think she gave it to him as he was the most special person in her whole world, and she trusted him of all people to remember.'

'And instead of gardening, Lola started collecting things.' I finished the tale as the rain grew heavier and we sheltered temporarily under the overhanging branches of an unkempt tree. We'd not made it back to the house, becoming caught up in Lola's tale, and I welcomed the necessity of huddling close to each other as the boughs moved in the breeze and we had to stand very close to avoid rain falling on exposed shoulders.

'I suppose. I don't think it was a conscious thing though. She just hates to see lost things. She comes home with all sorts as you've seen.' He glanced back to the house, smiling affectionately. 'Some of it she makes use of.' I was reminded of the different hue and design of her slippers. 'Some of it she passes on. She'll wash clothes and scraps of material and use them, make new things or even donate them.' I pictured her patchwork shopping bag. 'She now says that she's going to unpick everything in the house that's woollen and knit socks for the troops.' Gabe tried to lift the mood. 'I'm not sure how many socks or jumpers I'll have left when she's done.' I smiled but struggled not to think of the red war clouds that were gathering over places and people, ready to unleash a mighty and bloody storm; and so I returned to the gifts, the talents and bequests sacrificed willingly by those who were lost. My aim, too, was to lighten our spirits and move to a subject heartening and reassuring to Gabe.

'And you have your music,' I ventured tentatively, regretting my words even as I said them. Gabe looked uncomfortable and breathed quietly. Immediately, I wanted to take my words back, inhale them so they would remain unsaid; I'd seen Gabe flinch slightly as I spoke and it now felt too personal, and still too raw even, a subject for me to have broached.

He sighed gently again and his voice was soft. 'By the time I knew I could give it, I couldn't get close enough to do it. Then it was too late, and they were lost to me.'I thought that was it, the end of his story and of our conversation. Then he took a deep breath and straightened his back. 'It seems you don't have many years before the memory of you is just too distant for those you've left to recapture. When that time comes it's pointless to continue trying to resurrect it. You may as well turn away and move on in a different direction. Lola found me when the time for me to return to them was already slipping away.'

I noticed his breathing speed up and his mood appear to slide from a resigned sadness to anger. I'd not seen him like this before. His usually tender eyes looked hard and distant and his lips tightened. His hands had balled into fists, but his arms still hung by his sides. 'If I'd been able to get there, close enough, I would have given it, Eva, without a moment's hesitation.' His face clouded over even more, mirroring the sky. Then he took a deep breath and calmed, his features and demeanour visibly relaxing. I reached out my hand to him, but he didn't notice and I quickly pulled it back again.

Now the story of Gabe's music and his feelings towards it started to make sense.

In a few moments alone, while he was fetching logs from the garden store, Lola had watched Gabe go then spoke of him. She'd told me that Gabe's piano was the only thing that seemed to truly bring him peace, if not happiness. Lola had confided to me her belief that the solace she thought her company gave him could only ever be superficial and that his true peace came when he was sitting at the long row of black and white keys. Although, she'd shared, that had not always been the case, as it was months after they'd met that she'd first seen Gabe touch the ivory keys. She thought he may have been angry that he still had his gift, as though it had let him down, and should now be denied or punished. I hadn't understood what she meant until now.

Lola and I had sat at her kitchen table, as usual one of the few places where enough space could be made to sit down, as she'd told me the story.

'Gabe helped me to take some things to the church hall for the summer fete. I was assisting the good and noble ladies of the Women's Institute in setting out a stall.'She smiled conspiratorially. 'I'd found some lovely bits and pieces to donate.' I smiled back and could only imagine what she may have brought forth with a flourish for the ladies of the WI. 'I turned to look for Gabe, who carried my boxes, and he was standing near the piano in the corner of the hall. He was looking at it with both contempt and love, if that's possible. He was half turned away as if that very thing'd called his name as he was leaving and he'd started to turn back in response. I watched as he walked slowly over to it and lifted the lid cautiously from the keys. Eva, he ran his fingers so tenderly across those keys that I just knew he could play even though he didn't touch them hard enough for them to make a sound. It wasn't so much a touch but the gentlest of caresses, like the stroke of a lover. But I watched that caress and I watched his face. Then he saw me.' She looked wistful as she recalled the event, before she looked back at me. 'The lid was replaced and that was that.' She said it abruptly as if to illustrate the moment, then continued as before. 'But still, it was enough for me to know.'

She stopped as Gabe returned with an armful of wood, passing through the kitchen on his way to the sitting room. Lola's face gave away much as she smiled, clearly remembering an event she held very dear. Gabe soon passed us again en route to load up with more logs and kindling. I wanted to know more and was glad when, once more in Gabe's absence, Lola continued.

'I wanted him to play, but I didn't press then. I didn't say a word. The time wasn't right and I felt he would need privacy for it. I could see the effect that piano had on him. Anyway... 'she shifted her position and I waited, intent on hearing the rest of the story '...his room was upstairs then, the small bedroom. The room downstairs wasn't used as such – I just stored things in there, some of my bits and bobs.' She clearly meant more hoards and stacks and piles. I think she must have known what I was thinking, as she added 'I admit that the room was a little... '– a pause – '...busy. To be quite frank,' – a smile – 'no-one would have known that there was actually a piano in there. So I set to work and moved some bits and bobs around. I freed the piano and a stool and I left the door open. I knew he would have seen it but he didn't say a word about it for days. Then one day, at breakfast, he said he knew what I was doing and looked at me like I was a naughty schoolgirl! But then he thanked me. Weeks later, when I came home, I could hear him as I walked along the path. I knew it was him straight away. It was marvellous. He has a talent for the piano, but I don't just hear him play the mechanics of a tune. He *loves* the piano. He lives through it. It's as though it's not just the melody that he wants to coax from the keys, he loves the act of playing if that's the way to put it. Anyway, that first time, I waited outside for as long as my old legs would allow me in case the sound of the front door disturbed him. I wanted him to play and I wanted to listen.'She stopped and I nodded, urging her to go on. 'There was power and strength in the music, but also love and tenderness. The piano was charmed into singing out such beautiful music and it lifted my spirits to know that Gabe had something so special to comfort him and take him away for a while. I was surprised that when I opened the door he didn't stop. But then I understood, when I thought about it some more. He was utterly immersed; and immersed for hours. Every day after that, when he came home from Harry's, he played. Weeks later, when I felt brave enough, I pushed open the door to the room a fraction and watched. I have to admit, Eva, that I shed a tear or two. It was quite beautiful to see.' She smiled at me again. 'I decided that room should be his, in there with the piano. He plays every single day.'She'd laughed then. 'When he's playing, this little old house could burn to the ground and I'm not sure Gabe would even know. I see him sitting there, still playing, surrounded by ashes, charred splinters of wood and scorched red bricks!' Her eyes sparkled. Oh, how she'd laughed at the image in her mind and I'd laughed along too, not realising at the time how accurate the verbal picture she painted had been and what a big part of Gabe that this was.

‘Oh, I’m so sorry,’ I gasped to Gabe suddenly, shocked when I realised that I’d been carried completely away; I’d been taken, not by my own thoughts, but by Lola’s earlier recollections of Gabe and I’d been smiling to myself.

‘It’s fine.’ Gabe smiled and I could see that the cloud which had hovered over him had lifted and been blown away with the storm while I’d been daydreaming. We left our leafy shelter and walked back inside.

In a small room, as the rain tapped a rhythm against the window, a girl sat confused as she stared at her reflection in the mirror. She asked herself why she didn’t know who she was or what had happened. There was a memory of running, a bus journey. She wondered if she was sick – but did she need a doctor or the police? Even though she couldn’t find the answers, she somehow knew that a doctor or a policeman couldn’t help. But she didn’t understand why.

I wanted to ask Gabe what happened when memories returned to loved ones – was it really as if you’d never been away? I supposed it was, as when you were lost it was as though you’d never existed. I didn’t ask because I didn’t want to see his mood blighted again with his own sad memories. Maybe it would have been best if the lost didn't remember their lives either, so they didn't yearn for something they couldn't have.

I didn't ask exactly what happened if you were eventually welcomed home, but I wish I had. I wish for that every single day.

Plans

Now that I had come to an uneasy truce with what had happened, I was able to think a little more clearly. I couldn't spend any more time indulging myself with talking and tears, although I had a feeling the tears would continue to catch me unaware anyway. Days had passed and now it was time to stand back for a moment, do a quick mental stocktake, check my facts and come up with a strategy to put things right.

Despite my resolution that I would wait no longer and action was now urgent, we hadn't made any firm plans at Lola's the previous day – it had turned out to be so emotional and draining that, after returning from the garden, our conversation had naturally evolved and moved to lighter places. I had drawn the subject back to Annie but, once I'd been offered the promise that the next day we'd come up with a search plan, I allowed myself to be carried along by whatever topic presented itself.

Gabe and I had sat in the kitchen, watching Lola bustling about contentedly. She seemed to thrive on Gabe's company and we all chatted easily. I think our emotions must have needed a rest as our talk became gentle and airy. We discussed the weather, our locality, mine and Gabe's jobs, favourite places and foods, likes and dislikes. Lola prepared lunch, not allowing Gabe or me to help, but she did let us clear up after much pressing on our part. She disappeared for one of her naps and Gabe and I continued to chat over the dishes, packing away all the mis-matched lunch things.

As the time wore on, and Lola joined us again, our talk turned to more political issues and Lola's eyes saddened as we talked of the country's young men. Lola, of course, remembered the last war with clarity and voiced her fear for Gabe who reassured her. Such issues and horror seemed far from us, especially with other fears being so close and immediate.

My head was tired; although I was pleased that so much had been explained, my mind was still muddled and full. Despite the fresh wind and the dampness in the air, the outdoors beckoned and I excused myself for a stroll. Gabe said he'd join me and looked a little crestfallen when, with a touch on his hand, I stopped him rising from his seat to join me.

'No, thank you. I won't be long. I'd just like some fresh air and a few minutes to think. I really won't be very long.'

I returned to the sloping field with the magnificent view and pushed open the gate. I walked to the bench and sat down, looking once more across the fields towards the town. The gentle sunshine of my last visit was gone, replaced by silver grey clouds. The previous warm touches of colour that the sun had woven into the trees and houses were replaced by a pale grey wash; the view, although just as beautiful, now had a dreamier feel.

I sat with my hands either side of me on the old bench and became lost myself. Only I was lost in my past, not to my future. The warmest of memories held out their arms and I went to them willingly. I was so immersed in them that nothing else existed – even though my eyes were open, I didn't see the view. I just saw my past. I sensed it and smelled it, feeling its warmth and hearing its voices.

I saw my uncle teaching me to ride a bicycle, laughing as he ran along behind me holding the back of the wobbling machine – the sun shone and I saw our conjoined shadows on the grass. Then I saw his shadow hand lose contact and my cycling shadow leave him behind as he stopped and I cycled on unaided. I heard Annie, Kathleen and Bob clapping their hands and laughter leaving my lips in happy response.

I felt my hands kneading cool pastry as my aunt, smiling, watched Annie and me in the kitchen. We were spending the morning baking bread and cakes for my uncle's birthday. 'Cool palms make better pastry' my aunt advised. I tasted the sweet raspberry jam that we 'tested' for supremacy as we filled jam tarts.

There were warm blankets covering me as Annie and I snuggled together in my bed on Christmas morning. Too early to wake Kathleen and Bob, we waited, giggling conspiratorially, eyeing up the stockings that sat patiently at the end of our beds and guessing at what wondrous delights might nestle within.

Fear bubbled within me as Annie fell. She fell from high up in the apple tree at the edge of the allotments. As she lay on the grass, scratched from the branches and unmoving, I cried and tried to cradle her. I called out for help as two of Uncle Bob's allotment neighbours hurried to our aid. They sent me for Bob and Kathleen and I ran.

My cheeks felt the slapping of the wind and I saw leaves swirling up into a miniature tornado as Annie and I struggled to control our kite in the park, laughing as it whipped and dived in the wind and Uncle Bob called encouragement and instruction.

I felt splashes on my face as an argument over who was to wash and who was to dry the dishes descended into a water fight between Annie and I, culminating in wet faces, a puddled floor, dripping hair and raucous laughter.

My damp eyes were smiling as they once again saw the town and my memories gently set me down again in the present. I realised then that the recollections I had, weaving their way through each day, moulding my character, affecting decisions and choices and giving me my past were now only mine. No-one else shared them anymore, not as I saw them anyway. Annie's presence in them was painted over for everyone else – her role, her part, was blank, brushed away. Their memories were similar, but minus one important person. My past, so completely entwined with Annie's, was changed irrevocably with her disappearance from it. If she didn't return, I couldn't share these memories with anyone again.

Now that I recognised that there would be no help from Annie's parents or friends, I knew I was alone. Even though I still had Aunt Kathleen and Uncle Bob and all my friends and acquaintances in my life, I felt empathy with Annie, Gabe and Lola as I too was isolated and frightened. My thoughts stayed with these newest friends and I suddenly appreciated how much I needed them, something I hadn't consciously acknowledged before. I knew no-one else who could tell me how or where to start looking for Annie, or who would know how I felt.

I knocked on their blue door and waited.

Edie's Story

Lola wasn't verbose. She spoke when she needed to. I supposed it was all those years of solitude; not necessarily physical solitude, but emotional loneliness because she was indeed alone in the world. Despite her frequent silence, and absence, she was warm – just her presence was comforting. The touch of her hand told you not to worry, and her smile reassured you that everything would be alright. She was warm and caring, gentle and grandmotherly.

There was much going on around us – the whispered promise of change wove itself into the bullying threat of war, which nestled unwanted beside all the things I was discovering about these people who were lost to their families, their lives and themselves. The lost lives of all these people somehow eclipsed worldly events and I was drawn into their lives, their loss and their fear.

Despite all this pain and uncertainty, or maybe because of it, I felt safe here in Lola's kitchen surrounded by countless objects she'd collected in eighty or so years. These things were somehow comforting, each with its own tale to tell. The only things missing in this home were photographs. It was obvious now why there were no pictures, but it had taken me some time to register their absence consciously. I'd looked at the empty frames numerous times, but never really *seen* them. Now that I had, the sense of the house being incomplete started to bother me. Each time I saw one of the many frames that were scattered or piled around the house – some even hanging on the walls – I was reminded that Lola's warm and welcoming home had something missing. *She* had something missing. It was a past, a history shared with another (like I'd had, and might lose, with Annie – only for Lola it was magnified a hundredfold) and that made me sad.

Feeling so at home at Lola's in such a short space of time surprised and pleased me. Lola had answered the door and ushered me in and I didn't hesitate to head to the kitchen and put the kettle on to boil as Lola followed me and sat down at the table. She smiled and knowingly asked, 'Did you sort some things out?' I nodded. 'I thought you would. Gabe had to get back to the gardens; he was very sorry to go. He looked a bit lost himself, to tell the truth.' I smiled inwardly at her use of the word lost – she'd used it here in the sense that normal people used it, like you might inadvertently ask *do you see what I mean* when explaining something to a blind person. 'He wanted to come and find you, see that you were alright, but I said to him, *'leave that poor girl alone'*, I said. 'She'll be back when she's ready'. And here you are.' She waved her hand at me with a flourish.

As I found cups and saucers and filled the old teapot, Lola watched me. She looked relaxed and peaceful and I regarded her with the truest and most genuine affection.

'Not long after I met Gabe, we found another poor lost soul. She was a lovely girl, had a real talent for drawing and always had a pencil and paper with her. Always drawing Gabe or me, or the cottage. Her name was Edie.'Surprised at this sudden disclosure I looked up, waiting for her to continue. 'She was twelve and she took to Gabe straight away, adored him like a big brother. And he loved her. She followed him around like a little puppy.' I was surprised by this tale, as though I should have already known. She paused and looked at me. 'He has a little sister.' She stopped then and I sensed she was waiting for me to speak as she stood to bustle about the kitchen, opening a tin and emptying biscuits onto a dainty plate edged with tiny blue forget-me-nots.

'I didn't know. He doesn't really... you know... talk much about himself... or before.'

Lola sat down and pushed the plate towards me. 'No, I suppose he wouldn't. But I think he will. Edie stayed with us and we all took care of each other. We loved her as though she was ours, like she was Gabe's little sister. She was part of our home for almost a year. I hoped that her family would find her but there was a part of me, a very selfish part of me of course, that hoped she wouldn't leave.'

I couldn't imagine Lola being selfish.

'She was happy with us after a while, but I could still see the broken look she had in her lovely brown eyes. I knew how much she longed to go home. We found her family and, thankfully, eventually, her family found her. When they took her back, we were lost.'She sighed and smiled. 'We haven't taken anyone else in since then. We've helped a little, but it's like having a kitten that you don't hold in case they scratch you. We don't get too close and because of that we can be pleased if someone goes home. I'm sure it's different with you because you're not the one who's lost. We couldn't lose someone we love again, not like we lost Edie. Mr McCabe still takes people in though, and that seems to work out for him.' Lola had revealed much in the last few minutes.

'Mr McCabe? Chris McCabe, the teacher?' Now I felt dizzy.

'That's right. He lost his family some time ago – over twenty years back. Became a teacher. And he helps where he can. He's made a new life that suits him very well and he's happy. Miranda and Fletcher Page live with him. They're brother and sister, about your age or Gabe's, I imagine. You might have met Miranda; she works in one of the shops in the town. It's funny, I always forget which one. And Fletcher's a park keeper. Always working, that boy, a good lad.'She leaned forward and lowered her voice conspiratorially. 'I think Miranda is quite keen on our Gabe. Gabe doesn't know it. You know what men are like – walk around with their eyes closed much of the time.' She straightened back up, pursed her lips and raised her eyebrows. 'Mind you, Miranda's not his type.' And then she winked at me.

My mind wandered yet again; I wondered how many people I had met or known who were lost and were just making their way as best they could in their new lives, without those they had known and loved before. Maybe some were content, as Lola said, and had found a way to move on. Maybe some had been lost but were now reunited, with a huge secret hiding in their chest. Then I wondered if it was possible that some had actually been *un*happy before, and maybe this meant they'd been given a new and happier start – I supposed that could happen too, at least I hoped that could happen. And how could Miranda and Fletcher be lost together? Gabe had said that there was no pattern to any of this, so

I supposed that two people being lost with each other was also possible – as was virtually anything else apparently.

And I chose to ignore Lola's comment about Miranda.

I hesitated before asking another question, not sure what she would view as necessary confidences and what might appear as her betrayal of Gabe's secrets, so I tentatively asked 'Can you tell me more about Gabe?'

There was a hesitation that felt like an hour and I wondered if Lola was deciding how much she should tell. She breathed deeply. 'We met in Galton. He was twenty and he'd been lost for some months, but not just physically.'

I had to ask. 'What do you mean?'

'His body *and* his mind were lost. To start with he hadn't known why he was where he was, or who he belonged with. The poor dear boy. By the time we met he'd figured out his past, knew what it was, but he didn't know what had happened to it or what to do with the future. He had no idea where he was going or why. He was living by his luck and not by any judgement or sense, drifting from place to place just like the lost soul he was.'She lowered her voice as if to share a secret observation. 'I think he was drinking too much and living rough much of the time. When we met, I just knew he was lost. He was so relieved to find someone who *did* know their way about this situation. We lost souls do seem to have a knack of finding each other – we're almost like little lost magnets to each other. In your drawer full of bits and pieces –everyone has one – you can bet your life that the magnet and the pins will always find each other. But it's best to keep contact with those who are secure to a minimum, not to get too intimate. It's just easier that way, kinder to everyone, less pain.'

'Secure?'

'People who aren't lost.'

'Oh, right.'

'Gabe soon realised I wasn't a mad old lady and heard the truth in what I said to him.'She was more astute than I'd given her credit for. Maybe she actually knew that she appeared to the world like an eccentric but harmless little old lady, collecting her 'bits and bobs' and mostly keeping herself to herself. I started to wonder whether that mantle of eccentricity was in fact her armour, the thing that allowed her to be left alone. 'Gabe came home with me and got cleaned up. The inside of his head needed as good a clean as his body and his clothes –anyway, I burned *them* when he was in the bath! You should have seen his face when he saw what I was doing! He was so cross.'

She started to laugh and I couldn't help but join in. I pictured a damp, towel-swathed Gabe standing at the kitchen door, watching Lola burning his clothes in the back yard and resembling a Shakespearean witch dancing around a cauldron! 'Oh dear.'

'Oh dear exactly! Anyway, he soon calmed. I fed him proper food and let him rest. He stayed for several days. I told Gabe that he had about three years or so to get home, before the memories were likely to have no hope of being revived. That's the way of it usually. Then he told me it had already been two years. He left me then, the very next day. Was gone for fourteen months, trying so very hard for his family to find him. I'd only known him a few days, but I did miss him very much.'

She looked at me as if waiting to see if I'd worked out the sums, which I had. He'd been lost at about eighteen then met Lola at twenty, five years ago. It was seven years since he'd had a family. The story went on. 'When he came back, my heart broke for him. It took me back to my own childhood. He cried. He wept for his family and I wept for him. I'd missed him – it was nice to look after someone – but part of me was even sadder when he came back, as I knew his chance was gone and I knew the pain that waited for him around every familiar corner. You learn to live with the daily loss; you get used to pushing it away so that it doesn't hold you in an embrace so tight it feels like it will suffocate you, but shakes your hand instead. Then there are days when it's stronger than you are – special days; birthdays and such. You brace yourself for those, hang on tight and wait for it to stop.'She shook herself slightly. 'Anyway, now he looks after me as much as I look after him. There are no tears anymore. We get along just fine... but it's an empty kind of 'fine' sometimes. People like Chris McCabe do very well, but for many it can be a hollow life. There's no meaning, you see, without family.

No goal and no past.' Seeing my sad face looking back at her when she looked up, she smiled and squeezed my hand reassuringly. 'But we've made a little past together of our own. And Gabe is much happier now.'

She'd emphasised the *now* and was watching me, waiting for my reaction it seemed, and it took me a while to realise what she meant. I tried not to blush, but this was pointless; I could feel the unstoppable heat rising from my neck where the warmth threatened to colour my cheeks. She turned away then and I felt an even greater affection for her as she looked in the opposite direction to my embarrassment. Her warmth and possible encouragement made me question myself because I thought she'd previously been warning me away from getting too close to Gabe, the secure and the lost, but now I wasn't so sure.

I was still in a strange place, where all I knew had been completely changed. All that I had always thought normal and right had been thrown up into the air, and dropped back to earth. It was just like the child's game I used to play – with the collection of thin sticks that you drop then have to retrieve delicately, one by one. All you have is a jumbled mass of sticks all touching each other, although you can't be sure of each one's effect on its neighbours until you try to move it. Just like the sticks, my world had been rudely shuffled then thrown back at me. And I didn't know what effect each piece would have on another. Before, I had hoped and prayed I would wake up to find that all this had been a dream. And yet now I was scared and safe at the same time. I felt safe with Lola and Gabe and this was because I trusted them and, I now realised, felt a fast-growing affection for them.

Now, however conflicting, I was guiltily thankful that all this wasn't a dream as I couldn't imagine my life without my new friends in the cottage at the end of Mill Street; the house that Lola called a cottage, the peeling blue door that signalled sanctuary and the jumble of things that whispered 'welcome home'. I asked myself if I felt this way because of the reassurance Lola and Gabe gave me. Would I still feel this way about them if Annie weren't lost and I'd met them when all was normal?

The answer was yes.

'I have to find her, Lola. I can't bear the thought of her out there somewhere, frightened and all on her own. Just like you were, and Gabe, and the people Chris McCabe helps. Where do I start?'

Lola reached across the table and took my hand. 'Where indeed. I've never known someone to be looking for the lost,'came the cryptic response. I hesitated before asking more in case Lola was going to continue, but she just sighed and stood up. Walking to the back door, she turned back to me as she took her apron from a peg and proceeded to put it on. As she tied the strings around her soft maternal frame, she turned back and started gathering ingredients. I watched as she found flour, eggs and a small cube of butter. 'It's not so much a 'where' really, as a 'how'. You could start by visiting each town and village around about, then moving farther afield. But *how* do you look? You can't possibly search every home and business in every town. There would be quite an element of luck to the whole thing, even if you knew where to start.' The protective blanket of optimism I'd cast over the future was slipping off. I could search for a lifetime and not find Annie if she'd not found refuge somewhere known to us both. I had to hope that she remembered enough to come home. I would be the one who would recognise her and she'd fall into my arms with relief that someone still knew who she was.

'A needle in a haystack then? Gabe said we would make plans and you both promised to help me. Are you saying it's useless to try?'

'No dear.'She stopped her baking preparations and the measuring of flour and came to my side, placing a floury hand on my arm. 'No. It's *never* useless to try. I'm just saying that it will be hard to find her and you should be prepared for that.' She moved away again and I looked down to see a floury handprint on my sleeve. 'When Gabe gets home from the gardens we'll decide where you should start. In the meantime, we'll busy ourselves here and time will fly.'

Looking for the Lost

'It's the wrong way around, Lola. I've been trying to put it to one side, but how *can* Eva be looking for Annie, rather than Annie looking for Eva? Should we try to answer this before moving on, or do we let it go?' Gabe was standing by the fireplace with his arm resting on the only spare inch of the mantelpiece not obscured by Lola's collections of strange items. His arm was almost grazing a tiny milk jug and an old clay pipe and I wondered if one would soon be dislodged and end up in a hundred pieces on the hearth.

I was sitting on one side of the fire and Lola on the other. It was a rare event to be in the sitting room, as we mostly roosted in the kitchen, and an experience brought about by a considerable amount of shuffling and re-arranging.

'I've been thinking about this a lot,'she mused, 'and I'm sure now that it's because Eva isn't actually Annie's blood relative or indeed just a friend. Family, friends, acquaintances all forget – what about those who aren't any of these or who are all of these? Eva and Annie are family by heart, just not by biology. Eva's adopted in all but the formalities of paperwork.' She turned to me to sanction her statement. 'Isn't that right?' And she wrapped her deep red shawl tighter around her shoulders.

Gabe noticed this action and stepped forward, crouching down to put some more logs onto the dwindling fire. With his back to us I couldn't see his expression. I shivered as his body blocked the warmth, even though I could hear the crackle as the flames were excited by the new additions and fresh wood fell victim to a multitude of fiery tongues.

When Gabe moved aside, the warm glow returned to the room and I could feel the side of my face that was turned towards the fire warm instantly, almost burning, but pleasantly so. Without thinking, I raised my hand to the other cheek which was still icy cold.

Gabe had moved a pile of papers to the floor and was now perching on the arm of the copiously cushioned, but threadbare, armchair in which Lola sat – he pulled the slipping shawl up over her shoulders once more.

Although he hadn't pursued the matter I felt the need to explain, guilty that I'd obviously had such a candid conversation about my heritage with Lola rather than with Gabe, especially after trying to gently tease his own history out of him. I looked at him. 'Kathleen was my mother's closest friend. She and Bob raised me like a second daughter,' I offered, almost apologetically.

'You don't need to explain…' Gabe began, but I didn't let him finish and continued with my explanation.

'My mother passed away when I was three and my father was killed in an accident not very long after that. I've been really happy – Aunt Kathleen and Uncle Bob always treated me as their own and I've never known any different. I never felt displaced or separate and Annie's like a sister to me. They're my family and always have been as far as I'm concerned. I really don't remember life before them. They're my parents in almost every sense of the word.'Gabe didn't take his eyes from mine as I explained – they were soft and looked pained by my story. 'Kathleen was so close to my mum, she and Bob took me in without hesitation.'

'I'm sorry,' was all he said, but he didn't actually need to say anything as I could read a thousand words in his eyes.

Breaking the subsequent silence, Lola spoke. 'The thing to remember is that Annie actually has someone looking for her. Who really knows, or needs to know, why. Let's just be thankful that she does and she's not alone in this.'She puffed out her cheeks. 'It's unlikely that Annie's still in Rushton, or even Fielding. We need to consider our approach.' As I already knew, most lost people relocated further from home, whether by choice or necessity or confusion. But that was most people and I was still unconvinced that Annie would have gone far.

There remained a little part of me that believed I alone might be able to find Annie and that she would have stayed close by. I didn't see Lola or Gabe over the next two days; instead I returned to all those places I'd already tried. This time, however, I didn't stop there; I also revisited every local place I'd ever been with Annie or that she'd ever talked about. I hung around friends' houses, made surprise visits, dropped in on acquaintances. I adopted a casual, questioning approach which soon became as natural to me as breathing, providing leading questions and prompts and gently nudging people in casual discussion.

No-one mentioned Annie. Some asked after Kathleen and Bob, but there was no following enquiry after Annie which had always been normal and right. Somewhere deep inside me I wasn't surprised.

No-one mentioned Annie, no-one remembered the girl with the large brown eyes, the chestnut hair and easy smile. But she was starting to remember them. Forced to be practical if she wanted shelter and food, she'd stumbled into a market job on a stall that sold fruit and vegetables. As she twisted the corners of a brown paper bag for her first customer, the smell of the earthy produce and freshly harvested fare stopped her in her tracks. She breathed it in again and felt butterflies of excitement and recollection inside. She recalled an allotment and vegetables and a smiling face above earth-covered hands.

I knew that Lola and Gabe wouldn't judge or say 'I told you so'. I imagined they knew that I had to discover for myself that in their words there was wisdom. I had to trust them. I had to put Annie's, and therefore my own, fate completely into their hands; hands that I anticipated would hold themselves out openly with kindness and patience.

Miranda and Fletcher

It had been a week since I'd lost Annie and I couldn't keep talking about taking action, then taking none. I'd even told myself *that* before, and still been unable to take any forward steps. I'd re-visited, searched locally and made phone calls, but I needed to do so much more. I'd talked and questioned until I couldn't any longer.

There was a gentle rapping on my bedroom door, then Mrs Burgess' soft voice spoke.

'Eva, there's a telephone call for you.'I opened the door. 'A lady asking after you.'

'Oh, right, okay. Thank you.' I was surprised as I hurried down the stairs. Aunt Kathleen? No, Mrs Burgess would've said. Annie? No, I wasn't that deluded anymore.

I picked up the receiver in the hallway.

'Hello?'

'Eva dear?' Lola.

'Hello Lola, yes it's me.' Lola gave an audible sigh.

'Oh Eva, thank goodness.' I could hear the relief in her voice. 'Gabe and I have been so worried about you. Are you alright dear?'

Smiling, I replied. 'Yes, I'm fine Lola. Where are you calling from?'

'Ah, I'm at Mr McCabe's using his telephone. Never liked them much, but they serve a purpose.' I smiled again, visualising her holding the receiver with suspicion and a little distaste. 'Look dear, are you free this morning? Would you like to meet me for a cup of tea?'

'That would be lovely Lola, yes please.'

'Well, that's good. Let's see, it's about nine o'clock now I think. Shall we say ten o'clock at Betty's?'

And the date was made. I hurried back upstairs for my bag and shoes and left to catch the next bus to Rushton.

As the bus juddered along, I resolved to be gentle but firm; Lola and Gabe could either help or not, but I would wait no longer. If I had to I'd leave my job and, using my small collection of savings until they ran out, would head further afield in my search. If it came to it, I'd find a way of convincing Kathleen and Bob that the strange tale I had to tell was true.

Unexpectedly, Lola met me as I stepped down from the bus and we strolled arm in arm to the tea shop. Gabe was working until twelve o'clock, she said, so we could be girls together – I smiled at the little nonagenarian 'girl' who walked beside me. So it was indeed true that the body aged much faster than the mind – Lola was probably still a young girl inside.

We settled ourselves at Betty's and ordered our tea.

'Now then.' Lola sounded decisive and I watched her expectantly. 'I've asked Miranda to join us. She should be here soon.'

After learning about Miranda and Fletcher from Lola, she now introduced me to Miranda. It was a little odd that Gabe hadn't talked of her and Fletcher, even in passing. And although I couldn't quite get the reasons straight in my head it almost felt as though he'd intentionally kept them from me, or me from them.

The three of us had a nice, safe chat and made small talk until Miranda had to go. After Miranda bade us farewell, kissing us both on the cheek, Lola leaned towards me and suggested that the more friends one had who could understand us the better – even if you should always take care to 'handle a hedgehog with gloves'. Her use of words made me smile and I assumed she was referring to her previous disclosure about Miranda's apparent romantic leanings towards Gabe. Lola confided that, although Miranda was at heart 'a good girl', her actions may be influenced more by her 'romantic desires' than they should. Whilst she agreed that one could not have too many friends, one should also choose and confide in these wisely. I smiled inwardly at Lola's doubts about Miranda's scruples, but nodded sagely.

Lola confirmed that Miranda knew all about my search for Annie, although I had already assumed this from the subtle hints Miranda had dropped while chatting. Lola pointed out that our *situation* was best discussed privately at home, but that she'd wanted me to meet Miranda, who might aid our search. She explained how it had just worked out that Betty's was a good spot as it was 'close to where Miranda works, wherever that is. I've forgotten the name of the blessed shop again'.

All my resolve to be firm with Lola was washed away on our walk back to the cottage, when she held my arm slightly tighter than needed. There was more weight than there should have been from her arm as it linked though mine and I was keen to get her home. I was relieved to see that Gabe was already there by the time we arrived, coming to the door as we made our way up the path. He must have seen something in our faces and demeanour, as he rushed to us and took Lola's other arm.

'Don't make a fuss Gabe, I'm just tired.'

'Whatever you say, Lola.'He dismissed her reassurance. 'Come on, we need to get you indoors.' Lola tutted, but didn't argue.

Once Lola was resting upstairs, after admonishing us for fussing, I had no hardness left in me with which to speak to Gabe. The moment was gone and yet another day had passed. I was letting Annie down, but my hands and my tongue were tied. I was torn between my concern for Lola, and Gabe's obvious concern for her, and my missing friend.

Once again I felt alone, unable to press Gabe or Lola for help. Help soon came, however, from an unexpected direction.

After meeting Miranda, she seemed to have taken it upon herself to orchestrate the finding of Annie. The two of us, at Miranda's calling, met three times over the next two days, to Gabe's obvious consternation. Miranda made lists and suggestions and had even started making telephone calls on my behalf. Her sudden and complete absorption in my problems surprised but lifted me and I dismissed Lola's cautionary tale as well-meaning but erroneous.

I visited the cottage briefly on Sunday and Monday to check up on Lola and found Gabe there on both occasions fussing around her, as she affectionately berated him. When I said I was meeting Miranda for Sunday lunch, Gabe took me aside and asked me not to pin my hopes on her wisdom or to believe all she said. I caught a draught of frustration in his voice, which confirmed that he didn't like me meeting up with her. He obviously had doubts about her motives and her sincerity, just as Lola did, but I wasn't sure why.

I liked Miranda but couldn't help feeling that, if my world had still been normal, we probably wouldn't have naturally become friends had our paths ever crossed socially. The only thing we had in common were our strange, disconnected situations and our shared acquaintances. I suspected that his friendship with Miranda and her brother was a determinedly casual one on Gabe's part, borne also from shared experience rather than any deeper connection.

Miranda had introduced me to Fletcher on the Monday, as we walked through the larger town park during her lunch break, and I was surprised at the lack of sibling similarity.

Miranda was very confident, and it was clear that she was not only sure of her views and ideas but also of her looks. She was always perfectly presented and had a physical confidence that I'd never have. She didn't have more funds than anyone else in these austere times, but it was apparent that she took much care with her appearance and I imagined she must save hard to buy little indulgences, such as a new lipstick or scarf. There was no denying that she was very pretty; a heart-shaped face framed by long, wavy chestnut hair and large grey eyes protected by the most beautiful lashes I'd ever seen. She was slender and graceful with a poise that came naturally.

Her elder brother, Fletcher, was a gentle man of more reserved appearance and quiet opinion. He was gentlemanly, pleasant and kind. Fletcher was tall like Gabe and of average build and, although nice looking and with the same grey eyes as his sister, had clearly not inherited whatever genes were responsible for her considerable appeal. I liked Fletcher, but couldn't shake off the feeling that he wasn't as keen for me to find Annie as his sister was. I wasn't too bothered by this, as my problem wasn't theirs to resolve; it was therefore lovely, but quite unexpected, for Miranda to be so concerned. For whatever reason, Miranda cared that I should find Annie and wanted her to be restored to her family as soon as possible. I was grateful for that. With the mountain that I needed to climb, any helping hand to pull me a few steps higher and closer to the peak was welcome.

Miranda only briefly touched on her history when I gently enquired, preferring to talk of my search for Annie rather than her own story. She told me she liked to paint and Fletcher liked to take photographs, and that he was 'sometimes wet, but I do love him'. She did reveal that she and her brother had been alone for over ten years, but she didn't think of them as being alone as this was their life now, stating 'we've been without our family longer than we were with them', and they had people like Chris McCabe and Lola and Gabe as their friends. She soon shook off the subject and returned to me. 'Anyway *you're* not lost, you're here to find someone and I want to help.'

On the Monday, nine days after I lost Annie, Lola (who thankfully appeared much recovered) invited Miranda and Fletcher for tea. Miranda had seemed delighted at the invitation when she'd told me about it at lunch. I realised that this invite was a rare one, the siblings being acquaintances of Lola and Gabe more than friends despite Miranda's claim, but they had happily accepted and the evening soon came.

We all shared a nice meal together and talked politely, edging around the subject closest to my heart. Every time it appeared that we were getting close to it, Gabe steered the conversation skilfully away in a new direction. My frustration was growing by the minute and I was sure that my disdain must be apparent to all. I was becoming more cross with Gabe with each passing second.

However, Gabe's conversational skill was no match for Miranda's determination to reach her own goal. She wanted to help me find Annie and she was clearly tired of waiting to discuss it. Brushing aside all other conversation, she announced: 'This dilly-dallying has to stop, Gabe.'He looked up, surprised. Then she turned to me. 'You must go to see Randall Boyes.' Her focus turned to Gabe again. 'Mustn't she, Gabe? That'll be the quickest way to find Annie.' Miranda's demeanour reminded me of an animal, darting eyes full of focus with a definite prey in sight. Gabe's look of surprise moved to annoyance, but he nodded.

'Well, yes, we could try. But I'm not sure he'll want to help.' He hesitated as though as he was going to continue but then said nothing more.

We were all seated in Lola's living room, having cleared ourselves some spaces to sit. It was early evening and our elderly host had already excused herself and headed off to bed. Gabe's features had betrayed concern as she left and he'd followed her to the door, offering to help her up the stairs. Lola, smiling, playfully reprimanded him for treating her like an old lady and she winked at me behind his back. However, she didn't fool anyone and we could all see how stiff and unyielding her dear old legs were as she left the room.

'You must try.' Miranda almost ordered Gabe. She turned her attention to her brother. 'Fletcher, you'll take Eva won't you?' Fletcher, resembling a startled animal about to take flight from Miranda's confident and nimble one, didn't have time to respond as Gabe cut in. A momentary glance and Fletcher's eyes told me his answer wouldn't have been a yes.

'No.' The sudden force of Gabe's reaction surprised me and, I think, Miranda and Fletcher too. His eyes flashed. 'I'll take her.' I felt like a little girl listening in on the adults' conversation at a party from a secret listening place on the stairs, and not understanding a word of it.

'Um… excuse me. Can someone tell me who Randolph Boyes is?' All three faces turned to me with surprised expressions, as though they'd forgotten my presence.

'Sorry,' Fletcher offered. '*Randall* Boyes,' he gently corrected, 'holds the stories, if you like, of all us lost souls.' He almost said the last two words with contempt. Then he softened. 'But I think you should exercise caution. You might find out more than you bargained for…'

'Fletcher, don't,' Miranda interrupted quickly. 'Mr Boyes is Eva's best bet. Don't scandal monger.'

I tried not to smile at the accusation she'd thrown at her brother. Given all the things I'd discovered in the last few days, I didn't think that anything could cause me more concern than the situation I was already in. This feeling gave me a sensation of déjà vu – my 'situation' somehow had the ability to be rendered more complex on a regular basis, just on the strength of a few words offering half exposed information. I'd been here before, tensing every fibre, waiting for a bomb to drop.

'It's high time we sorted out this mess, and got things back to normal. Annie needs to be found, so that she and Eva can get on with their lives as before.' I was caught by the passion in Miranda's voice, and reminded how she'd taken my cause to heart. Maybe she wanted to put right for someone else what she hadn't been able to do for herself and her brother.

I'm sure the surprise was visible on my face; it was wiped away by disbelief when I looked at Gabe and caught his fleeting glance at Miranda – a glance which could only be described as contemptuous.

The turbulence in my poor head welcomed more reasons to twist and turn. Gabe's scathing look at Miranda and my new knowledge of this Mr Boyes aided my cerebral hurricane. And, if Mr Boyes had so many answers, I wondered why his name had only just been given to me.

While lost in my thoughts, Gabe had moved to my side. He laid his hand on mine and, for a split second, I saw Fletcher's eyes dart to our touching hands. 'Fletcher's right – I'm not sure Randall is the answer. But we will go and see him.' He looked pointedly at the siblings and added, 'Eva and I.'

I wondered what I might have missed during my few moments of recollection. It seemed almost territorial, the way Gabe had moved and spoken, but I quickly dispelled such absurd thoughts and replaced them with a fresh optimism that Randall Boyes was the man who had some answers.

At last – at long last – Annie was getting closer.

The Bookkeeper

Randall Boyes was a strange looking man. Although I've never been good at judging people's ages, I guessed he must be about fifty. There were round, wire rimmed spectacles perching on his long nose and his wild hair was reminiscent of Albert Einstein, although Randall's was mousy brown with only the merest frosting of white. His checked shirt was buttoned to the neck and partly covered by a threadbare brown wool cardigan. The ensemble continued down to light grey corduroy trousers and dark brown shoes that didn't look as though they'd seen polish for some considerable time.

I felt very uneasy that Gabe hadn't been the one to suggest this visit and, on the way to our appointment with Mr Boyes, I had to ask him why. It bothered me that he'd not added this particular avenue to our search map and I voiced these concerns to him.

'I'm sorry. I just didn't think of it. I guess my head didn't think it was an option. Randall has never, as far as I know, been approached for such a task. Before you, I'd not known of anyone searching for someone who was lost. You know, lost in the way that I'm lost and Lola and Annie and all the others. It was only ever the lost themselves who searched out their families, not their families searching for *them*. Randall hadn't even entered my head as a possibility.' He looked at me guiltily. 'Miranda's seeing things from a different perspective I guess. She's very... strong willed. I'm sorry it wasn't me who thought of it. And I'm really surprised that we're getting to see him. He's a stickler for rules and convention and isn't known for being particularly, ah... cheery.' A warm feeling of relief enrobed me and I knew he was telling the truth. 'Just don't get your hopes up.' He smiled carefully. 'Please.'

We followed Mr Boyes down a long corridor which sprouted doors on both sides, all closed. We didn't stop until the corridor did and Mr Boyes beckoned Gabe to him with one inviting motion of his hand. I knew the invitation didn't extend to me, so I stood still as Gabe followed. Gabe and Mr Boyes moved a short distance away, but it was far enough that I couldn't hear all they were saying. Mr Boyes spoke in quiet tones but I thought I could pick out the words *discretion, confidential, shock, revelation.* I couldn't decipher any of Gabe's words, although I tried hard to. Whatever we were doing here, it was clear that Gabe saw it as important but that Mr Boyes viewed the whole exercise with trepidation, and possibly some fear.

We'd travelled some way to Little Stanton, changing buses twice, before I finally found myself in a nondescript building. It could have been a large house, but when we entered it became apparent that it was more of an office or library. Randall Boyes had been there to greet us, but there was no smile or welcoming hand, outstretched and warm. He'd met us with a serious, almost begrudging demeanour and a curt, 'We'd better get on with it then,' before turning, after which we'd followed him into the depths of the building from which I wasn't sure I'd find my way back if unescorted, such was the maze of corridors and rooms.

I waited while they talked. They turned back and walked towards me, with Gabe taking my hand as soon as he was by my side again. Mr Boyes unlocked and opened the door nearest to us and we followed him inside silently. The room was musty, like an old museum, and the colours inside were muted and dark. There were no windows and the only lighting was from numerous table lamps, being switched on one by one by Mr Boyes, dotted around the many desks.

As my eyes adjusted to the dim lighting, I looked up to see shelf after shelf and row upon row of books reaching up to the high ceiling. There were hundreds, possibly thousands, of books. I scanned them quickly; they ranged from ancient-looking dusty tomes, heavy with their gnarled leather bindings, to books that seemed newer, thinner, lighter in colour and more delicate. The newer volumes were lower down and within easier reach; those higher up could, it seemed, only be disturbed by an old wheeled library staircase which ran around the perimeter of the room, tethered to the shelves by a brass rail. From what I could see there didn't appear to be titles on the books, just numbers or possibly dates...

'What are all those books for exactly?' I leaned in to Gabe as I whispered, so that Mr Boyes might not hear. Gabe opened his mouth to speak, but it was Mr Boyes' voice that I heard.

'Those, my girl, are the books of the lost'. I must have frowned or revealed an expression that gave away my confusion, as Gabe felt the need to explain further.

'Each book up there covers a period of years. And each contains details of those lost during that time, a record. That's why Mr Boyes is a bookkeeper, not a librarian. The books aren't here to be borrowed. It's not a library, it's an archive. But it's an active archive as the more recent books show those *currently* lost, so we know Mr Boyes as the bookkeeper.' Mr Boyes coughed, then Gabe added 'Or curator.'

'So Annie's in one of them?' I croaked, but I knew the answer already. I could hardly force the words from my lips, they seemed to stick in my throat as the magnitude of it hit me. There were so many books, indicating that countless people had been, or were, lost. All these people. So many years and lost lives, broken families and broken hearts. My eyes filled and I tried very hard not to blink as I knew that would force the tears down my cheeks. They started to fall silently despite my effort to contain them and I tried to wipe them away without Gabe seeing. Gabe took hold of my damp hand and kissed it tenderly.

'Don't cry. Please, don't cry. I should have thought of this days ago; I'm sorry.'He whispered his words, and I knew that this time the bookkeeper hadn't heard, as he'd already turned away and was leafing through a hefty book on the desk farthest from us. 'This will help us find Annie,' Gabe whispered again.

Us. He'd said 'us' so naturally and so easily. It wasn't my search alone anymore, but ours together and I smiled through the damp streaks on my face.

Mr Boyes was now lifting one of the newer books from a shelf. I shook myself from my thoughts and returned mentally to the library-which-wasn't.

Straight to the point, Mr Boyes was walking to us opening the book. 'Here it is. Annie Carter.'He offered the book to Gabe, not me. I moved closer to him and tried to peer at the open page. Before I could, the bookkeeper snapped the hefty tome shut again. He looked at Gabe. 'She mustn't... as I said.' He lowered his voice, cupped Gabe's elbow with his hand and turned him away from me. 'There will be others' – I didn't like the way he stressed the word *will* – 'that she doesn't know were, are, lost. I don't know what would happen if she saw those pages and those names. You know we've never had anyone here, in this room, who wasn't lost themselves.'Gabe nodded. 'The natural way of things could be overturned and I really think...'

I saw Gabe touch the older man's shoulder to reassure him. It amazed me that anyone could think this disturbing and almost imaginary world, where people disappeared but could be found in some absurd, almost fairytale, book room could be natural.

'Caution, my boy,'Mr Boyes' summarised. 'Caution.'

In his half whisper he clearly thought I couldn't hear, but I heard every word. I wasn't upset or offended, I wasn't even curious. I'd learnt enough in these last eleven days to know that I really did not want to see what was in that book.

At Betty's

Gabe smiled at the waitress as she came to our table. 'Tea for two, please.'

As she turned and walked away, I couldn't help but giggle. Gabe tilted his head and frowned, a smile hovering on his lips in the spirit of camaraderie, even though he didn't know what I'd found so funny. 'Tea for two, and two for tea?' I explained my mirth.

'Oh, I see.' He laughed quietly as his head lilted from side to side and he mouthed a few words from the recent song without any sound leaving his lips.

'Sorry, I think it's the relief of being able to find Annie. It's making me act a bit giddy.'

His smile was lost and he quickly grabbed my hand across the small table. 'Hang on Eva. Don't get excited, we *haven't* found her. And even when we do, there's still the matter of bringing her home. We have to find a way to get her parents back.'

'Yes, but you said when, not if.' I smiled, as if winning a point, and tangled my fingers in his.

'Okay.' Resigned, he grinned, allowing me my brief, victorious moment.

I like Betty's and it felt right to come here in our small celebration of triumph. I always feel relaxed in the warm and welcoming little tea shop. It's been here as long as I can remember and has been a favourite haunt of mine ever since I was old enough to have one. Sometimes Annie and I would find ourselves here, sometimes I'd come in alone or with Aunt Kathleen; on a few occasions I'd popped in to buy treats to take to Annie's or as a surprise for Mr and Mrs Burgess when a special occasion, or even just a special treat, beckoned. There is always a little bunch of fresh flowers on each table and there are pretty curtains at the window bridged by a thin cotton curtain on the bottom half; thick enough for privacy, yet transparent enough to indulge in some people watching if you're sitting at one of the two tables that hug the window. It was at one of these tables that we were ensconced, but I had no time or inclination to look away from Gabe or to consider anyone but him, Annie or our plans to find her.

'Can you tell me all that was written about Annie in the book?' The waitress returned with a tray and silently placed a pot of tea and cups and saucers on the table. Gabe paused while she did so and I watched her put the items in front of us. It was a novelty, given my recent dining habits, to drink from matching cups and saucers and I smiled, thinking of Lola's pre-loved and odd homewares. I preferred Lola's.

'Thank you.' He watched her leave then turned to me 'She's in Exley. We'll have to go to Exley.' Gabe absentmindedly played with my fingers as he watched my face for a reaction. Exley was a good eighty miles away. 'The book really just has places and dates, not much else.' I wasn't sure whether this was true or not, but the books frightened me with their lost worlds, lives and loves.

'How does Mr Boyes get the books and how do you know to trust what's in them?'

'That's yet another question I don't have the answer to, Eva. It's one of the many things we just accept; the books are there and we assume they always have been. I don't know how they get there. Randall is the latest in a long line of curators. I don't know any more. Just like I don't know how the lost are singled out to be lost, why some people and not others. I don't know how all record or sight of them disappears, just to reappear if they're found. There are more questions than answers. We all know so little. I don't know whether anyone will ever find all the answers or where those answers are; maybe they're lost too. The one thing I do know about those books, though, is that Annie's isn't closed. If the entry's underlined, then that's the end of the story.' He paused to let me catch up. 'Annie's story hasn't ended yet.'

Enough.

'When can we go to Exley? Can we leave now?' I stopped, thoughts racing furiously in my head. 'We'll be gone more than one day. I wonder if I should ask Miranda to come. What will people think otherwise? You and I, I mean. We couldn't go, just the two of us.' My hand lightly pulled away from his and I scraped my chair backwards a little, getting ready to stand, but at my hand's withdrawal his fingers tightened round mine and I was forced to remain seated. Gabe's lips curved into a rueful little smile and brought me back to reality. I was reminded for a second of the day we met, when I'd tried to leave and Gabe's eyes had begged me to stay. I gave in to them again.

I was keen to get going, yet I knew it wasn't going to be as easy as just catching the train, meeting Annie, then bringing her home. Life was different now.

'Slow down. We'll start tomorrow,' he soothed. 'It's getting late now and *we'll* need somewhere to stay when we get there.' He emphasised the *we'll*, as if to discard my suggestion that anyone should be going except he and I or that anyone could catch even a whiff of impropriety. 'We're not just going to walk into her the moment we step off the train. It'll take time. We need to pack, sort things out at work. And I need to speak with Lola, make sure she'll be alright for a few days.' Then he added, 'And *we will* be going on our own.'

I hadn't noticed until he'd spoken that the sky was dimming and the signs of early evening were showing. I was glad one of us was thinking straight and was silent as he began pouring the tea.

'Why do people always think a cup of tea makes things better?' he asked, as he carried out his task. 'When someone dies, when there's an accident, a person loses their job, when a baby's being born.' He paused. 'Or even when war breaks out.'He looked at me. 'We all stop for a cup of tea.' It was the first time Gabe had offered much to me in the way of traditional small talk, or his views on normal life without the conversation already being there. Another breakthrough. Then he continued. 'I will go; if I'm called up to fight I mean. I would join before being called, if I had to. If there was no reason to stay.' I was surprised at the change of direction in our conversation, but wasn't worried by his statement – it was the patriotic and right thing to do. His words held no real concern for me as everyone was confident the war would be over in a matter of months this time, with minimal disruption to our lives. But his comment about having a reason to stay was odd, then suddenly warming as I realised he might be talking about me.

‘I would be very proud of you. But I don’t think you’ll need to go,’ I confirmed genuinely, believing every word I spoke as I took his hand.

‘Don’t be so sure. If there was nothing to keep me here… ‘He stopped talking and pushed my cup towards me. ‘Anyway… cheers.’ He smiled lifting his cup in a toast.

‘Cheers.‘I smiled, doing the same, then taking a sip. I nodded, thinking that tea was nice but a long soak in a bath was much better. ‘I feel better already.’ At my slightly sarcastic comment, he tilted his head and smiled – it was the warmest and most beautiful smile I’d ever been offered and I could have revelled in it forever. For a brief moment, I hadn’t a care in the world.

Finding Annie

Sleep felt like it would be difficult, so I packed instead of trying to go to sleep. That task done, I sat on the end of my bed feeling restless. Eventually I went to bed; sleep took a long time to find me but it finally caught up.

Restless slumber made my mind shuffle through thoughts that had temporarily lain dormant just waiting for such an opportunity and keen to show themselves again. I saw Miranda and Fletcher, although they were just small children. And there were others too, and trees. The view over the fields to the town flashed by, along with six trees numbered in big black letters and lying on the field. Then the trees were logs and the logs were burning as Gabe, Lola and I sat around the fire. The numbers on the wood fell prey to the blaze; one, two, three, four, five, six. The piles of Lola's collections were so high that the three of us had to either stand up to see each other or peer through small gaps in the teetering towers of lost belongings. An owl, or maybe a hawk, with Randall Boyes' face sat on top of a pile of books, leafing through them one by one and looking at no-one.

Glad to welcome the new day and leave my strange dreams behind, I rose early. I left a note for Mrs Burgess with some white lie as to my whereabouts outlined briefly – visiting a friend, short notice, may be gone a few days, not to worry.

Leaving the bus stop in Rushton and walking through the town, I was preoccupied with thoughts of the trip ahead. I was so deep within them that I didn't see Aunt Kathleen until I was so close I could have bumped into her. Thankfully, she was turned away from me, delving into her shopping bag. I quickly dodged out of sight into the closest shop doorway as she turned and walked towards me, where I leaned against the slightly recessed shop door and held my breath trying to mould myself into the wood and glass. I felt a nervous sort of fear at the thought of my discovery, and a guilt that I should be hiding from the person who'd raised me. I closed my eyes, like a child believing that not seeing means not being seen. Peeping through my lashes as Kathleen passed by, I saw that she was intent on heading towards whatever chore was next on her mental list of jobs to do. A sigh of relief escaped my lips and my body relaxed against the door.

Suddenly I took an unexpected step backwards as the door that supported me opened with a jingle of its bell.

'You'll be found out you know,' the smiling voice behind me said.

'Oh, Miranda.' I turned to see her standing just inside the door, her fingers wound around the handle.

'I thought it was you. Are you hiding from a jilted suitor, or do you owe money?' she asked flippantly, as she took my arm and guided me into the shop. At first I didn't hear the jesting note in her voice.

'Oh no, I... 'Flustered to be discovered, I was lost for words for a moment. 'I confess I was dodging my aunt. I just couldn't... you know... it's difficult.'

Her smile was lost and she appeared immediately contrite. 'I'm sorry, I shouldn't have joked. I'm sorry Eva.'

'It's fine, honestly,' I offered genuinely.

'Where are you off to then?' She eyed my bag and I caught the momentary rise of a perfectly-arched eyebrow. Oh no, what to say? Gabe wanted us to leave town without Miranda and Fletcher knowing. It didn't worry me if they knew our plan, but it seemed to bother Gabe so I hesitated. Subterfuge, however, has never been my forte and I was unable to summon a feasible excuse at such short notice.

'We're going to look for Annie.'

'We?'

'Gabe and I.'

'So Randall was a help then? I'm glad. I did call round twice to see how it had gone, but no-one was home. I stopped by at Harry Stanley's too, but no sign of Gabe. Anyone would think he and Lola were avoiding me.'She smiled, unaware, or possibly not, that her words may be more truth than jest. 'The sooner you find Annie the better. Is she far? Did Randall give you what you needed? Would you like me to come? I'm sure I can get some time off.' She glanced towards the back of the shop and I was worried she was going to ask her boss's permission there and then.

'That's really kind Miranda, thank you. But we'll be fine. It would be a great weight off Gabe's mind to know you're here if Lola needs anything.' So, the odd white lie wasn't so difficult to come across after all. The air was lost from Miranda's sails and her shoulders appeared to drop a little, before she smiled.

'Of course. Good thinking. Well, I wish you luck. Where are you going? Just in case I need Gabe, in case we need Gabe,' she quickly corrected as she probed again.

'Exley.' No point lying now.

'Oh, right. How long will you be gone?'

'I'm not sure, not long I hope.'

'You'll let us know where you're staying?'

'Yes, of course.' I wasn't too sure of the plan, but I was more than happy to provide reassurance as a means to escape. Miranda took hold of my hand.

'It's really important that you find her, Eva. Don't give up. If you want my help, just let me know. Alright?'

'Thank you Miranda, that's very kind. I will, of course. Thank you for the refuge, but I'd better be off.'

'Of course, go, go.'She shooed me out of the shop then and, on the doorstep, gave me a kiss and a very tight hug. As I walked away from her, I turned to smile. 'Please find her,' she called. Although Miranda could be a little overpowering, knowing that she cared was a nice feeling and it was good to have gained her as a friend.

Despite my brief sojourn with Miranda, I was still at the little red brick house much earlier than I needed to be. As soon as I was inside the front door, details of my conversation with Miranda spewed forth and I apologised repeatedly.

'It's alright.,'Gabe reassured me. 'It's not your fault. I just didn't want her getting involved or, worse still, inviting herself along. She'd complicate and confuse things, and take over. I hope she doesn't go running off to tell Fletcher, but I don't suppose she will. He doesn't share her opinions, so I'm guessing she'll see the news of our trip as being on a need-to-know basis.'

'Because he thinks we should leave things alone?'

'Yes. Look, can we not talk about it? It's just Fletcher's superstition, let him deal with that.'

Conversation closed.

Gabe had spoken with Lola at length the night before and as we outlined our plan of action again that morning she listened, nodding, having agreed wholeheartedly that we should both go in search of Annie straight away. She emphasised the *both* in her endorsement, then surprised me with her worldliness when she made some suggestions of places to stay.

I realised I'd been picturing her as always being in and around Rushton, thinking she'd not ventured much further than this town she'd called home for so long, and forgetting she'd been born elsewhere. It gave me a little jolt and reminded me how much I didn't know about her and how much I wanted to know. I was looking forward to a time when life was restored to normal and we'd be able to sit and talk about all these things, getting to know each other better. I already felt that I knew her quite well but there were such big holes in her past which, with her permission, I wanted to learn about. I knew the person she was now, but hoped she'd reveal the journeys which had shaped her into the Lola I was growing fonder of day by day.

As Gabe retreated to his room to collect his bag for our trip, Lola patted the seat next to her in invitation. It was unusually clear of any hindrances to my settling so I sat down and she turned towards me and placed both of her hands side by side on my forearm, smiling.

'Now Eva, do what you need to do and don't hurry back on my account. Bring Annie home where she belongs and take as long as you need to do it. I know Gabe worries about me, but please try not to let him. He fusses about and doesn't need to. Concentrate on the job you have to do; let Gabe share the weight that you have on your shoulders. He wants to look after you.' She leaned towards me and lowered her voice. 'I see happiness in Gabe and a new contentment, deep down. His smile isn't just on his lips anymore, it's in his eyes too.' Then she whispered as she took my hand and placed it over her heart, 'And I think he's smiling inside.'

I was stunned by her candid approach and the observations she thought she'd made and obviously believed. She clearly noticed through my eyes that my thoughts had wandered away from her words, as she squeezed my arm gently to gain my attention once more. 'I can't wait to hear all about your adventure. It's such a long time since I travelled. Look after each other, won't you?' She glanced towards the door as if expecting Gabe to return.

For some reason all her apparent reserve about contact between Gabe and me, and her comments about the lost and the secure, were crushed and forgotten. Before, she'd urged caution and hinted at the pain that would be caused by mixing our two worlds. But now, she was openly encouraging our friendship, even nurturing a romance.

All her words started to sound more like a final goodbye than an expression of good luck for our quest, but all I could think of in surprised reply to her instruction to take care of each other was, 'Yes, of course'. Then I could say no more as she squeezed my arm again and I turned to see that Gabe was back and carrying a small leather bag, the unfastened strap hanging down as if forgotten in haste.

I kissed Lola's cool powdery cheek and retreated to the hall so Gabe could say goodbye too. I tried not to intrude but couldn't help turning my head towards them as I waited, seeing Gabe kneeling in front of Lola and she quietly speaking with him as he nodded several times, her old hands cupping his chin like a mother soothing a child. As he rose I turned away guiltily, wondering if this was the first time they'd parted since their long separation just after they'd met; when Gabe had left alone in the hope of recovering his family and returned to Lola who then filled that void. I hoped this parting didn't resurrect more pain for him.

Gabe stopped next to me to pick up the small case I'd brought and, with both bag and case in one strong hand, he opened the front door and stood back for me to leave first. The air was mild and the sky clear as we headed down the leafy path towards the gate, the town, the train and, I prayed, Annie.

I couldn't find any words which felt right for the situation as we waited for our train, then boarded, found seats and sat down. Lighthearted banter seemed superficial and I couldn't shake off a feeling that we were being naughty, playing truant like schoolchildren. There was small deceit involved in arranging my absence, but I tried to convince myself that my dishonesty with Mr. Grayson was justified. I didn't know what Gabe had needed to orchestrate in order to be here, but I didn't want to be party to any more deception so I didn't ask.

Eventually I broke the silence. 'It really would be nice to know how Mr Boyes gets all those books.' Gabe looked away from the window and turned his gaze to me as he straightened in his seat.

'Yes, it would. He doesn't give anything away, as you saw when you met him. Lola says that there are things that just *are*, like love and trust. There are things that have no explanation, and we shouldn't try. I've only met Randall once before and I would never ask him. I don't think there'd be any point. You see how closed he is.'

'Is he lost?' Gabe nodded. I started to feel my indifference, and slight disdain, towards Mr Boyes evolve into tentative sympathy. 'But who writes the books?' Gabe shrugged. 'And I don't understand where every sight and sound, every belonging, goes Gabe. How on earth does that happen?' Gabe shrugged again.

'I'm sorry Eva, I told you before, I don't know. I really don't. I'm not keeping anything from you. I honestly don't know these answers. It's another of those things that none of us understand. It just... is.'

I wasn't getting anywhere and we fell back into silence.

As the train pulled into Exley station, after a mostly silent journey spent watching the fields and towns rush namelessly past the window, Gabe rose and collected our bags from the overhead rack. We stepped down into the crowds of people milling around and I noted numerous uniformed young men, far reaching events being much more apparent here than in our secluded little home. Gabe took my elbow as I stood there, quite conceivably looking like someone on their first city outing, and guided me through the throngs and out onto the street.

It was late morning and Gabe suggested we find somewhere to stay before doing anything else. Lola had provided a list of names; guest houses and small hotels that she hoped were still in business – I hadn't a clue how she should know, but supposed that nothing should come as a shock anymore. Gabe was keen to find a telephone when our lodgings were established. Lola had no telephone, so he'd arranged to call Chris McCabe who had promised to visit Lola and let her know that the searching pair were safe and sound.

The first name on the list of prospective lodgings was the Sea Trout Inn; the name gave the impression of a public house, but it turned out that it had ceased to be such a long time before and was now purely a guest house. We entered what I assumed was once the bar but which now housed neatly dressed tables, complete with little vases of flowers, each encircled by three or four chairs. At the rear of the room was a desk on which sat a small bell next to a closed ledger, titled 'Guests'.

I wondered when Lola had been here, or whether she'd heard of this place from someone else. I questioned if her name was on a page in the book, turned over long ago, the visitors forgotten. And I pictured Lola as a young woman, sitting at one of the tables.

Gabe rang the bell, bouncing me back to the present, and a few moments later a middle-aged gentleman appeared through the door just behind the desk. He smiled as he saw us, asking how he could help.

Gabe asked for a room and I felt the warmth of blood rise to my cheeks, sure that this heated glow would be immediately obvious to both him and the man behind the desk. *A* room, he'd said, not *two* rooms. He booked us in as Mr and Mrs Adams. At these four words, I instinctively slid my left hand into my coat pocket. I'd seen this in films. Did people really do this? What on earth was he doing? And what was *I* doing? Although I trusted Gabe completely, I couldn't help but feel a little confused.

The man bent to take our bags, but Gabe said it was no bother, he'd carry them. We were shown to our room from a door in the far left corner. This immediately took us up a flight of stairs and we were shown along a short corridor to the second door on the right. After unlocking and opening the door for us the man was gone. I entered the room first and Gabe followed, closing the door with his foot then depositing both bags on the floor at the foot of the bed. I moved to the window, which overlooked the front entrance of the guest house and the street beyond, and then I turned to survey the room properly.

Small but welcoming; there was delicate floral wallpaper and a pretty chair with a hand embroidered cushion in front of a small dressing table. In the far corner was a sink with two dainty towels draped over the edge. The double bed, with sunny candlewick bedspread, stretched ominously between Gabe and me as he stood unmoving from where he'd stopped not many footsteps inside the door. He must have registered the look on my face as he remained rooted to that spot, making no movement towards me or to venture any further into the room.

'I'm sorry, I thought one room would save funds. You know, the train, the room, food. I don't know how long we'll be here. And I thought it would make it easier to make plans if we're in the same room, you know, at night. You know, to talk. Just to talk.'He quickly added, 'I'll sleep on the floor. I'll bet there are extra blankets somewhere.' With that it was his turn to flush a little as he quickly turned away from me and moved towards the wardrobe, opening the doors to search. I knew he meant every word and I smiled to myself at his sweet boyish blushing.

Blankets located, Gabe suggested we start our search immediately after he'd called Chris McCabe. We made our way back to the front desk and I absentmindedly picked up a little menu card from one of the tables while Gabe used the telephone. I looked up at Gabe as he spoke; the affectionate smile which had spread across my features as I looked towards him dissolved the instant I registered the expression on his face. Menu forgotten, I was at his side as he was hanging up. I touched his arm. 'Is everything alright?'

'It's Lola.'

My breath wouldn't come.

'She's had a fall. In the garden.'

My heart beat faster.

'He says she's fine, resting at home. He and Miranda are keeping an eye on her.'A pause. 'I don't know why Miranda's involved herself, but Chris said Lola has instructed him to tell us she's fine with Miranda and not to come home until we've found Annie.'

I sighed in relief that Lola was alright and I sighed with warmth when the word she'd used registered; she'd told us not to come home - *home.* Theirs was my home now.

'But is she really 'fine' do you think?' I asked and Gabe shrugged, matching my doubt.

'Who knows? But, either way, if we go back straight away we'll get a good telling off from her.'He smiled. 'Let's stick to the plan for now. I'll phone again tonight and in the morning to check up on her. If I sense that Miranda or Chris aren't telling us everything, then we'll go back and risk the wrath of Lola together.'

'Safety in numbers?'

'Always.' And he squeezed my hand.

That first day took us methodically from guest house to hotel, bed and breakfast to employment agency. I could sense that Gabe was still thinking about Lola and was worried more than he was letting on, but I said nothing. It was six o'clock when I realised that we hadn't eaten all day and suggested we head back to the Sea Trout for food and rest.

After the constant activity of our first day, strolling silently back to our temporary home was nice. We held hands as we walked along the unfamiliar streets, watching unfamiliar people getting on with their lives. They all looked so normal and I wondered whether they might be thinking the same of us, that our lives and loves must be unremarkable and routine. How wrong we all could be about each other; how little we appreciated what paths others trod. I started to view people with a suspicious camaraderie. Perhaps they were lost, or had lost someone but didn't even know it. Maybe they were a member of this horrible club that I was now part of.

After a call to Chris McCabe, which provided some reassurance, we could wait no longer to eat. Once seated, we ordered our food. Gabe didn't drink alcohol and we both had water with our meal. We chatted over the events of the day and our plan for tomorrow. Other patrons arrived, two couples were shown to their rooms and three other small groups had come in just to eat. There was the low murmur of people talking and the occasional sound of glasses clinking or plates moving as people carried on with their evenings around us.

As the population of the small restaurant gradually dwindled, there came a point when we both found ourselves looking around uncomfortably and then back to each other. There was an awkward silence for a fleeting moment, as I think we both realised that we should head up to our room.

History

Gabe unlocked the door and held it open for me. I entered and collected my wash things, hastily saying that I'd be back in a moment then heading for the bathroom.

When I returned a few minutes later, Gabe had laid out blankets and pillows on the floor as far as was possible from the bed. I smiled inwardly but said nothing. It was then his turn to leave the room and by the time he returned I'd changed at incredible speed and was sitting up in bed with the covers pulled over my bent knees and right up to my chin. Gabe smiled broadly and I suspected he was laughing at me.

'Are you sure you're alright sharing a room?' he asked.

'Yes, it's fine. Are you sure you're alright sleeping on the floor?'

'I've slept in worse places, believe me.' My thoughts pushed themselves briefly into his past, imagining the places he might once have been; the nights he'd slept rough, scared and alone, cold and hungry. I felt fraudulent, knowing some of Gabe's story without him having told me himself and wondered whether Gabe knew that Lola had confided some of his past to me. I wanted him to be the one to confide in me and tell me all about his family and his life before Lola, before ending up in Rushton and creating his life there. Before meeting me.

Once again he was standing still and I eventually realised he wanted to undress so I turned away, blushing slightly at my ignorance. I heard him moving about for a few moments. 'It's okay you know; you can turn around.' I could hear humour in his voice once again.

Smiling, I had to break the awkwardness so I turned to face him relieved that I hadn't caught him half-dressed but in pyjama trousers. 'This is daft, isn't it? We're acting like children. I don't mind sharing. I wouldn't be here if I didn't trust you. Not just in this room, but in Exley, or even at Lola's house. I believe you and believe in you.'

He climbed into his makeshift bed and sat there watching me, also smiling, but looking a little embarrassed.

His tender smile was soon replaced by a cheeky grin. 'You're lucky I'm a gentleman, young lady.' He winked and the awkward moment had passed. I wasn't ready for sleep and relaxed, crossing my legs, folding my hands in my lap and sitting there in bed as he sat on the floor.

Although no words of confirmation had been spoken, Gabe and I had grown close. There were little touches, a squeeze of the hand, the comforting tenderness, a reassurance in just being with him and the unspoken pact that finding Annie was our task, not just mine.

'Gabe?' He was lying on his side, looking towards me, his head resting on his hand and his elbow propped up by his pillow. 'Can I ask you something?'

'Anything.' Now there was an invite.

'Will you tell me about your family?' I waited for a reaction, but there was none that I could see and I was drawn to fill the silence. 'Do you mind?

You don't have to, of course. I just wondered... I hoped...' Thankfully he stopped my stuttering.

'No, I don't mind. Not with you. I'm happy to tell you anything you want to know about me.'He hesitated, his eyes briefly falling towards the floor. 'But it's not something I would talk about with anyone but you or Lola. Although there's really nothing to talk *about*, it's just the telling of a story. One day that life will have been so much smaller than the one I live now. It's already just a short story, in the past. It won't be long before it'll be a very tiny part of me, like Lola's past is to her, and the story since that time will be the bigger part outweighing it by years.'

'But does it have to be?'

'Yes it does.'Then I saw the reaction I'd waited for earlier, which had taken until now to show itself. He sat up straight, took a deep breath and looked at me. His eyes locked into mine as if connected by an invisible thread or a magnet, and he didn't look away. Although his eyes met mine and didn't waiver, at first he seemed to look straight through me. Then his eyes narrowed a little and he sighed, his smile returning once again. 'Lola told you about Edie.' It was a statement not a question, but I nodded anyway. Maybe Lola *had* told Gabe that she'd been telling me about him. His eyes released me then and they were elsewhere, seeing and reliving the past maybe, as he started to tell his tale.

'Edie reminded me of my little sister Ruby – Ruby was about her age when I left. I don't know what words to use, to explain how it felt for those first few evil weeks. I didn't know where I'd been or who I belonged with, or if I belonged with anyone at all. I convinced myself I'd knocked my head somehow –maybe I'd been in an accident and had amnesia. That could be the only explanation. I was so confused; I was so confused it physically hurt. And there was this pain.' He touched his hand to his chest. He didn't look at me, but I hadn't taken my eyes off him once. His voice caught on the last words. If it's possible to actually feel your heart hurt for someone else's pain, I felt it then.

I wanted to reach out and touch him, or put my arms around him, or kiss him; I wished I could stroke his hair, murmur gentle words of reassurance in his ear. But I didn't, I just watched and waited, until I gently asked 'What was it like when you did remember?' He ran one hand through his hair, leaving a little boy tuft sticking up to give him an air of vulnerability. He still didn't raise his eyes to mine.

'It was slow, gradual over a few weeks. Little things started to come back to me. My memories crept out bit by bit, sometimes because of something I saw or touched, or even by a smell, a sound or a taste. Then I was rushing home. I was relieved, excited, believing they'd be looking for me and worried about where I'd been since I'd cracked my head and disappeared.'

'What did you do then?' I asked cautiously.

'When I got home?' I nodded. 'I frightened my little sister like you wouldn't believe. I didn't know that she wouldn't have the slightest clue who I was, but she was the first person I saw and I carried on as normal. I thought I'd been confused after banging my head, losing my memory. I imagined they must have been looking for me everywhere. When I first saw her, I scooped her straight up, swinging her into my arms and spinning her around with joy. Until, in that split second, she started to struggle, then pull away from me, then scream. She shed no tears of joy.

I put her down and... and I stood there as she ran away. I couldn't move. I couldn't think. Then I realised that Ruby hadn't run to me with open arms and eyes crying tears of relief; she'd looked at me as if I was a stranger. I should have known immediately that there was something seriously wrong. Despite all that, it took me a while to work out that she actually didn't know me. No one knew me, not even my mother. When I did grasp it, although I hadn't a clue how it had happened, I tried to convince Ruby that I was her brother, not a stranger. But I'd scared her off by then. She was so frightened; she must've thought I was a madman. I probably looked like one.' He stopped and inhaled deeply. 'I looked awful, Eva, unwashed, unshaven. I hadn't eaten or slept properly, and I was wearing the same clothes I'd left in. I was scared too. Yes, I'd forgotten them, but then I'd remembered and gone home, only to find that *they* didn't know *me*. It didn't take me long to leap from scared to angry – I was really angry Eva. I got into some brawls in bars and even in the street. But anger didn't resolve anything and then the only emotion left was despair. That's where I was when I met Lola.

Eva, if despair had been a place on a map I would have been one of the locals. And there was still that pain.' His head lowered and he rubbed his chest for a moment, as if trying to ease an ache. 'I was in such a mess. It had been almost two years and I'd followed my father in a way I swore I never would. I was useless. Drinking, working barely enough to survive, not even that sometimes. I'm ashamed to admit that I stole food. I was a physical and emotional skeleton. I couldn't fall any lower. Who would take me on or trust me in that state?'

'Lola.' I offered. He smiled and nodded. I wanted to cry, but that seemed like pity and I dug my nails into my palms really hard. What right did I have to cry someone else's tears? 'I can't imagine how it must have been, losing your family like that.'

I imagined that death might be easier to cope with than this no man's land where no one knew you. At least with death there was an accepted grieving process, one which people understood and where there could eventually – hopefully – be acceptance. To lose your whole family to a loss of memory and have no-one to confide in, or seek comfort from, was inconceivable. How did you live with the rejection of all those most dear to you? I now understood the fierce strength of his devotion to Lola, the Samaritan who'd taken him in without fear or question, then welcomed him into her home a second time and saved him from himself.

He didn't speak for a few moments and I didn't interrupt; I could see that he was struggling with his memories. Finally, he continued.

'It was worse than just being apart and missing them so much. I also knew that if I wasn't with them I couldn't protect them.'He looked at me then and, before I could ask him to explain, carried on without prompt – he must have seen in my face that I didn't know this part of his story. 'My father liked a drink, Eva, he liked lots of drinks. After work he always went to the local and then rolled home when it closed, or when they threw him out. He could be…' he hesitated to find the word, 'rough. I was the one who stood between him and my mother.'

I didn't know what to say to show how I felt – that I was sad, that I was horrified, that I was desperately trying to understand how he must feel. Again, I think he knew the feelings I wanted to communicate to him, knew the words that wouldn't form but that couldn't ease his pain even if I could find them. I didn't know if he was incredibly intuitive, or if it was because he knew me very well already.

'You don't have to say anything.'Another pause. 'If they suffered, it's because I wasn't there; but there was nothing I could do about it. I had to leave. If I'd stayed, I wouldn't have been able to stop myself trying to bring them back to me and that would just cause more pain for them. I tried to give them a bequest, gift, whatever. After Lola had told me that I could do such a thing and I went back, I tried to do it. I needed to give it to Ruby – we were so close I knew it would work if she could have it. She would've remembered, I know she would've remembered me. But I'd scared her off and I couldn't get the physical or emotional closeness to do it. Lola told me that the door to the past seems to lock at some point. She said that, before then, the door is closed but it can sometimes be opened. Three years, or thereabouts, seems to be when the key is finally turned. It all becomes too distant then.

No-one goes back when it's been that long. I think the memories are too pale, washed out. It's pointless to keep trying, or hoping. You just have to accept it, and learn to live with it. Or maybe die without it.'

I gasped without thinking.

'What's the alternative Eva?' he questioned. 'Believe me, some people take that route.'

I was shocked, sad to think that some lost and frightened people had no option but to consider the route that Gabe had intimated. I had to force such thoughts away. 'Did you go straight back to Lola then?'

He nodded. 'It was the only place to go. She received me with the warmth you'd expect. Somehow she managed to straighten me up. She gave me a home, fed me, found me a job. She helped me to stand up again. And burned my clothes.' He smiled at the memory and I reciprocated.

'Have you been back to your family since?'

He nodded again. 'Just once.'

Again, I waited. 'Are they alright?' I asked cautiously and had to wait a few moments for his answer.

‘My father’s dead.‘Emotion cracked his voice on the last word and he looked away for a moment before clearing the sentiment from his throat and carrying on. ‘What will you think of me if—’

I panicked, tension racking my muscles, sitting a little more upright than before. How did his father die? What was he about to tell me?

He continued. ‘Will you think less of me if I say I’m glad?’

I relaxed into my pillows. *Stupid girl, what did you think he was going to say? You know him so much better than that.*

‘The drink finally got its revenge. He died as he lived. He went to the pub one night as usual and didn’t come back. They found his body in a ditch the next afternoon. I think things got very tough for my mother and Ruby with the loss of my father’s wages. But I would say that living without his wages must have been better than how they were living *with* my father. They’re free from him now, although I know my mother would have been heartbroken. He was a good man once. Apparently. And she loved the man he used to be, despite what he’d become.

I don't know why he was like he was, or when he changed, but she always defended him to me. If I was still there I could be looking after them. I'd be providing for them and smoothing their path a bit, maybe helping to make it a happy home at last. I saw Ruby when I went back, and the woman she is now. She's beautiful, bright, and full of the sun. Despite everything.' His eyes glowed with the thoughts he had resurrected of his sister, and his face relaxed. 'It's a cliché, but it's true that the most valuable things in life are actually completely free. It's very sad that so few people realise this until it's too late.'

I wanted to ask many more things; what exactly had happened to his father, did his mother work, where did they live, what was Ruby doing now. But Gabe had bared so much of his soul, dredged his feelings for me, that I couldn't ask any more of him now. So I said nothing. He looked tired and, without thinking about it, I hopped out of bed and walked around to him. He looked startled, almost concerned at what I was doing. I sat down next to him and, although clearly taken aback at my sudden change of location, his left arm rose and curled around my shoulders as I leaned into him. I could feel him relax as I moulded into his chest and he kissed the top of my head. I draped my arm around his body and his other arm curved around and held my hand. I breathed in the warmth of him as we relaxed into the silence.

The next thing I was conscious of was the light as it poked itself though the curtains and danced across the room, coming to rest on my face. I'd obviously slid down during the night and was now curled up in the makeshift bed on the floor, with Gabe nowhere to be seen. Blinking, I sat up slowly, disappointed to leave the warmth and surprising comfort of this snug little nest. Once upright, I could see Gabe at the little dressing table writing something. My movement must have alerted him to the end of my slumber and he turned to face me.

'Good morning interloper' he smiled.

'Good morning.'I returned his smile. 'What are you doing?'

'I'm making a list of more places we can try. I borrowed the telephone directory from the front desk while I was calling Rushton.'What on earth was the time? 'Lola's fine, in great spirits, but a little put out that Chris is keeping her at home. Apparently she was quite unsteady after her fall, but the doctor's happy that she's alright; just bruised, a little achy. And old. It'll take her a while to get back on her feet, but Chris says she bright enough and fed up with being in bed.'

I felt as relieved as Gabe looked. 'Thank goodness.' I realised I'd released a huge sigh and it made me aware of just how much Lola had been on my mind, even though it was almost crammed to capacity with so many other things. I stretched, trying to wake myself properly, as I still felt as though my brain hadn't fully woken.

'Did you sleep alright? Were you uncomfortable on the floor with me?'

'I was fine. Did I cramp you?' He shook his head. 'Can I suggest, though, as comfortable as the floor is, that you sleep in the bed tonight? It's really daft for you to be on the floor when there's a good bed to be had. I mean no offence, I do appreciate your gallantry, but you really should share the bed.'

'No offence taken,'he smiled, 'but the floor is fine.'

After breakfast, our search resumed and we carried on in the same vein as the previous day. Our hopes went up and down but, each time I felt despondent, I also felt the squeeze of Gabe's hand. Although we'd not made any progress Gabe's mood was optimistic, at least outwardly, and he dragged my spirits kicking and screaming up with his. In Rushton, he'd been the one trying to temper my fevered optimism with medicinal doses of reality, but now that reality had landed heavily in my lap it was he who kept my spirits up and encouraged me to be positive. Returning from the ladies' that afternoon I did catch Gabe rubbing his face in his hands, but as soon as he saw me he'd straightened and smiled.

Two more days of searching passed.

The awkwardness of the evening routine was gone and, although we politely turned our backs for each other to change, we were relaxed in each other's night time presence. I perched on the side of the bed talking to Gabe while he straightened out his bed on the floor, on which he was still sleeping.

Although we were in Exley with the mission of locating Annie, there had been situations which demanded humour and lightened the grey clouds of despondency which threatened to unleash their contents on me every now and then. I laughed as Gabe received a gift on his shoulder from a passing bird; and I'd been so preoccupied with talking that I'd almost tripped over a dustbin, giving Gabe his merry revenge. Gabe loved the stories I recounted of mine and Annie's childhood exploits and I delighted in his enjoyment of them. For the first time we were able to laugh together openly and delight in a shared joke, with no hovering secrets or missions. We knew what we were doing now and we knew each other.

The night came once again and we were back in our friendly little room. Once changed, I climbed into bed, still talking. After Gabe had arranged his bedding on the floor, he pulled the chair away from the desk and towards the bed and sat there instead, his feet resting on the bed with ankles crossed and his fingers linked together across his stomach. He looked the picture of relaxation.

And there we stayed for hours, discussing, comparing, talking and laughing and me crying a little. The time ticked by without me noticing; until Gabe pointed out that it was past 2am. With more than a little reluctance, I agreed that we should sleep. Gabe returned to the floor and I slid down under my covers. I wanted to offer to share again, but didn't. I'd mentioned it twice now and couldn't do it again. I soon thought I could hear Gabe's breathing turn steady and slow, to that of a person captured by sleep, so I shoved the thought of sharing petulantly from my mind willing it to stay away and not bother me again.

Sleep wasn't going to come so easily for me that night, a problem I'd grown used to over the past two weeks, and I lay in the darkness, turning thoughts over and over in my mind. Two weeks ago, I would have laughed if anyone had suggested I would soon be playing truant from my job and sharing a room with a man in a strange town.

I recounted the day to myself. I planned the next day. I thought of Aunt Kathleen and Uncle Bob. I worried about Lola. I felt guilty about Lola, as the week before I'd ventured uninvited into her past. An intruder. My best intentions had been my excuse at the time, but now I was having doubts about the sense of my actions.

Despite the mess of 'Annie confusion' I found myself all tangled up in, I couldn't shake off the thought of a young Lola and her story. The vision of her was stuck in the back of my mind and refused to leave. I found it hard to believe that nothing could be done for a lost person, even after such a long time. I still believe that the invisible ties of a family are strong enough not to come undone even in the hardest of circumstances. This thought kept poking at me, not letting me forget it was there, as if it had a life of its own. It was close by all the time, even though it might sometimes be buried under other thoughts; frequently it struggled to the top and forced itself on me, an uninvited guest.

The day before Gabe and I visited Randall Boyes, I'd done some investigating of my own.

As I'd sat on the bus watching the countryside go by, I experienced three emotions. I was nervous, unsure and excited. Nervous of what I may find and of the reaction I would get from Lola and Gabe, unsure of what I was looking for or what I would do if I found it and excited that

I may be able to do something wonderful for a lady who'd become a very dear friend.

I hadn't told Lola or Gabe what I was planning – I didn't want to upset Lola, or to raise any unfounded hope. I also didn't want my plans to be thwarted. Lola already tried all that was possible many years ago, and surely she would tell me that the passing of such time would make success impossible. I didn't confide in Gabe either as I had a doubt, nibbling away, convincing me that Gabe wouldn't approve of my quest.

When I arrived at the county archive a few minutes before my appointment time, I explained to the lady at the front desk what I was looking for and she led me through to a reading room. It was a little like a library, where she beckoned me to sit and advised that she'd return shortly. I sat at the large wooden desk with my hands flat on its surface. I ran my hands over the smooth brown wood and imagined all those who may have been here before. The wood was beautiful to look at and touch and I pictured all the years of use, hands and paper, books and elbows that had worn the desk to this beautifully smooth and tactile form.

My romantic reverie was ended abruptly when the lady returned with two large tomes containing parish records. I thanked her and waited for her to leave before opening the first book. I don't know why I waited, unless I was somehow expecting everything I wanted to leap out at me from the pages in a loud explosion of revelation. I visualised Pandora's Box and quickly pushed the thought away, nervously opening the first cover.

Once alone I pored over the pages, lingering on some longer than others. It felt like I was intruding on the lives of these people a little even though, for many, their lives had long since passed. The pages were stiff with age and crackled as I carefully turned them, reading the names and years that passed before my eyes. 1860, 1859, 1858, the years continued to roll back.

Lola's name flew out at me as if it was painted in red.

I was momentarily stunned, amazed that I should find her. I didn't know why Lola still appeared in ink and on paper. I still don't. Just another phenomenon that I have no way of questioning.

She was there and that was all that mattered – a new baby's birth recorded here in front of me. I was smiling to myself; not because I'd found part of what I'd been searching for but because I was picturing Lola as a new-born, maybe swathed in a white lacy robe and held lovingly by parents, aunts, uncles. I knew it was a dreamy image but I hoped it was accurate. I knew that the romance I'd dreamed up didn't have a happily ever after, but it was nice to think that Lola's early years could have been idyllic, in some way storing up happiness and memories for the lonely years that followed.

The task I'd set myself was to find out what had happened to Lola's family. Were siblings or cousins still alive, had they had children, grandchildren maybe – and if so, could I find any of them? What I wasn't so sure of was what I would do if I could find any of these people. I knew that I should confide my secret to Gabe and seek his advice, but with so many unknown and varied outcomes I was convinced he'd tell me to leave well alone. Deeper inside were fears that he would be angry at my intrusion into something I knew almost nothing about. I pushed these worries away – that discussion was a long way off so, for the moment, I could swathe it in denial, store it away for later and maybe forget it was there.

The time passed quickly as I continued my research, branching out into newspapers to further my investigation. Lola's family were beneath my fingertips – so close and yet so far. I could see that their lives seemed to have carried on without any major incident, at least nothing apparently newsworthy enough to be documented in bold script in the papers and books lying in front of me. They were silent and still and yet willingly offering me their secrets, holding open the past for my prying eyes.

I wrote down some notes and then folded these away in my bag. My prying done, I left the records office thanking the lady who'd been so helpful.

I mentally sifted through all the details I had. Maybe letting my search take me to Lola's family *was* a step too far. What else could I do? Tell Lola? No, too painful for her. Talk to Gabe? I couldn't admit my duplicity. Contact Lola's family in some way, jog a memory somehow? Surely if it was that easy we wouldn't all be where we were now. And neither would countless others.

A noise outside in the street returned me to the present. I couldn't turn on the light to check my watch and confirm the extent of my insomnia, but guessed that dawn couldn't be very far away. I sighed quietly, turning on my side away from Gabe and towards the window and pulling the covers up to my chin; maybe feeling the warm cocoon of the covers wrapped around me would help me drift off to a sleep where no worries or guilt haunted me.

My next awareness was of moving, tilting backwards slightly, and it took me a few bleary half-sleep moments to understand that my movement was due to the springs in the mattress behind me being depressed with the weight of another body. There was no alarm or uneasiness, just the feeling of my body relaxing as Gabe gently curved his arm around me and we moulded together comfortably and both fell asleep.

Success

After a few moments of that delightful in-between place where neither slumber nor consciousness are really yours, I was awake and enjoying the warmth of Gabe's arm around me. We'd stayed in the same position until dawn.

I felt better today; maybe the result of being held in Gabe's lovely warm embrace, maybe because it was time to starting looking up not down, or maybe I had an intuition that success would soon surrender itself to us - whichever it was, I smiled, stifling a yawn in an effort not to wake the man who slept soundly behind me. I decided to indulge myself for a little longer before sliding out of bed to head for the bathroom. When I got there, I smiled at myself in the mirror.

Our breakthrough came on our fourth day in Exley and purely by accident. Gabe and I had paused for lunch in a tea room away from the business of the main streets. While Gabe paid our bill, I looked past the other patrons assembled at their tables and out into the quiet street. On the opposite side of that street and perched on the corner of the next one was a sign announcing the Old Toll House and there was a second sign, in the window, which confirmed that there were vacancies. It was another guest house and therefore worth a visit.

When Gabe was done, we ventured across the street to the Old Toll House. A young woman was behind the reception desk, diligently tidying papers. I smiled as I approached and she stopped her shuffling of paperwork and smiled back. I began my well-worn introduction and offered her Annie's photograph to look at. If the spoken word could become faded through exposure or be diluted by limelight, as a picture can, then the words both Gabe and I had spoken to so many people in our search should have turned from a rich and shining gold to a watery, rain-washed yellow. They held no less importance to us but, unintentionally, had become so familiar a spiel that they were now a well-worn mantra, recited without needing to think.

As the young woman held Annie's picture, she smiled again.

And nodded.

'Yes.'She spoke as I was almost reaching to take back the picture before turning to leave. I turned to Gabe in startled surprise at her answer. 'Yes, that's Miss Carter,' she offered. Too stunned to speak, Gabe took my part.

'Does Miss Carter have a room here?' he smiled and took the picture as the receptionist offered it back.

'Oh no, not any more. Miss Carter was here for a while, but she's moved on I'm afraid.'

'Where did she go?' I'd regained my voice and leapt in with my interrogation. The receptionist looked a little surprised. Gabe touched my arm to calm me.

'I'm not sure. I think she found somewhere more permanent. Can I give her a message when I next see her?'

Next see her? I could hardly breathe – my breaths reduced to shallow, jumpy starts. This girl would *see* her?

'That would be very kind, thank you.'Gabe smiled his response; he was composed and had taken my hand discreetly, possibly in an effort to pull on my reins, slow me down. 'Can I ask how often you see her?'

She smiled. 'It's only occasionally. We got on really well while she was here and sometimes when she's passing she'll drop in for a chat. She even brings cake some days – very kind.' Gabe and I both now smiled at her.

'When will she next be here?'

'Oh, I don't know. It's unannounced, just when she's in the area.'

'If we leave her a note, would you mind passing it on?'

'Yes, I can do that.'

Gabe motioned to a writing desk on the opposite wall. 'Might we?'

'Go ahead.' The girl smiled once more and offered me some paper and an envelope from the desk she'd been bringing to order.

I hesitated as I sat down to write. There was so much to say, but I knew that just a few words to Annie could convey all they needed to at this point. My hands shook as I composed the most important note of my life. A few moments later

I sealed the envelope, hoping that it contained a future.

We chatted animatedly that evening as we ate our meal, tripping over plans of how we'd first see Annie, what I'd say, how we'd tackle Aunt Kathleen and Uncle Bob. Gabe didn't try to temper my exuberance this time, letting me have my evening of joy. Each day had been much the same until that one; a telephone call home, searching, asking, a quick lunch, more questions, more looking, then a meal at the hotel and another telephone call before we headed for our room where we'd talk and make more plans.

This evening flew past like all the others, but with an added thrill; the new promise of success. We talked happily all the way up the stairs and as we dressed for bed. Without any awkwardness or question we both climbed into the bed only pausing once as, on opposite sides, we appeared like mirror images lifting the covers to climb in. We laughed quickly at each other before sliding in and resuming last night's embrace. Our happy discussion gradually waned, as the day's success and the last few days' activity and planning forced weariness upon us and we both relaxed into sleep.

A gentle *tap tap, tap tap.* In my half-sleep I didn't know what the noise was. Another nasty dream? I fell back into slumber. *Tap tap, tap tap.* Not the dream about the nurse again, surely? *Tap, tap, tap.* It became louder and more urgent, insisting it now be acknowledged. It's the door. There's someone at the door. It's real. I'm awake. Not a dream this time.

'Gabe. The door,' I whispered quickly into the darkness.

I turned towards Gabe and could tell he was awake too, even though there was no light to show me. I felt him lean away from me to switch on the lamp which stood guard on the night table and my eyes were shocked by the sudden glare. The tapping was insistent, begging for response. Gabe was across the room in an instant, opening the door a crack and speaking with the person outside it. He closed the door and was hurriedly putting on his trousers over pyjamas as he spoke.

'There's a telephone call. For me.' His alert eyes locked into mine and I could immediately tell what he was thinking, what I was thinking.

The only reason someone would call at this time of night. It wouldn't be Annie. It would be Miranda or Mr McCabe. I'd hopped out of bed and was also grabbing at clothes. Gabe left the room and hurried down the stairs, with me a few paces behind. The manager was behind the desk when we got there and handed Gabe the telephone with a grave expression, no doubt knowing the implications to anyone of a telephone call at this hour.

Gabe took the receiver with a 'thank you' and the manager nodded, before retreating tactfully from the room.

The darkened room was silent for a short time after and I strained to hear the caller's words, while trying to read Gabe's face as he spoke. I was standing right next to him, but couldn't hear what was being said to him or by whom.

'How?' A hint of anger.

'Alright, ok, yes.' Calmer.

'What do *you* think?' Sarcasm.

'First thing of course.' Stating the obvious.

The receiver was replaced. I watched him and waited. I'd never seen such pain on anyone's face before - pain he was battling to contain. Then it escaped. 'Oh God, oh God,' he cried as he turned to me and his handsome face was broken.

Back in our room, we sat side by side on the edge of the bed. We'd walked very slowly back up the stairs we'd flown down just minutes earlier. I'd looked at my watch when we returned; four o'clock. Nothing could be done now. As soon as we could, we'd be packed and at the train station boarding the first train back to Rushton.

'However ill she is, she'll wait for you.' I leaned into Gabe, bridging the small distance between us and lifting the heavy silence at the same time. 'It's my fault you're not there. I'm so sorry I dragged you away.' I was responsible for his absence from Lola's side.

He spoke for the first time since replacing the receiver whose news had broken him and smiled kindly through empty eyes. 'Eva, don't. We're here together because we should be. I wanted us to do this together. Lola wanted us to do this together.' He took a deep breath and put his arm around me, pulling me closer, and kissed the top of my head. 'Come on; let's see if we can get some rest for an hour, then we'll get packed.

We'll be at the station in plenty of time to catch the first train home.'

I knew he was polishing his fear into optimism for me even now and I nodded, loving him all the more for his attempt to buoy my spirits at the very moment his life was collapsing around his feet for a second time.

As we lay in bed once again, with me curled under his protective and comforting arm, we didn't sleep. We didn't move. We didn't speak. We both lay there, silently navigating our way through our own thoughts. Mine ran over and over the past few weeks, a twisting and turning hall of mirrors where nothing was as it seemed or as it should be. I imagined the turning pages in Gabe's head were of the last five years with Lola and the increasing sunshine after an all-consuming hurricane. I wondered if the warm and giving eyes I loved, now staring and empty, saw a darkening sky which threatened to unleash a tempest once again.

Lola

I pushed open the door to Lola's room just a tiny bit, whispering Gabe's name as I did so.

'Come in,' a sure but cracking voice offered. It wasn't Gabe but Lola who bade me enter. I peered around the door. 'Come in,' she repeated.

I shut the door gently behind me and ventured over to the bed. Gabe was sitting in a chair to her left, holding her hand, and she raised her right hand beckoning me closer and patting the faded floral bedspread.

Gabe's head was bent, but he looked up as I perched gently on the bed next to Lola. She turned to him. Although her voice was quiet there was no doubting the force behind her words as she spoke them, mother to child. 'Gabe. I will have none of this moping and whispering. Go on downstairs and put the kettle on. Have a cup of tea or something, for goodness sake.'

Despite the sombre mood I smiled as Gabe stood obediently, then kissed Lola's cheek and left the room. She smiled the smile of a devoted mother as she watched him leave.

She was clearly waiting until he'd shut the door before speaking; as he did so, she turned her attention to me. 'Now.'She patted the bed closer to her in invitation and I shuffled along a little way. 'Eva. I've never been one for fanciful notions of deathbed outpourings—'

I interrupted. 'Lola, please—' but she interrupted back.

'Eva, dear.'She patted my hand to silence me. 'Let's not pretend I'm sixty years old. That was a few years ago.' She smiled cheekily. 'Please don't be sad, or let my Gabe be sad. I'm not even sad. I'm just tired. Don't you mourn a lost and lonely life because it hasn't been like that, not for many years.'Again I tried to speak, but she raised a finger to her lips. 'Now who's to say that my first life would have been perfect?' She looked tired and old, but not at all troubled by any distant memories which might have stirred. She smiled. 'If things hadn't happened the way they did, I wouldn't have met Gabe and we wouldn't have met you. Fate's a funny thing. I *have* had my family and my children; it just took me longer than expected. I had a second life, instead of a first. How many people get two?' She chuckled quietly, but there was weariness behind her smile and the bright impishness in her blue eyes wasn't there. 'Eva, look after Gabe won't you? Look after each other. There are still things you need to know, what might happen if you find Annie. But I think it could just all be alright this time, because it's different. I wouldn't have encouraged you so much, if I'd thought… I hope…' Her voice trailed off and she looked frail and faded.

'Lola, please don't. You just need some rest. You have years left with us yet. We're here to look after you, whatever you need. The doctor said you—'

Despite her physical fragility and weariness, her mind was firm and her words cut into my keen reassurances with a blade of realism. 'I know what the doctor said. I know what he said to you and I know what he said to me and the gist of it is that I'm worn out. It's not the kind of worn out that sleep will cure, Eva, but it's alright, as long as we're honest about it. Let's not start fibbing with each other now.' She patted my hand. 'I might have a little rest for a while now, but I need to talk to you again later.' She squeezed my hand, gave it another pat and nodded and I was taken back to that first visit to her kitchen. She was still finding ways to reassure me, even now, giving me the bravery I lacked. 'You go and find that man of yours downstairs.' A cheeky little sparkle shone at me once more from childlike eyes.

She closed her eyes while shooing me away with her hand. 'I love you Lola,' I said, and kissed her as Gabe had. Then I left her to sleep.

Downstairs, Gabe was sitting by the empty fireplace in the one clear chair. He watched me cross the room and, without thinking, I curled up on his lap feeling strong arms enveloping me warmly. 'Well?' he questioned into my hair.

'Girls' stuff,' I offered.

'Oh, right.' I could sense acceptance in his voice and maybe a little disappointment that he'd been excluded from something.

'She's worried about you,' I added and he laughed very softly. We sat curled together until the daylight was covered by darkness and I rose begrudgingly to pull the curtains, shutting out the darkening sky. I turned around to see Gabe disappearing from the room.

While he was gone I kneeled down to set the fire, absentmindedly laying kindling and striking a match. I stared into the fire as the small flames licked their way around the edges of the wood and became hungry for more; they grew strong as they devoured their first feed. I nourished them from the log basket and gazed at the graceful dance of the flames, a gold and yellow ballet in the hearth; beautiful but dangerous, delightful yet deadly. Gabe returned to advise that Lola was still sleeping and we both sat down on the floor and watched the ballet together. The only light in the room was that of the fire, giving the room a sleepy warm glow and casting waltzing shadows on the floor and walls.

After some time, Gabe squeezed my hand and I turned to his fire-lit eyes.

'Stay the night. Please.' It started as an instruction but softened into a request. I nodded, knowing that I couldn't be anywhere else that night.

Lola's Farewell

The warmth and light I could feel on my face before I opened my eyes promised it would be a lovely bright May day. The days before had been dull and bereft of sun and I was glad that today's weather was different. Rain and darkness would only make today that much harder. I was worried for Gabe. I hadn't stayed over at the cottage for several days, even though I'd visited daily. Gabe was distant and closed, stricken with a grief I couldn't soothe. I sat up, took a deep breath and swung my legs out of bed.

I hesitated before I knocked on the door of the red brick house. There was no music. Although the sun shone like an old friend trying to offer reassurance, the world was a much sadder place without Lola and the sun's warmth didn't bring the optimism it once had. Then I heard it... just a few tentative notes at first. My knuckles stopped short of the door.

I picked my way carefully through the pots of dead and dying flowers, unwatered and unkempt, under the overhanging willow and the once heavily-laden forsythia – which had dripped bright yellow spiky blooms a couple of weeks ago in spite of its neglect – to the side of the house. I knew this was where I would find the window to Gabe's room. I'd never been in his room. The first night I'd stayed, we hadn't left the living room, sitting in silence as the fire danced then died, apart from trips upstairs to check on Lola. I'd stayed twice since but, again, we'd remained in front of the fire where we talked, dozed and sat in silence in equal measure. I'd never even peeked around the door to Gabe's room before, despite all the times I'd been to the house. The window was slightly ajar. I didn't move far enough to look in, for fear of revealing my presence, but I could hear every note as clearly as if I was standing right next to the piano. I knew Gabe could play. I knew Gabe could play well. It was only now that it registered just how gifted he was.

The music I heard was beautiful yet sad. Gabe had lost his family for a second time and I didn't know how on earth I would be able to help him fill the space Lola had left. The piece of music he played was one I'd heard him play before, but only through walls and closed doors. I'd had a handful of piano lessons from a friend of Aunt Kathleen's when I was a little girl but, like so many pastimes, this was tossed aside when other things came along. I couldn't play a single tune or read a solitary note.

Hearing the music stop I walked back to the front of the house, hating to knock and disturb Gabe's mourning. But before I could tap on the door, it opened and he stood in front of me. He looked different. I realised then that it was his clothes; a sombre dark suit and tie over crisp white shirt. Just as I'd chosen a dark blue dress in recognition of the occasion, so had Gabe picked out the clothes that society would expect. He might have guessed what I was thinking, seeing my eyes linger on his attire for a little too long. Reaching up, he pulled his tie contemptuously from his neck and tossed it into the nearest bush just outside the front door.

'When did Lola ever see *me* wear a tie?' I could see the hint of a smile; it hovered at the edges of his mouth before disappearing again as quickly as it had arrived. He bent down and picked a delicate frond from a little plant, still bravely growing right on the edge of the path. Standing, he tenderly pulled my hair loose from its own severe ties and entwined the tiny cluster of blue flowers into it instead. 'Forget-me-not. Seems appropriate,' he smiled. Then he took my hand and we walked to the church.

The only mourners at the grave, we stood side by side. Gabe swayed almost imperceptibly backwards and forwards, the way you might while soothing a child. I continued to hold his hand but we didn't look at each other, both staring down into the earth at the plain wooden box as the reverend said the words he must have said many times. I noticed then that one of Gabe's shoelaces wasn't tied and yet another wave of tenderness for him washed across me.

I didn't really hear what the reverend said – my mind had returned to the day I sat in this churchyard and thought of Annie and of all those buried here. I remembered that I had hoped they were tenderly left here by their families in the shadow of a church that had watched over many other souls for hundreds of years. I knew then that Lola had also been laid here by her family – Gabe and me. She had been, was still, truly loved and would never be lost again.

After the short service ended we shook hands with the reverend, murmured our thanks in response to his soothing words and I turned to leave. Gabe didn't try to keep my hand in his as I slowly moved away, our little fingers staying loosely linked for a few moments longer as the distance between us grew. I left the churchyard and he moved away from the graveside. I looked back as I stepped through the old wooden gate and saw that he was sitting beneath the oak tree which had looked after me – its branches curved above him, strong and unmoving. His head was bowed, deep in thought, and I knew he was with Lola somewhere.

As I turned away to close the gate, my eyes were caught by an old gentleman standing by the churchyard wall. A younger woman held him firmly by the arm. My eyes were drawn to his weathered old hands and the little bunch of bulbous purple-blue flowers, like tiny hyacinths, that nestled there. He was looking towards Gabe. And towards Lola's resting place.

A tiny spark ignited inside me as I recalled the letter sent so many weeks ago; a hopeful letter sent by a well-meaning friend to a little boy now grown, aged with the passing of eighty years. A letter enclosing a purple-blue flower folded gently in tissue paper. It was such a big task for such a small flower – not only to flout the unwritten rules of those who are lost but, now, possibly, after all this time to reverse the failure of memory that the passage of time can sometimes leave in its wake.

I didn't venture over to the kind-faced old gentleman with the white hair and boyish sparkle deep in his watery blue green eyes.

I went back to the red brick house to wait.

It was dark when Gabe returned. I'd already lit the fire, drawn the curtains and tentatively laid the table in preparation for some soup, in case Gabe felt like eating. The door clicked as it closed slowly behind him and I walked into the hall. He didn't look as he had earlier. Although his mouth didn't smile, his eyes did as he wrapped his arms around me. We held each other gently and silently for some time.

When he finally pulled away, he took my hand and led me to his room. He sat down at the piano and tapped the space next to him. I joined him on the stool and could hardly breathe for the anticipation fluttering in my chest like a little trapped bird. The fluttering turned quickly to hammering and I feared that this insistent beating inside my chest might take over my whole body, rendering it impossible to see, do or hear anything. I was excited at the prospect of seeing him play and honoured that he was going to share this with me. He lifted the lid from the keys and I knew that he was taking me somewhere he'd not taken anyone for a very long time.

As his fingers caressed the keys, I watched. The timeless and beautiful sounds that he was able to coax so lovingly from the instrument at which we sat lifted me up and danced away with me. I danced away from that moment and into a place I didn't know and couldn't describe.

Gradually my eyes absorbed not just his fingers, but his wrists and his arms, then his shoulders, his neck and, finally, his face. I could see that not only did the instrument respond to his almost sensuous touch, but also he to it. It was as though he and the piano were one. His head occasionally moved very slightly, sometimes dipping forward and sometimes tilting a little to the side. His body leaned forward and his movements were fluid and tender, a mirror of the melodies he played.

When I could drag my eyes away, I looked at the piles of music stacked on the piano and could just make out the name of a piece that lay on the top; Beethoven's Piano Sonata #14. I couldn't see the names of any others and he didn't have any music in front of him, playing piece after piece without prompt or hesitation.

My eyes roamed to each part of his face; his jaw was strong and his lips full and smooth. His nose was straight. I looked to eyes which were gentle, with lids swept by dark lashes and framed by brows that were currently bridged by a shallow crease as he concentrated. His eyes closed then as he continued to play. A few locks of dark hair fell across his forehead. My eyes returned to his hands and the notes of the music took me with them, floating weightlessly and unthinking.

We sat there for a long time, he playing and me mesmerised. Lola had been accurate when she'd described Gabe's playing. I couldn't say how long it was before he stopped, momentarily, his fingers poised just above the keys. He started playing again after a short silence and I heard the tune I recognised from that first afternoon when Lola found me, and from numerous other snatched moments since, including that very morning when I'd hovered unseen outside his window. I thought of the times when the door of his room had been closed to me, along with the door to whatever we were sharing now. My questioning thoughts as to the piece he was playing were answered when, without missing a note, he said 'Bach's Ave Maria' so quietly he almost breathed the words. When the last note had been taken away by the evening air, I waited.

At last, he turned to me and took my hands. 'Thank you. For today. For last week.'

I smiled. 'Thank you for everything.'

He smiled back. 'Thank *you* for everything,' he winked. 'I'll walk you to the bus,' he added and stood, pulling me up from the stool. I stretched the stiffness out of my bones after sitting motionless for so long. I was disappointed he hadn't invited me to stay, but he had to deal with this loss in his own way and that clearly meant solitude tonight. My body and my emotions screamed at me for sleep and I was aware then of how tense I'd been all day. What Gabe felt was much greater. I knew that he hadn't slept properly for some time. 'I'll get you a coat or something'.

As we walked in the early evening, with me wearing his overcoat and holding his hand, I had the feeling that something had ended but also that something had now really begun. Although we'd said our last physical goodbye to Lola we'd also shared something that we hadn't before, even in Exley. I'd been allowed into Gabe's most intimate and private world – the place he retreated for comfort and reflection and where he'd now taken me. I was happy. I was more than happy.

And someone else was happy. Brown eyes smiled tentatively back at her from the mirror as she brushed her long hair. Her happiness came carefully, borne of hope and optimism; hesitant steps towards home. She recalled a sleepy picture of a water fight. And a picnic. And a kitten. And mater-

nal arms rocking a small child to sleep. The smell of fresh laundry and an open fire. She knew she had a family. Somewhere she had a family.

As I climbed into my bed, I was smiling to myself. I felt very peaceful when I discovered and admitted that in a strange way I felt happy for Lola. She'd been happy for me and Gabe too, and reassured that he wouldn't be alone without her. My little room didn't feel so solitary now. It was strange; I hadn't realised it was lonely until it wasn't anymore. Although I was on my own, I didn't feel alone.

In my head I could hear the delicate notes of 'Ave Maria' beginning to float though Lola's house – gentle notes played by expert hands. I closed my eyes and pictured Gabe moving gently with the music, his own eyes sometimes closing as he played. Curling up and hugging the covers to me, I thought of Lola and Gabe, how they'd become a family and I'd joined them. Annie's temporary, and it would be temporary, loss of *her* family had given *me* one. Although Annie and her parents had been my only family until then, they'd now become my *extended* family and it felt right that Gabe and Lola had become those closest to me instead.

My room at the Burgess's was now somewhere I kept my things and returned to for sleep. As homely and welcoming as it was, it was now just an interim abode for me; a stopping off point until I could return to Mill Street. My real home was there, at first with Lola and Gabe and now just with Gabe. He occupied as many of my thoughts as Annie, and more of my heart. He and Annie were now the two most important people in my life. I couldn't wait to introduce my past to my future and knew that Annie would see, and share, my absolute and all-consuming joy.

I was sad that there wouldn't be another person sharing in this wonder that I'd found. However much solace came from knowing that Lola had eventually been happy, her passing meant that I'd never get the chance to talk with her about all she experienced in her long life; to learn more about her, to laugh with her about silly things, to see more of that mischievous sparkle in her eyes. I'd realised some time back that she had the sense of fun of a young girl, and a playful streak that I would have loved to be a part of. I wished we'd met long before, as time had now run out for our worldly friendship. I knew that Lola wouldn't have told us not to cry or be sad; she'd have said it was alright to cry, but not for too long. She knew that nothing could be gained by wallowing and that, if nothing else, you learnt from every experience. She told me she believed in fate and now I did too.

The day after Lola's funeral, we'd met with Chris McCabe, Miranda and Fletcher. Although Gabe had asked that it just be he and I at the funeral, we all gathered for a farewell wake as convention demands. It was a celebration of Lola's life; but of a second life, not her first. We met at Lola's and Chris had brought a bottle of sherry which we'd sipped politely from odd glasses while hovering around the traditional sandwiches and cake.

Gabe couldn't eat anything, looking low and preoccupied, and Chris was clearly moved by the loss of a dear friend; as he left, Fletcher said it was time that he and Miranda made a move too. Miranda seemed reluctant to go, but Fletcher eventually steered her out of the door and down the path. Gabe lingered in the garden after saying goodbye to his guests and I left him to his thoughts.

I wasn't sure what to do after clearing away the remnants of our small buffet. I surveyed Lola's kitchen collections as I slowly returned each piece of unique crockery to its home, absentmindedly wondering where each piece had originated before being saved by Lola. One dainty cup had tiny trios of roses dotted all over, another sported pansies which covered every inch, one more was white with a border around the lip of blue and golden filigree, edged with posies of papery pink roses... the variety went on, the saucers all different, the spoons angular, rounded, baroque, deco, plain...

Gentle notes whispered into my ears once more and I smiled. Rather than disturb Gabe I found myself strolling through each room except his, pausing to take in Lola's things and trying to commit every part of her to memory. In her room, I sat on the edge of the candlewick bedspread for a few moments, saying my own little goodbye as my eyes scanned over piles of folded linens, a stack of books, a pile of little boxes, a jar of pins.

The nightstand held books (the Bible, Vice Versa, Little Women and three of poetry, although the weightiest of these appeared to have been used for flower pressing as a few paper-thin petals peeped out at me from between two almost transparent sheets of tissue paper), some pieces of paper (a shopping list and a 'to do' list) and a jam jar with fresh flowers standing proud. These were too fresh to have been there long and I knew that Gabe must have been the benefactor. I picked up and scanned the shopping and 'to do' lists, smiling.

And in Exley large brown eyes were also reading – and smiling.

As I stood to leave, I was surprised to see that one of the numerous empty picture frames on her wall was now occupied. I stood up and took it from the wall to look more closely. I hadn't noticed it before. It held a photo of Lola, Gabe and I – I'd completely forgotten that Fletcher had taken it. Miranda had, strangely, admonished him for taking the picture which I hadn't really thought about at the time. I was now so pleased that he had – he'd clearly given it to Lola not long after, enabling her to finally show faces in a family's frame. It was a touching gesture and I smiled at Fletcher's quiet kindness. I realised then that there was a similarity between Fletcher and Lola; Fletcher collected photographs and Lola collected 'things'. Miranda seemed to view Fletcher's hobby with an indulgent humour, as if he was a child collecting insects. He took lots of photographs, of anything and everything, then he developed them and kept them. I wondered if this was his way of keeping his memories safe. I hung the picture back in its place and then, instead of leaving, I sat back down on Lola's bed and thought of family.

My mind was back at the churchyard, with the old gent standing by the wall. I wept for him and I wept for Lola; she'd missed him for eighty years and he'd missed her by a matter of days. When the time was right I'd speak to Gabe about it, but not now. And when I did raise the subject with him, I would talk about his mother and his sister. If Lola's brother could remember after all this time...

Gabe was still playing and, returning composed to the hall with secret tears wiped away, I lingered by his door. I couldn't resist any longer so I ventured in and sat next to him once again. He smiled as I sat down, but continued to play.

A short while later, he stopped mid-piece and turned to me.

'Annie,' was all he said. I'd forgotten about Annie, momentarily, for the first time since she'd disappeared. My mind was saturated with Lola and Gabe; there was grief at losing Lola, worry for Gabe and a fear of the future. I'd wondered what would happen to the red brick house, Lola's cottage, and worried about what Gabe would do and where all Lola's things would go. I prayed Gabe wouldn't have to leave his home. Not again.

'Yes,' was all I could muster.

'We should go back to Exley.' His tone wasn't questioning or suggesting, but decisive and firm.

I was stunned. 'What?'

'We should go back to Exley.'

'But Gabe, we left Lola's address for Annie, as well as the name of the Sea Trout. She'll be able to find us. And, you're forgetting, she knows where I live – she can always come home to me.' The thought of a return to Exley hadn't crossed my mind with the events of the last week or so.

‘I think we should go back and carry on looking. How long has it been?’

‘Twenty-four days,’ I replied without hesitation, knowing exactly what he was referring to and surprising myself with my accuracy. She’d been gone for twenty-four days. And had I really only known Gabe for that long?

‘Look, she may still not know what’s going on. She can’t come home if she doesn’t remember you. And if that’s the case, even if she does get your letter, would *you* follow the instructions in a note from a complete stranger? We just can’t rely on that. But if she was to see you…’

I thought Gabe should have time to grieve without being forced to continue trying to resolve my problems.

‘Really Eva, we have to keep up the momentum. We’re so close. If we stop looking now, Annie might move on and we’ll be back where we started. Randall Boyes won’t welcome us back a second time.’

Now *that* I believed.

He hesitated. ‘It took an awful lot of convincing from Miranda before he finally agreed to see us the last time.’

'What? You didn't tell me that. I thought you'd telephoned him and arranged it.'

'There was no need to tell you how it came about, Eva. I did speak with him. He was quite definite in his response and said no straight away. I couldn't talk him round. You heard him when we were there; no-one ever looks for a lost person and certainly no-one has ever been allowed access to the books before. I didn't know what to do next, and then Miranda turned up while I was trying to think of a way around it with Lola. Miranda took it upon herself to deal with it and went to see Boyes without even telling me until it was a fait accompli. I suppose she turned on the charm.'

I was stunned.

'She actually went to see him?' He nodded. 'Why would she go to all that bother?' I was amazed at the newly-discovered depth of Miranda's friendship and devotion to my cause.

'She wants you to find Annie – simple as that. Don't get too caught up with her, Eva, please. And don't be too grateful. She has her own reasons.'He shook himself as though he'd felt a shiver and started again. 'Look, what I'm trying to say is that it was really hard to get access to the books and to find out where Annie was last. We won't have that help again. I told you what Randall's like. If we lose Annie now, I don't know how or if we'll get this close to her again.' Taking my hands in his, his eyes implored me and I was torn. 'We have to go.'

This had all started with Annie – she'd led me to Gabe when my sole purpose was to find her and make her safe again. Now I wanted to protect Gabe as fiercely as I needed to continue my search for Annie. I couldn't let one be to the detriment of the other.

'Eva, listen.' He squeezed my hands. 'If we stay here, what do I do? Work, eat, sleep, work, eat, sleep. Let's do something positive. I don't need to be here to remember Lola, or to grieve if that's what's worrying you.' He smiled warmly. 'Let's be naughty – we'll skip work on Friday, go back to Exley. We'll come back Sunday evening. We can go back there every weekend if we have to. Besides, being here, in this house, all weekend without Lola…' His voice trailed off then he smiled again. 'Call it therapy, taking me away from all this.' His eyes grazed the shadow of every corner in the room to highlight his point. 'And I also need some time alone with you – when we find Annie I get the feeling you won't want to leave her side for quite some time.' He chuckled for the first time in a week, then locked his eyes on mine. 'We won't get this chance again.' I knew he meant our chance to find Annie, but his words sounded final.

'Alright, alright, we'll go.' I succumbed to his reassurance, his eyes and his apparent need for a purpose. I couldn't ask about the house and his future now, when his loss was so raw. I just knew his arguments were genuine and assumed he knew what was best for him and Annie. I couldn't use this delicate time to highlight his future's uncertainties. The practicalities of our next trip were a safer subject. 'We should let Miranda know what we're doing.'

'What? Why?' He looked dismayed and the positive and boyish glow to his face dropped away.

'Because she's been trying so hard to help, that's even clearer now, and someone needs to know that we're going. She knew last time and it didn't cause any problems. She's been so encouraging Gabe, give her a chance. Can't you just trust that she's genuinely kind?'

'No, I can't. Please just leave it Eva. We might be back before she even knows we're gone. I'll let Harry know and you tell Mr Grayson that you need a day off. Tell Mrs Burgess you're going away for the weekend by all means, but let's leave Miranda and Fletcher out of it.' Now Fletcher was included too.

His mind was set and his plans so definite that I was happy to acquiesce, to soothe his concerns. So, as suggested, we made our hasty arrangements with our employers and I wished away the next two days until Friday morning came and we left once more for Exley.

Truth

The journey felt very different this time, as the roots we had previously left behind in Rushton were no longer there. Our maternal anchor wasn't waiting at the red brick house for our return. The fields and houses rushed past the window of the train just as they had before. My mind wandered as I watched the scenes of green and blue pass the window like an impressionist's painting.

I started to understand Gabe's need to continue our search so soon, to fill his mind with other things. But I still didn't understand his sometimes thinly-veneered distrust of Miranda and Fletcher. I liked them both; Fletcher with his gentle hesitation and quiet ways always seeming to be thinking deeply about things; Miranda, spontaneous and dynamic with strong views and confident ideas.

I knew Miranda had a soft spot for Gabe and, just as Lola had discerned, maybe more than that of a friend. But she seemed happy about our friendship and encouraged us in our search at every turn. Fletcher, as much as I liked him and felt that I was more *like* him, was tentative in his encouragement, unsure whether what we were doing was right. He encouraged caution and questioned our faith in the outcome. It seemed that he was concerned about upsetting some invisible balance between the lost and the secure. I felt Gabe's hand touch mine and turned to him as he smiled reassuringly, nodding his head towards the window as the station came into view.

We stepped down into familiar territory and walked well-known steps to the Sea Trout, wasting no time. As soon as we'd checked in with the manager, who smiled in kind recognition, and left our bags in our room we hurried to the Old Toll House with anticipation.

I was disappointed to see a different girl behind the desk and she told us that the young woman we'd seen previously wasn't there as it was her day off; disheartened and deflated, we left. Wanting to speak with the young woman before searching anywhere else, we made superficial small talk over our lunch in a nearby tea shop and then strolled by the river which wound through the town.

Despite the anti-climax, the afternoon went quickly and we didn't find ourselves back at the Sea Trout, hungry, until the early evening. We were greeted immediately by the proprietor who advised that there had been four telephone calls for Gabe, with the caller sounding quite agitated. He passed Gabe a slip of paper and retreated. Gabe looked at me questioningly, then at the slip of paper. It was a message from Fletcher.

'Why don't you get a table and order us something to eat. I'm sure this won't take long.'I wasn't sure whether he was trying to get rid of me or reassure me. I hesitated. 'Really, it's fine,' he encouraged and kissed my cheek and I got the impression that this signalled the end of the discussion.

'Okay, I might just pop upstairs. I'll be back in a few minutes.' He nodded, smiled and turned towards the reception desk. I couldn't stop myself. I turned the corner of the stairs just out of sight, then hesitated, thankful that the small restaurant was quiet this evening and hopeful that I might be able to eavesdrop on Gabe's conversation. Fletcher had clearly answered the phone quickly.

'Well, good evening to you too.'A short pause. 'Exley.' Long pause. 'Why? Is that really anything to do with you, Fletcher?' Another pause. 'Well, I can figure that one out.' Somewhat sarcastic. 'Look, we're staying put for now, we'll be back on Sunday. Miranda?' A mocking laugh, brief and insincere. 'You know what she's like Fletcher. No, she hasn't. We hope to. Yes, I will, thank you.' More sarcasm.

It was impossible to work out the conversation from what I'd heard and I was surprised to hear the tone of Gabe's voice. He sounded impatient, annoyed.

Fletcher was a kind, quiet man and I couldn't imagine why he'd been so keen to speak with Gabe or how he could have upset him so much. Even his reserve and apparent reluctance to interfere with the way things were in this warped world shouldn't be enough to get Gabe so upset.

I left my hiding place.

'What did Fletcher want? Is everything alright?' I asked as we were seated and offered menus. Gabe didn't look at me, but continued to survey his menu, clearly dwelling on the telephone call.

'He thinks we should come home,' he replied, without looking up, 'that we should stop looking. Miranda, however, is all for us carrying on until we find Annie and bring her home.'

'Oh,' was all I could muster. Gabe started to laugh; I started to get cross. 'What? Why are you laughing at me?'

He smiled at me, put down his menu and took my hand. 'It's lovely that you can't even see it. Fletcher has a crush on you – I don't think he likes the idea of us being here alone.'

'That's ridiculous. He's just cautious, he's a worrier. He doesn't want to 'upset the apple cart'.'

'Eva, this is nothing to do with him or Miranda. Look, there's no need for him to be cautious or worried. I think it's as simple as him not wanting you and me to be here; all this time alone together, being so close. Getting closer.' He sounded so sure that I started to wonder if he was right.

'And he's fallen out with Miranda?' That was the only thing I had guessed at from the one-sided conversation. Gabe didn't pick up on the fact that I'd clearly been listening in, or if he had he didn't mention it.

'Yes. She's been doing her own research at home, looking up numbers, telephoning people again.' I was touched once again that she'd do so much for me, a stranger until recently, and Annie, still a complete stranger to everyone but me. 'Fletcher told her to leave well alone, but you know Miranda. What Fletcher wants her to do will have no influence at all on what she actually does.'

'That's so kind of her. She's really trying to help isn't she?' Gabe nodded. 'She's been so nice. Every time we meet, she's encouraging and sweet.' I hesitated and watched Gabe as his eyes roamed up and down his menu, his jaw clenching – seemingly at my words. He must have felt my eyes on him because he looked up. 'Please don't be so hard on her.' His face hardened into an unasked question and I had to explain. 'It's alright. I know.'

'Know what?' His eyes darkened and he put down the menu, just as a smiling waitress approached us. The smile dropped from her lips as Gabe turned to her.

'Shall I come back?' she offered.

'Please.' I smiled quickly as she retreated.

'Know what?' Gabe pressed.

'The other day, when I met her in town, she told me all about you and her. It's alright, she explained everything.' Gabe's soft eyes turned to steel before me.

'Eva, there's nothing for her to tell. There's never been a me and her.'His voice grew louder with each word and I sensed heads turning towards us. 'I'm not hungry anymore, let's go.' He stood and took my hand as we left the table, his face still tense and mine smiling an apology to the waitress.

In our room I sat on the edge of the bed, hoping he'd sit beside me to talk, hoping I could reassure him that it was alright, that there was nothing to be upset about. Instead he leaned against the window with his arms folded, his face stormy.

'Alright, what's she been telling you?'

I felt like a naughty child, even though his anger was with Miranda and not me. I told him exactly what Miranda had told me, recounting our conversation as accurately as I could.

Smiling in the midday sun as she ran long graceful fingers though her hair, Miranda had giggled then linked arms with me; she'd exclaimed 'What luck, seeing you! We can have lunch!' and pulled me towards the baker's. There, she'd insisted on buying our lunch and we'd strolled arm in arm the short distance to the park, where we sat on the grass and laid out our simple picnic. She'd asked lots of questions about Annie and our growing up together. She asked about Kathleen and Bob and their home.

Gabe watched, emotionless, as I talked.

Miranda had asked about Gabe and me; how we were getting on, whether he ever talked about her. 'Ah, when we were together...'she blurted as her hand darted to her mouth in horror. 'Oh Eva, I'm sorry I didn't mean to say that!' Miranda took my hand as immediately as I was struck dumb. Maybe there was more to Miranda's infatuation than Lola had thought. She patted my hand and smiled 'It's alright, it's completely alright.'I nodded, still unable to speak as an invisible spoon stirred everything in my mind to a pulp. Maybe it was Miranda who was holding that spoon. 'Really, it was when we first met a few years ago. Gabe and I were drawn to each other. You know, we have so much in common.' She emphasised the *so*. I nodded again. 'We comforted each other.' Her expression was soft yet her eyes, almost siren-like, appeared to recall a secret but wonderful memory. Horrible visions invaded my eyes, visions I didn't want to see; they were powerful, passionate and intense and I was scared to blink lest they sink into my eyelids and remain forever. She paused, watching me.

I tried to speak, but croaked instead. I coughed gently and continued. 'I see.' It was the best I could do.

'Really Eva, it was nothing. I realised that Gabe was relying on me too much, and me on him of course. So I decided we should just be friends and he was fine with that. It was our shared history, you know, that brought such...intimacy. We understand each other deeply. But now, he's like another brother to me.' She patted me again like she was reassuring a child that the tooth fairy would come and smiled gently. 'Honestly.'

Gabe closed his eyes for a moment and I waited. And waited. Until I could wait in the silence no more.

'It's alright Gabe. She was very candid, very kind.'

'And you think I kept this from you?' he asked through gritted teeth.

'It's not important.'

'That's not what I asked. Do you think I'd keep something like that from you?'

'Gabe, it doesn't matter.'

'But it *does* matter, it *is* important.' He moved to sit beside me and we turned to each other. 'If something had happened between us, really happened, I would have told you. She's lying.'

I didn't know whether his face was angered or exasperated. 'But why? I don't understand.'

'Eva. I know that you understand how terrible it is to be lost. But, as beautiful and lovely and kind and caring as you are,' he smiled and touched my hair, 'you can't *feel* what it's like. And I'm glad.' I nodded and he sighed. 'When I met Miranda and Fletcher, we got on alright. I think Fletcher and I were fairly indifferent to each other. But Lola said that Miranda had a... a thing about me.' He raised his eyebrows a little and sighed again. 'I thought it was rubbish, and told Lola so. But Miranda and I kept bumping into each other. She was very pleasant, but I just wasn't interested. I wanted to keep myself to myself. Lola and I were doing just fine on our own.'

I smiled and squeezed his hand, hoping it would provide reassurance without interrupting him.

He took a deep breath before he continued. 'Anyway, the day I went back to watch my mother and my sister, after I knew they were gone for good, I came home to Lola's so low; and vulnerable, I suppose. Lola didn't know where I was going and she wasn't there when I came home. She would have been if she'd known.'

I saw the scene as Gabe painted the picture for me.

'At that moment, I was back in the dark pit that Lola had helped to lift me, drag me, from. But Lola wasn't there to haul me up. Guess who was?'

I didn't need to answer.

'I don't remember whether I'd said anything that might have led her to guess where I was going. Lola certainly didn't know. Anyway, she was there in the garden when I got back. Maybe I misled her. I don't know. I hope not. But nothing happened, even though she made her feelings clear. She initially masked them as concern, camaraderie, but under the polish it was clear. She tried to... 'He stopped his explanation of Miranda's actions and straightened his back. 'Anyway. Lola came home and that was that. She shepherded Miranda down the path quite firmly.' He smiled at the memory. 'Lola knew what was going on – she's not daft. Wasn't daft. And that was it. Miranda didn't get what she wanted.'His anger spent, he looked at me with boyish eyes. 'Nothing happened. I swear to you Eva, nothing happened.'

And I showed him I believed him.

* * *

Explanations completed, we left the guest house and walked once again through streets that felt like ours. We eventually found ourselves sitting on a bench overlooking the river. The water was still, except for the ripples caused by three ducks as they passed by. I watched them absentmindedly.

A few moments passed before Gabe spoke – I followed his gaze to a ladies' brown leather glove lying forlornly on the footpath. 'Oh dear,'was all he said as he stood up, retrieved the glove and returned to the bench. He flattened the glove carefully and placed it on the bench next to him. 'Do you think she'll be back for it, the lady who lost it?' His hand lay on top of the glove.

'I don't know.'I knew he was thinking of Lola. The glove would be in her shopping basket by now, ready to head back to Mill Street to join other discarded, lost or lonely objects. 'What will you do with all Lola's things?' I probed gently and naturally, sensing that the moment was right to ask.

'There's no hurry,'he sighed. 'Let's find Annie first and worry about that another time.' It sounded like denial. I would help him with Lola's things when the time came, of course, but I didn't relish the thought of such a final task; of removing the traces left by Lola. Although most of her collections were of no use to anyone, how could either of us bear to throw any tiny piece of her away? I still couldn't force myself to ask about the cottage, to question whether, in the near future, he would even have somewhere to live. I didn't know if the cottage was even Lola's. We sat there for a while longer, making plans for Saturday instead, and then we left for the guest house.

We smiled to the manager as we passed through the dining area. 'You know,'Gabe whispered into my hair, 'we could always give Fletcher something to be jealous about.'

I blushed.

The Old Toll House

I was so desperate to get to the Old Toll House and resume our search that Gabe and I were dressed and ready for the day by half past seven the next morning. As we left our room, me first and Gabe locking the door behind us, he admonished me, 'You know, breakfast isn't served for another hour and it's too early to go to the other hotel.'

'I know, but I just can't sit and wait.'

'So what do you plan that we do young lady?'

I paused on the stairs. 'Find somewhere nice, like a park?' I suggested.

'So we can sit and wait?' he smiled, teasing me.

'Okay, point taken.' I returned the smile and we left.

Spring had agreed to let summer practice its art for the day and outside it was mild and clear, hinting at warmth to come. The world seemed truly friendly for the first time in weeks and the weather suited our spirits which were bright and positive.

The town was waking up with a few people on their way to work and deliveries being made. A paper boy whistled a nameless tune as he passed and shopkeepers opened shutters and rolled out canopies. It was nice to see these routines, which must have been played out almost every day, carrying on as normal. I tried to push the thought from my mind that any of these people might be lost, or have lost someone without even knowing, as these feelings made me once more question the truth of my own existence; whether I had lost someone other than Annie and if this person had tried to rebuild my memory unsuccessfully, becoming lost to me forever.

Someone else was asking questions too. The brown eyes that read the note yet again narrowed in thought, while the heart that had squeezed tightly shut started to open in hope. A note. Some answers. More questions. A door had been opened, but did it lead to sunshine or rain?

'Are you alright?' Gabe had stopped me walking by taking my arm. 'Eva, what's wrong?'

'Sorry. One minute I was enjoying the normality of everything and then I, then I just drifted. Sorry.'

He wrapped his arms around me in a warm embrace, then he pulled away slowly, took my hand and we continued on our way. 'There's no need to be sorry. We're in this together.' He pointed down a small alley. 'Come on, there was a baker's down that way I think. We'll see if they open up early to make deliveries – we may be able to get something for breakfast.'

We were indeed able to buy a breakfast of freshly baked bread rolls, and strolled quietly down the pretty streets looking for somewhere to sit. I kept checking the time, willing it to pass so that we could be on our way back to the Toll House to see if Annie had returned since we left the note. Eight… eight-thirty. We found a bench set back a little from the shopping streets and perched there for our impromptu breakfast, even though my hunger had been chased away by anticipation.

Suddenly.

'It's her, Gabe. It's her!' I smacked my palm down onto Gabe's leg as I lurched from my seat and into a run.

I reached her in seconds and grabbed her arm. She spun around to face me, surprise and fear in her eyes. I smiled as I saw the light of recognition slowly push the shadow of fear from her face.

'Hello again. We met at the Toll House some time back. I left a note for my friend, Annie?'

'Oh yes, hello.' A startled little bird, she looked from me to Gabe who was now standing beside me.

'Did Annie Carter call in? Have you seen her?' Any social graces I might have possessed were forgotten as I grilled this poor girl in the street.

'Yes, she dropped in a few days ago. I did give her your note.'

A hundred butterflies danced inside me and I hardly dared to ask more. But, tentatively, I began. 'Did she say anything when she read it?' The girl shifted slightly as though keen to leave and looked tense and apprehensive, eyes darting between Gabe and me. Realising then how I had abruptly accosted her on her way to work, I softened, apologetic. 'You must be busy, I'm sorry. I just need to get in touch with her so much.'

She smiled kindly in response and seemed to relax. 'She didn't say anything. I'm sorry. I said I'd seen her friends and they were looking for her and then I gave her your note. She read it and put it in her bag. That's all.' The butterflies were slowing.

'Oh,' was all I could manage. The butterflies died.

'Thank you for passing our message on.'Gabe had stepped in. 'I don't suppose you found out any more about where she might be staying, or working?'

'No, I'm sorry. I think she's moving on, she said she'd be leaving Exley soon, but that she hoped we might catch up again some time. I said anytime she was passing it would be lovely to see her. She didn't offer me an address or anything, honestly. But even if she had…' I admired her candour and believed that she knew no more.

Gabe thanked her again as I struggled to form any more words and we let her continue her walk to work in peace.

There seemed nowhere to go now and we both stood silently in the street as people moved around us and the girl disappeared into the distance. My mind stood still, butterflies gone and hope sliding. Eventually, Gabe took my hand and led me to a small restaurant whose owner was just opening the doors and turning its sign to 'Open'.

We sat in silence over yet more cups of tea, this time untouched, until Gabe spoke.

'Maybe Annie's moving on because she's going home.'I hadn't thought of that. 'Now I'm sure we really have done all we can in Exley.' The finality of his statement stung like a betrayal and anger started to wake within me. He reached across and wrapped his fingers over mine, but I didn't look up. To me, leaving Exley now meant giving up and I was the one who felt lost. And sad again. And angry.

'What do we do now then?' The feeling that we were being disloyal to Annie weighed me down.

'I don't know. Go home? Sit tight and hope the note did the trick.'

'But Gabe, you're the one who said we had to keep going, keep looking, that we were too close to give up. Stop changing your mind. How can we 'sit tight'. How can I 'sit tight' and wait?'

'I know it'll be hard. But now we know for definite that she's seen the note. And you heard what the girl said – she thinks Annie's moving on. It's changed now, Eva. It's unlikely we'll just bump into Annie. If we knew she was definitely still in Exley, there might be the smallest chance, but what if she's already left? Maybe she's on her way to us at home. There really is nothing more we can do here. I think, if we stay, we'll be in the wrong place. Honestly, I do. Now she's seen the note, we have to go home and wait for her.'

I was sad and dejected and without the power to argue; my head was trying to convince my heart that his words made sense. The words I didn't want to say tasted sour but they came anyway. 'Okay; you're right.'I sighed. 'Let's do that.'

'One thing though.'

'What's that?'

'Tell Mrs Burgess you're leaving and come and stay at Lola's with me.'

Home

Sitting once more in Lola's home, I didn't know how I felt. I loved the house, the feeling of being home, but the warmth I felt at being there with Gabe had shards of ice piercing it – we both missed Lola and I felt unsettled at not having an action plan to follow. Our inertia felt like failure, saying *what will be will be.* Gabe insisted that we try to carry on with life as normal, whatever that was, so we went to work, we ate, we slept, we walked in the town, we sat on the bench overlooking the fields, and we saw Fletcher and Miranda just a couple of times. I visited Kathleen and Bob.

Miranda felt as I did, that our inactivity was wrong, and I caught sharp words between her and Gabe to that effect one day when I came home unexpectedly. The moment was quickly glossed over by both parties and nothing further said, even though the air was heavy with acrimony.

A few days later, I was home early from work and was on my own when the doorbell chimed. I answered the door to Fletcher, ever shy, and invited him in. It felt almost normal, having a friend drop by, as if I'd always lived in this house among these friends that I hadn't known for very long.

We wandered out into the back garden and perched on a low wall I'd discovered days before, amid weeds and overgrown plants.

We made small talk for a short while, before the conversation inevitably turned to Annie.

'Eva, I'm not going to go on and on about this or, I suppose, even expect it to make any difference. In fact, you wouldn't be the Eva we know and love if you just gave up looking, but please listen to what I have to say.' It sounded as though he'd rehearsed his plea and I was touched by his affectionate words.

'Go on.'

He took a deep breath before continuing.

‘I’d never forgive myself if I said nothing. Let her go. Let it go. It’s not as simple as just finding her.’

I interrupted him. ‘I know that’s only the start, Fletcher, that when she’s back we still have to get her home to her parents—’

Now it was his turn to interrupt. ‘No, it’s not that. You don’t understand. I lost someone, but not like you lost Annie. It’s you and Gabe. You need to understand what you’re doing, what you might lose—’ The back door burst open and Gabe was next to us before any more could be said. I stood as I saw his eyes flash with a fire that I’d never seen. His face was inches from Fletcher’s, his eyes burning.

‘What have you said?’

‘Gabe, I—’ Fletcher looked more surprised than concerned.

‘What have you done?’ Gabe spat the words venomously at Fletcher and I stepped forward to intervene.

‘Gabe, please.’ Not knowing what the problem was, I didn’t know what to say to pour cool and calming water on the fire. However, I did know that this wasn’t just about Gabe’s suspicion of Fletcher's 'crush' as he'd called it. Anyway, I had the feeling now that Gabe was wrong; that Fletcher had something else that he needed to say. It was clear that there was yet another fathom to the murky depths of this story. The more I learnt to swim in this ocean the deeper it went, and I wasn't sure how deep I could go and still manage to breathe.

'Just leave, Fletcher.' Gabe had calmed and stepped back, controlled thunder showing on his face.

'No Gabe, I won't.' My eyes snapped from Fletcher's face to Gabe's, worried ahead of his reaction. The words Fletcher wanted to say were clearly so important to him that they forced him to step from his quiet shadows and into Gabe's burning glare.

'What?'

At Gabe's seething response, Fletcher's demeanour changed once more and he straightened, looking tense and dark. 'I said no, Gabe.' I'd never seen mild and gentle-mannered Fletcher so defiant and solid. 'I came to talk to Eva and that's what I'm going to do, with or without you here. You and I both know that there are things that need to be said. It's me who has got to say them, because you won't.' He let out an involuntary chuckle. 'And you know Miranda won't, but then that's another story isn't it?'

Gabe stepped the few paces towards Fletcher and took him roughly by the arm. 'Right, that's it. Out.'

'Gabe.'I tried to diffuse the moment. 'Gabe, don't.'

'Eva, please, just stay out of this.' A scuffle started as Gabe tried to man-handle Fletcher towards the kitchen door and I almost danced around the edges, moth to flame, trying to stop him. Gabe's free hand gently held me back, whilst the other one, conflicting, forcefully pushed Fletcher towards the door. As Gabe momentarily turned to me, Fletcher wrenched his arm free and pushed Gabe backwards. He stumbled, righted himself and lurched upward in one fluid movement punching Fletcher square on the face. I'd never actually seen someone hit another person, except at the pictures, and I flinched at the hard yet soft fleshy sound of the impact as Fletcher tripped backwards to land on the stone step of the kitchen.

'Gabe!' I shouted at the same time as I bent down to Fletcher.

'I'm alright. I'm alright.' Fletcher repeated, to himself as much as to me, as the blood started to trickle from his nose. I looked back up at Gabe who was looking at me as if he was a naughty child. Fletcher winced as I touched his face.

'Come on, let's go inside and sort this out,' I soothed.

'No Eva. It's alright. I'll leave.'He looked at Gabe. 'It's not over Gabe, but it might be if you don't stop this searching. Don't end up like me.' He stood, turned to me and squeezed my hand. He gave me a small smile, wincing in pain as he did so. Then he left.

I looked at Gabe, who walked towards me. 'Don't, Gabe.' I turned away from him and followed Fletcher's path into the house, leaving Gabe standing in the garden just outside the kitchen door. Rather than stopping, I walked straight through the house, into the front garden and down the path. I heard Gabe call my name, but I ignored him and he didn't follow. There was no sign of Fletcher. I continued towards the town.

With no money or handbag, I found myself in an obvious place. The library welcomed me back with no admonition for my absence. I lost two hours, poring over books, reading their spines, scanning some half-heartedly. The longer I stayed, the more I was reminded of Annie, of the books in Randall Boyes' care and of how complicated my life had become. I saw how much had passed in so little time. I knew how days could feel like a lifetime. I felt how tiring fear and pain could be. I left to walk back to the cottage, not wanting to face Gabe, but knowing that my anger at his behaviour was gradually abating.

I remembered my aunt once telling me how, in protection of her young, love could turn a mother from a timid mouse to a roaring dragon, change timidity to the utmost bravery. I supposed fear could do the same. Fletcher had found a strong voice that needed to be heard and Gabe had reared up in protection of me, even though I hadn't heard Fletcher's words and didn't know what Gabe protected me from.

I could hear the music as I walked the last few steps to the front gate. It grew richer as I walked up the green-swathed path. Pushing open the front door which already stood slightly ajar, the smell of cooking reached me as the sound of music buffeted my ears – strong music, reaching a crescendo of such power and passion that I had to stop and listen. Then it ebbed and flowed into a smooth melody and swayed and lilted, like a dancer. I leaned against the sitting room door and, looking towards Gabe's room, was lost again.

I was sure that Gabe didn't know I was there. When I eventually made my way to the kitchen, still accompanied by music, I saw the table laid for two. He knew I'd be back. Something was bubbling in the oven. Grape hyacinths were in a white jug on the table. A pitcher of water stood waiting, next to two unrelated glasses, odd plates, mismatched cutlery. A hand was on my shoulder, making me jump. I turned and moved away from Gabe – I surprised myself with my reaction more, I think, than I surprised Gabe.

'I'm sorry.' His words were genuinely contrite.

'Tell that to Fletcher.'

'Touché.'

I stared, not stirring, into his eyes where the flash of fire was gone, extinguished and replaced by the usual softness and warmth. I didn't speak; why should I help him in his explanation?

He sighed. 'I'm sorry I hit him, it all got out of hand and I'm sorry.' No conciliatory reaction from me and he tried a different, more gentle approach. 'Fletcher lost someone once.'

'Yes, they both lost their family, I know that. They've felt that same pain of loss and you should appreciate that.'

'No, this was after that. Some time after. A girl. He's been through it twice and I know that he's still deeply troubled.' He hesitated and I got the impression that he was trying to guard against being too sympathetic. His voice hardened a little. 'But what we're doing really is none of his business. Or Miranda's.'

I ignored his final comments. 'I don't understand. How can it happen twice? I thought noone knew they'd lost someone, that I'm the exception.' I slumped down onto a kitchen chair, suddenly exhausted as I surrendered myself once again to further horrors, more deep water. How much more was there? I was so tired of twists and turns, dizzying me with their changes of direction. Gabe came to kneel in front of me.

'It's not like you lost Annie, it's different. Look, it's not important now. It's Fletcher's story and it's all in the past. This is your story, yours and ours. One day you'll understand, I promise.'

'Can't we help him?' Gabe smiled and brushed some hair from my face.

'You can't make everything right for everyone. Fletcher's story is done. The thing that matters most to you, above everything else, is seeing Annie again and bringing her home. I know that and you need to focus on that too. Anything else, any other sacrifice, has to be made to achieve that. So stop trying to solve other people's troubles and concentrate on Annie. Okay?' Some of what he said made sense. 'I would never ask you to sway from that and you shouldn't ask yourself to. She's the sister you never had. Annie means more to you than anyone else in the world.'

I couldn't correct him now as his plea was so heartfelt, but one day I would put him straight. It wasn't Annie who now meant more to me than anyone else in the world. But the person who did, who knelt in front of me, couldn't see it yet. There'd be plenty of time to put that right.

Sunlight

Although I couldn't bear to move anything in Lola's home, I felt I could in her garden. As she'd once had the joy of nurturing and caring for such things, I didn't feel bad about trying in a small and amateurish way to resurrect the green space she would have loved. I hoped she was looking down at me and smiling as I toiled happily in her garden. I'd borrowed the floppy straw hat I'd found hanging on a peg in the hall and Gabe was loaned some tools from Harry Stanley. Whenever I could I'd be weeding, digging, pruning, cutting and sowing. All new to me, I found that I enjoyed the time outside and was pleased with the little areas of progress gradually being seen in the garden. I hoped Lola would have approved of the small changes I'd made – nothing major, mostly tidying and freeing plants from the weeds that bound them. I did have thoughts of the vegetables that should be cultivated in an effort to be self-sufficient and made a mental note to speak with Gabe about this, more to seek his permission to make such a change than to ask his advice about the practicalities.

Weeks had passed since our final trip to Exley. Resignation to the waiting game had been hard, but had eventually come. Summer was now with us. The warm weather lent itself well to our positive and optimistic facade and our efforts at ordinary domesticity. We tried to mesh this outlook with our feelings about Annie and the continual rumblings of impending war that we read about in the paper and heard on the wireless; at moments like these, our eyes would be drawn to each other and we'd try to change the subject.

My regular visits to Aunt Kathleen and Uncle Bob had resumed – I had to keep pretending things were normal, but it was getting easier and my capacity for this veneer amazed me. Gabe and I had slipped into what might be considered the routines of normal life, almost starting to believe our own guise – but inside it still hurt and Annie was with me every day. The pulling at my heart to return to Exley was very strong, but the reasoning in my head along with Gabe's reluctance was powerful enough to keep me from acting on it.

Kathleen and Bob were unaware of my new lodgings and I was sure that was the best way for now. My aunt's path never crossed with Mrs Burgess, who thought I'd moved home to my aunt and uncle's. No-one knew that I now lived in the cottage, the red brick house, at the end of Mill Street. The house was a distance from any other dwelling and so overgrown was the garden, even after my efforts, that any comings and goings were sheltered and discreet. Miranda and Fletcher weren't party to my change of location either – my visits had been so regular before Lola's passing that we tried to maintain the impression that I just continued to visit often, without actually having to say anything or tell any untruths; in reality I'm sure they must have known but chose, thankfully (and surprisingly in Miranda's case) to say nothing directly to us.

The day after the fight between Gabe and Fletcher, I'd sought him out. I assured him that Gabe had told me everything. Fletcher had asked me what 'everything' was and all I could bring myself to do was reassure him, tell him I knew the whole story. I couldn't tell him that I knew something of his second loss and then to resurrect his pain by making him re-live the circumstances for me.

Despite my vagueness Fletcher seemed resigned to my assurances, obscurely telling me that he supposed it was my choice. I tried hard to push the suspicion, or maybe knowledge, that there was yet more to know from my already disturbed mind. I didn't think I could survive knowing any more of the cruel twists and turns these people suffered and, although some masochistic part of me longed to know, I didn't ask. Denial was wrong but it was also, in the short term, less painful than truth.

Of course, a part of me wanted to know his story; the natural human desire not to be kept in the dark wondered at the circumstances which led to him not only being the person lost, but having then lost someone himself. I was amazed that this could happen to someone twice; it had taken a lot just for me to believe in the phenomenon of becoming lost and now I felt additional anger at whatever reason or power let this awful thing happen to a person twice.

I wondered at Fletcher's capacity for survival, his acceptance of his lot and his ability not to succumb to being cruel and hard. I couldn't imagine the pain of being lost, albeit with a sibling, and not being with my family again. I couldn't imagine the joy of then finding a soul mate, as I had now done, only to lose them too. I didn't ask Fletcher how he'd survived, whether the person he'd lost was indeed the soul mate I assumed them to be; I didn't try to find any answers. I just assured him that I knew what I was doing; I was set on the path Gabe and I had chosen and was happy that I was doing the right thing, that Annie must come home no matter what intervention there had to be from me. I was sure Fletcher was concerned by my continuing interference in the way this lost thing worked.

Since our conversation, Fletcher seemed to be keeping his distance which both saddened and relieved me. Miranda was rarely seen, having tried hard to convince us we were wrong in our languid approach. There had been some harsh words and she now only dropped in very occasionally, still trying with any visit to force some action from our hands. Two warm friendships had recently cooled through disapproval, Fletcher's of our search and Miranda's of our inactivity, and I felt a little ashamed to admit to myself that I was, selfishly, quite content to have Gabe to myself.

Time ticked by; on occasion it seemed much slower than the hands of the clock. There were quiet moments when I would be caught by genuine doubt. It wasn't the uncertainty I'd experienced before, as that had always been underlined with the belief that all would eventually be resolved. The doubt, the hesitation, which now prodded me was saying that maybe I was wrong; maybe this was the way life would remain. Despite my happiness with Gabe and my all-consuming belief that I should always be here with him, the need for Annie's return clouded everything. It bothered me greatly that my optimism wasn't as strong now. I not only felt guilt at my increasing acceptance of the way things were but also superstition, as if my doubts could be self-perpetuating. If I believed she wasn't coming home, maybe she wouldn't.

Annie's birthday came. I visited her parents, sure that on this day they would recall something. Surely the wonder of giving birth, the marvel of holding your own new-born, which I'm told only a mother can truly understand, could not be forgotten on such a day. But, as Gabe had warned, it was just another day for them and I returned home with my heart bruised yet again. How much trauma could a heart take and still keep beating? Gabe could see that I was becoming more despondent with each few days that passed and so he promised that, if yet another week passed with no news, we would resume our active searching somehow. I don't know what he thought we could possibly do, but he must have been getting desperate to reassure me as he even suggested that maybe we could try to force some further assistance from Mr Boyes. Despite his optimistic words, I sensed the same doubt shadowing his eyes. I saw in them his fear that the words meant to buoy my spirits didn't have the strength to carry my heavy hopes. I clung to his words, despite my misgivings. We'd waited long enough for Annie to come to us.

The news of our decision obviously pleased Miranda when she paid us one of her rare visits. She said we'd been 'sitting around and doing nothing' for far too long and, accusingly, tossed in a comment about our 'cosy cottage arrangements' confirming my suspicion that she knew more than she'd voiced. Although she was still as encouraging as ever in our search for Annie (in fact, if anything, when she spoke of Annie I thought I could hear a note of near desperation in her voice as though Annie's return meant as much to her as it did to me) I noticed a barely concealed tone of malice, but said nothing of this to Gabe.

I still hadn't raised the subject of ownership or tenancy of the cottage with Gabe. There'd been no mention of Lola leaving a Will, or of any arrangements with a third party concerning the cottage. I couldn't bring myself to ask and had to assume, with so many weeks passing, that all had been addressed without my knowing; after all, it really was nothing to do with me. The inside of the cottage remained largely unchanged in Lola's absence. Lola's collections stayed where she'd left them and I consciously kept any visual signs of my own residency there from view. The few things I'd brought with me stayed out of sight.

The sun warmed my shoulders one Saturday afternoon as I toiled in the front garden, my back to the lane and my head bowed low. I reached for a large thistle which had been trying to hide beneath a shrub under the sitting room window, hoping my thin gloves would provide enough protection against the hostile plant. Lola's garden had been replacing my library visits for some time. The library saddened me and being in Lola's garden doing something that she once loved brought me close to her and lifted my spirits. It was my project when Gabe wasn't around – he couldn't bring himself to join me in my endeavours. For me it was therapeutic, for him it was painful. He was pleased for me to resurrect the garden, but memories of Lola hurt him still.

I knew Gabe would be home soon, so I wasn't surprised to hear the front gate open and close behind me. 'I won't be a minute,' I called without turning. Time to leave the gardening – just this one green prickly intruder to deal with.

'Eva?' I grasped the thistle involuntarily, tighter than I'd planned, and froze. I let go. Slowly I turned and, blinking up towards the shining sky, saw the shadowed figure looking down at me framed by the brightness. I closed my eyes, opened them again. She was still there.

I didn't have time to stand before she'd dropped to her knees on the ground in front of me, just inches away. I held her face in my earthy be-gloved hands, not wanting to let go in case she disappeared. She smiled through her tears as they fell from huge brown eyes and we clung to each other, still kneeling.

Crying turned to laughter, which turned back to tears. There was disbelief and joy, relief and delight. Among the tears, we both fell over our words as questions were forced aside by the happiness falling from our lips. It seemed such a long time before we were able to stand, but we couldn't let go of each other even then. I held Annie's hand tightly, almost afraid that if I let go she'd be pulled away from me and back into my imagination alone.

We moved to a crude little bench I'd recently constructed from some large stones and a plank of wood and sat down, still holding tight to each other, anchoring ourselves to the elation that we felt in the other's presence. Where did we start? What could we say? This moment that I'd lived and prayed for, begged would come and wept for, was here.

Annie spoke first.

'I've missed you so much,' she cried through her tears.

'Oh Annie, I can't begin to tell you…'

'I know. I know.' Was all she could whisper now, between the hiccupping breaths that come when you've cried every tear that you have and your eyes are left stinging, but searching for more.

All I could say was, 'It's weeks since the girl said you got my note.'

'Yes, yes, it is. It's been so long Eva, so very, very long and tiring, and sad and frightening.'I wrapped her in my arms and rocked her like a baby as she slowly continued between sobbing breaths and new tears. 'Your note, it filled in spaces for me. Eva – no-one knew me, no-one. And then I didn't know me either. I was standing in a strange place and I didn't know anything. And I ran. I didn't understand what had happened. Who was I? I just ran away.' I rocked and nodded and soothed. 'Then little things started to come back, and then bigger pieces did, then broken bits that it was hard to piece together properly. And I didn't know what was real and what I'd imagined. When I got your note it turned on a light. It put bigger pieces in the gaps, but I was still confused. It was as if I was in the middle of this great big lie and I didn't know what to do, what the truth was.'

I gently asked, 'Annie, why didn't you just come straight home when you got it, got my note?' Despite all Lola and Gabe's explanations, when face-to-face with Annie, I couldn't believe she hadn't known who I was.

'I didn't know if things would get better or worse if I came. It was all such a mess. You seemed to know things about me, but I couldn't get this feeling out of my head that something was wrong. I can't believe it now, but I just couldn't place us together; I didn't know how we fitted. It was like an itch I couldn't reach.'

I tried to understand but guiltily felt wronged, as though my note should have answered everything.

She grasped my hand. 'Until yesterday. Yesterday, Eva, it was like a waterfall emptying on me.' She smiled and held my dirty gloved hands in both of hers. 'I was walking past this little tea shop and heard a crash. I glanced in and saw a smashed teapot on the floor, then I heard someone in the street whistling 'Over the Rainbow', then I read your note again. I had it in my bag. Things that weren't there in my head before suddenly were. And I knew it would all be alright. If you were looking for me, it would be alright. I remembered it all. I was so relieved to know that—' She broke down and I embraced her again.

'I know. I know it all, Annie.'

She sobbed into my shoulder, and then looked up at me with huge brown eyes that dripped tears onto my shirt. 'You remembered me, all that time you remembered me, then helped *me* to remember. And I know what happened before I left, Mum and Dad… they…'

'I know, I know,' I whispered as we continued to embrace tightly, afraid to release each other.

'We'll work it out, I promise. We'll work it all out together.'

We sat there for some minutes and eventually the sobs of past despair and weeks of frustration turned to tears of relief, which then dried into smiles of happiness.

'I just can't believe you're home.' And I clung to her again, still with the fear that she'd somehow disappear. Stranger things had happened, after all.

With the slow calming of our intense emotions came the recollection of my own new situation.

'Annie, we have to tell Gabe.' Excitement was bubbling up in my chest, making it hard to breathe or talk, butterflies were resurrected. 'I have to show you to Gabe!' I stood and dragged her to her feet, barely giving her time to stand before rushing to the lane with her staggering and half-tripping behind.

'Eva, Eva who is Gabe?' I stopped and laughed as I turned to her, just outside the gate.

'Annie, Gabe is, he's...'

Annie's laughter stopped and she looked at me in mock reproach. 'I've missed a lot then.' She smiled, despite damp red eyes and runny nose. Then we were holding each other again.

'You have Annie; you've missed so much.' I smiled in return, feeling a little embarrassed, then added so quietly I don't think she heard, 'Gabe's the whole world.'

We half ran, half walked towards the market garden. Our legs hurried us towards my goal as we breathlessly exchanged questions, short explanations between the breaths of our exertion. We talked at the same time as each other, tripping over our excited enquiries. Annie begged for news of her parents, but I couldn't highlight how complete her parents' erasure of her was. I did verbally stumble briefly across my search for her, with my words alighting on Lola and Gabe with the briefest of butterfly touches. I asked Annie where she'd been, how she'd been, what she'd done; all our questions were rushed and brief between breathless gasps for air, all our responses too short for that which lay within our heads and our hearts. Then we stopped as Annie cried. Our rush to Gabe was forgotten for the moment as we stood facing each other in the lane and I listened.

Annie spoke of fear and loneliness, of the girl at the Old Toll House, again of the note. She told me once more how she'd slowly remembered parts of her life before Exley, stirred by some of the things I'd hastily written in my note. I held Annie's hands as she spoke and felt them tremble with recent memories. She didn't speak for very long, clearly finding it hard. She took a deep breath and changed the subject.

'Come on Eva. Let's not talk now, here. Let's find this man. He's the man who was with you when you left the note?' I nodded as Annie grabbed my hand tight and we started to run again. 'Then I have lots to thank him for.'

Our run, walk, run continued until we could run no more and a fast walk was all we could muster to take us the last few hundred yards to the gates of the market garden. Our flight to Gabe had taken twenty minutes and I couldn't wait any longer. As we pushed open one of the gates, adrenalin gave my body the strength to run again with poor Annie being pulled along beside me. I was shouting Gabe's name before I could see him. Then, at the sight of him in the distance we stopped at the end of a row of glorious lush green vegetation. He looked towards us. I couldn't see his expression from so far away, but I could guess. I saw him straighten up, lift his chin slightly as he strained to see. He hesitated, dropped what he was holding but which I couldn't really see, then he too broke into a run and was with us in moments.

When he reached us he stopped. He wiped a soil covered hand on his trouser leg and offered it to Annie, smiling. Instead of taking his hand, she reached up and wrapped her arms around him. He smiled at me gently over her shoulder as he held her in his sincere embrace. He winked at me, then his gaze travelled down to my hands and I followed it to realise that I was still wearing my gardening gloves. I laughed, then hastily joined Gabe and Annie in their hold.

Filling In

Keeping Annie firmly to ourselves, we spent the evening in happy disbelief at Lola's. We talked, we ate, we moved from kitchen to sitting room where we continued to talk. Annie wanted to know all that had happened from the day we'd all lost her until today, almost two and a half months later.

My words danced around the issue of Annie's parents until, encouraged by Gabe, I gently explained all that I now understood about their loss of Annie. I was surprised at the strength Annie had on hearing what I had to say, but I could see that her faith in her parents was such that this barrier seemed small compared to what she'd been through so far. Annie filled us in further, tearfully, on her experiences during the past few weeks; her loss of memory, her panicked flight which ended in Exley, her desperation, the gradual recovery of parts of her history, my note, coming home.

Gabe left most of the talking to us and we continued late into the night. I wondered whether Annie's story had refreshed some of Gabe's emotions and had once more made raw the feelings that he'd long denied.

Annie wanted to know how Gabe and I had met, how we'd known to share her story with each other, found her whereabouts. I hesitated, knowing that my explanation would eventually take me to Lola's story and to Gabe's. I stuttered as I tried to find the words to start, then felt Gabe's hand touch mine. I saw Annie's eyes drawn to the touch, then dart away discreetly and knowingly.

Gabe began.

'If I take you back to the very start right now, we'll be in for a long night,' he smiled. 'Being lost, like you were, are, isn't new.'Surprised, Annie looked to me for reassurance and I nodded. 'It happens. It happens to some people. There's an awful lot to tell but, for now, this story starts with Lola. This is Lola's house.' He looked around the room. 'Lola was my very good friend for a long time. She was lost too; and she looked after me when I was first alone. Lola was the lighthouse to which I swam. That's how we knew your story, through our own experiences.' I could almost feel Annie's sudden inhalation of breath at the revelation. 'Lola and Eva met on the day Eva found out that you'd gone. There are more lost souls out there than you might imagine; we were able to help Eva untangle things.' Humbly, he hadn't explained that he and Lola had thrown *me* a lifeline from their vantage point, which I'd grabbed gratefully and held tightly to for weeks while they, and now just Gabe, dragged me to safety.

'Gabe's being very modest Annie. I wouldn't have been able to do anything without him and Lola. I don't know where I'd be now, or where you'd be, without them.' I had to show Annie that Gabe and Lola's parts in the story were actually the starring roles and that our safety and our reunion was all down to them.

Neither Gabe nor I had explained Lola's absence and Annie's innocent question unwittingly dealt a stabbing blow.

'Where is Lola? I'd love to meet her.'

I faltered a little before explaining. 'She's gone Annie. She died in May.' I didn't look at Gabe, but watched Annie's face drop.

Gently she responded. 'I'm so sorry.'

I couldn't let our talk of Lola end on a low note. I felt that Annie should know more about Lola right now rather than leaving her even temporarily in Annie's mind as just a story-less name, a past acquaintance. Lola deserved more than just a passing mention.

'You would have loved her Annie.'I smiled and Annie did too. 'She was warm and kind and understanding, she gave hope and sanctuary. She wasn't a mother but she was the most motherly person you could meet.' My heart sent the words to my mouth and they tumbled forth without me needing to form them in my head. 'She had a cheeky sparkle in her eye. And she had a patchwork shopping bag. And wore odd slippers. And collected things. And she loved us.'I slowed. 'And she'd be as happy as we are that you're home.'

I was surprised to hear Gabe's voice then. 'I couldn't have introduced her any better,' he smiled.

When we were so tired that we thought we could talk no more, I showed Annie to Lola's room. It was the only other bedroom with any space to sleep and, regardless, it seemed appropriate that she should sleep there. I'm sure Lola would have approved. I showed Annie the picture Fletcher had taken and spoke of when we'd met. As tired as we were, Annie and I found ourselves sitting on the bed talking still; we held on to each other again for a long time before we could tear ourselves apart and I went to bed happy, complete and smiling.

Gabe and I were awake and dressed before Annie the next day and let her sleep; although I did silently open the door to Lola's room just to see her, to reassure myself that she was still there. It didn't surprise us that she was still sleeping, this being quite conceivably the first restful night she'd had for many weeks. I knew how I'd felt the previous night and could imagine those sensations magnified a hundred times for Annie.

I was smiling as I leaned against the kitchen table, watching Gabe scrape the dry mud from his work boots just outside the back door. He sensed me watching and, stopping, turned to face me.

'You know this isn't the happy ending just yet,' he warned.

'I know. I know we have to deal with Kathleen and Bob. I'm just so happy. No, I'm not happy, happy isn't enough. I'm *euphoric* that we have her back. I still can't believe she's here and she's safe.'

'I just don't want—' Worry creased his brow as he spoke and I interrupted him before he could dampen the moment with more realism.

'It's alright Gabe, don't worry; I know that we could have a mountain ahead. But I really think we're more than halfway up it already. Only yesterday morning, I couldn't imagine even getting *this* far.'Gabe watched me. 'I don't want to share her time just yet, but I suppose we should let Miranda know that Annie's back.' Now he turned back to his boots, scraping them more forcefully, as he muttered something indiscernible under his breath.

No more was said on the subject and I chose not to press the issue further. We should tell Miranda, but I could see that another day or so wouldn't do any harm and I let the matter drop for now.

When Annie woke and joined us downstairs she looked refreshed, which was a relief. Yesterday, she'd looked tired and drained of any energy or fight. Today, she seemed revitalised and hopeful and was Annie again. As I started making breakfast for her, Gabe said he'd leave us to talk and retreated to his room. I wondered whether it was the earlier talk of Miranda that had dampened his mood.

Soon the dancing notes of Gabe's piano drifted in to us.

'That's so beautiful,' remarked an entranced Annie, as she turned towards the melody. All conversation was forgotten as we listened.

After some minutes, I began to talk. Despite Gabe's very brief outline of his and Lola's stories to Annie last night, I knew from previous conversations that he was happy for Annie to know more. The sound of Gabe's piano had opened my thoughts to this and I told Annie about the giving of a gift. I explained Lola's gift to her brother and what Gabe had hoped to pass to his sister. These gifts hadn't proved positive for Gabe or Lola, and the last thing I wanted was for Annie to become more frightened that her situation was permanent, but I did want her to know more about the people I loved so much. She listened intently and I could sense her genuine compassion for them; but I couldn't tell whether I'd caused her any more alarm.

Return

Despite Annie's safe return and the relief this offered, for the next two nights I struggled to sleep. The night of Annie's homecoming gifted to me the deepest and most luxurious slumber I was sure I'd ever had. It seemed like a cruel joke now, being followed by two nights of fitful sleep and an overactive mind. I couldn't push from my head my worries about Kathleen and Bob and how we'd return Annie to them. It's true that the higher you fly on rapture the more painful it is when you fall back to earth. My restlessness was so bad that staying in bed was an ordeal; if sleep wouldn't take me I found it hard to lie still in the darkness.

The first night I'd sat in the kitchen for a while, had some warm milk, then wandered about silently. The second night I turned on a small, red-shaded lamp in the sitting room and curled into the one free chair. As I willed myself to relax, inviting slumber to envelop me in Lola's chair, my gaze drifted down to the floor to find a small gap between the chair and the hearth. Lola's red shawl lay there in a little puddled heap. Leaning forward, I picked it up. Without thinking, I raised it to my face and buried myself in its soft folds. I caught the faintest scent of a perfume I didn't know the name of, but which I knew instantly was Lola's. I shook out the creases and wrapped the soft wool around my shoulders. I wished Lola had met Annie, seen her safe return. I hoped that somehow, somewhere, she knew. My mind walked carefully around all my memories of Lola as I closed my eyes and drifted.

Gabe and I had insisted that Annie spend a few days resting before we worked out the next stage of her life. In truth, I'd been trying to plan it out in my own head continually since she'd come home. I couldn't bring myself to tell her how hard I feared it might be now the initial exhilaration had been replaced with realism, a word and a feeling I now hated. Changing the thoughts to words gave them more credence somehow. I didn't want to add power to the uncertainty by voicing it.

It was strange to me that the person with whom I once had no secrets was the person who I now kept the largest secret from. I shielded her from the most important thing in her world, her own life. We'd not ventured into town yet and I knew that I couldn't wrap her up in the safety of denial any longer. We couldn't protect her forever. We needed to decide what we would do next and I was sure that Gabe had also been plagued with the swarm of worry, ideas, plans and fears which had taken over every available recess of my brain.

The issue of telling Miranda the news was snatched from our hands, as she dropped in unexpectedly two days after Annie's return. On the Tuesday morning, I'd answered the door early and not been completely surprised to see her standing on the doorstep. She was groomed to perfection and wearing a fitted grey dress, trimmed tastefully on collar and pockets with black velour or some similar fabric. Her black coat was hung across her forearm, along with the handle of her tiny black handbag.

'Eva. I'm glad it's you.' She started over the threshold, speaking quickly. 'I've been thinking. Why don't we try the—'

I laid my hand on her arm to halt her words. I had to tell her, as I was sure she was about to outline another search plan. 'Miranda, she's here.'

'Who?'

I let out a blurt of a laugh involuntarily. 'Annie. Annie's here. She's home.'

'Oh dear God! When Eva, when? Where is she?' Her eyes glowed with an excitement and pleasure that was touching, if incongruous with the fact that she didn't even know Annie.

'Come on, I'll introduce you.' I led Miranda through to the back garden, where Annie was sitting on the wall reading the newspaper half-heartedly. She turned as she heard our voices and stood to greet this new friend.

Introductions over, we all sat in the garden drinking the ever-present mismatched cups of tea and looking, should anyone have peeped in, like three old friends chatting and enjoying the morning sunshine.

Miranda was the most animated I'd ever seen her; she radiated relief and delight, beauty and happiness.

Plans

That evening Miranda made it quite clear to Annie, Gabe and I that she felt we shouldn't delay and must immediately begin what she termed 'working on' Kathleen and Bob. I was grateful for her continuing enthusiasm but Gabe was, as ever, cool towards her and getting more so. I was sad that he wasn't more tolerant of her given her enthusiasm, and was slightly embarrassed by this, but he was always guarded around her and I couldn't change it. I knew Miranda cared greatly for him and several times had glimpsed it in the way she looked at him, betraying admiration, love and maybe even adoration. Gabe was clearly uncomfortable, even if he did believe that Miranda's infatuation was long past.

When Gabe and I were alone in the kitchen, I asked him again about this and he reassured me. His feeling was that we should consider our approach to Annie's parents, rather than rushing in unprepared and he said he wished Miranda wasn't always there to interfere. Hearing Lola's words in my ear about Gabe's ignorance of Miranda's continuing soft spot, I said no more. Gabe's insistence on caution with Annie's parents made sense and was fine by me; his approach was more cautious and considered than Miranda's. It was perfectly acceptable for him to get frustrated with her occasionally, when she constantly pushed for her course of action to be taken over his.

We'd all talked over the possibilities for quite some time that evening and when Miranda rose to leave Gabe, too quickly, offered to see her out. Annie and I continued talking in the sitting room. After a little while, I ventured into the hall. The front door was ajar and I could hear Gabe and Miranda talking outside. I knew I shouldn't, but I stood very still just inside the front door and listened. They were clearly at the end of their conversation.

'Fletcher's judgement is coloured by his own experience, Gabe.' Miranda sounded exasperated.

'Is yours coloured by anything?' Gabe's tone was accusing.

'I want what's best for Eva and Annie. Obviously.' She was indignant.

'Obviously,' he echoed. 'Can you just leave well alone, Miranda? Please? Don't rush it, you know it will happen. Just let Eva and I have a little more time.' He sounded saddened and almost defeated.

'You're deluded Gabe, the sooner Annie's back with her parents the better it'll be for everyone. Even you.' It was clear she'd ended the discussion as she flung out those words.

I heard her footsteps walking away from the house and I moved to the front door.

'Gabe? Has Miranda gone?'

'Yep.'

'What were you talking about?'

'Just asking her to leave us to sort this out. Too many cooks and all that.' He was distracted, but we returned to the sitting room and continued with our plans.

The days of delay and letting Annie settle in were done and now there were no excuses left. We were trying to put off the task that was so important to us as we were frightened of failure, and not knowing whether we'd succeed was better than actually finding out for sure.

We decided to tread very carefully, with further gentle nudging of Annie's parents, before attempting to change things by force. I had always liked the story of the wind and the sun and their battle, as they looked down on the earth, to see which one of them could rid a man of his coat the fastest. The force of the wind just caused him to wrap his coat closer around his body, clutching it to himself tightly. The gentle approach of the sun, however, offering the warmth of its rays in encouragement, induced him to remove his coat willingly and with a smile. I wanted to take the gentle and encouraging approach of the sun, before having to resort to a gale force wind.

I stepped into my aunt's kitchen to be met by her enveloping arms.

'Come in, come on in.' Then she held me back at arm's length and appraised me. 'It's been a good week or so since we've seen you. Have you lost weight? You've been eating properly, haven't you? It's so important when you've been poorly.'

'I'm eating properly, don't worry. Anyway, it's been weeks since I was unwell. You know that I'm fighting fit now.'

'Well, it can take a long time to get your strength back after something like that; you have to look after yourself. You need time to recuperate and it's my job to keep an eye on you. It doesn't matter how old you get, I still have to look after you.' I smiled indulgently and we were soon in the front room chatting casually, or so my aunt thought, over slices of home-made cake.

Sneezing a little too theatrically, I rummaged noticeably in my bag for a handkerchief. 'Ah, there it is.' I dragged attention to the bright orange square of cotton that I drew from the bag. My aunt looked at me as I did so, but she carried on talking without even the slightest hesitation or acknowledgment. The garish orange handkerchief, which had caused so much hilarity in the house two Christmases ago when Annie had given it to me in jest, had created no spark. Not a big enough prompt. 'I should have brought some cakes really, treat *you* for a change. Shortbread maybe, it's become my favourite recently; can't get enough of it.' The mention of Annie's absolute favourite treat again brought no spark. 'This will make you laugh. I've just re-read Gaston Leroux's 'Phantom of the Opera' for the umpteenth time; I know you won't believe that I've read it yet again. You know how Uncle Bob says he's surprised that there are no other books in the whole library worth reading!' Even the family joke about Annie's reading habits brought no flicker in my aunt's gentle, oblivious eyes.

Despair and Hope

'Nothing at all?' Annie's eyes were the saddest and emptiest chocolate brown pools I'd ever seen.

A gentle, 'I'm sorry' was all I could muster, but somehow words weren't necessary. Annie sighed as she bowed her head. I looked to Gabe for help. He nodded towards the kitchen and I followed. Speaking quietly to Gabe as we retreated to the next room, I voiced my frustration.

'Three days of casual drop-ins and nudges, Gabe, and there's been nothing at all, from either of them. I don't know, I somehow thought that with Annie so close it would change things. I think I kind of hoped they'd feel her presence or something. I've gone through everything again. Favourite foods. Nothing. Flowers. Nothing. Anecdotes. Nothing. Annie's poems. Nothing. Even perfume, then goodness knows what else. And still nothing.' I'd spat out the last two words of my frustration as Gabe's suddenly alert eyes moved from my face to look over my shoulder; Annie had appeared without my knowing. I followed his gaze and winced at the words she would've heard. I started to move towards her then stopped. She looked not to me but to Gabe and I could see hope in her eyes. I felt sorry for him, a man with two desperate women waiting for his wisdom with utmost faith that he would find a way to set everything straight again.

'Okay.'He paused. 'Enough of the subtle approach. Kathleen and Bob need to see Annie.' At his words Annie gave a little involuntary gasp. 'You need to touch their lives, Annie, it's all that's left.'

'What if it does nothing?' She almost cried the question and her hands went to her face. I continued my move towards her and wrapped my arms around her trembling shoulders.

'Let's cross that bridge when we come to it,' I offered, using one of Uncle Bob's favourite phrases, and she laughed and cried at the same time. I watched Gabe's face over Annie's shoulder as I comforted her. He held my eyes as he looked at me, expressionless. But even with no attempt to communicate, I knew the fear that sat within him. The same fear lived in me too; but Gabe's fear was borne of experience and his own loneliness, knowing all that could go wrong or just fail to go right. My fear was wrestling with optimism, defiant against a belief that there had to be hope; that this couldn't be the end.

With no reason or desire to delay, the long-anticipated contact between daughter and parents would come the next day. Thankfully, my aunt is very much a creature of habit when it comes to her shopping trips into town and you can be fairly certain of time and place. Our plan, therefore, was a simple one.

The next morning at about ten o'clock, ten weeks to the day since I'd first found Annie missing, we took a window seat at Betty's and waited. Gabe had arranged to have yet more time off from work and we'd all rattled around the house in silence earlier that morning, lost in our own thoughts with no-one being able to speak the words I was sure we were all thinking; what if it didn't work? We'd all risen early and found needless tasks to fill the time before we could sensibly leave and begin our short walk to town. I had cleaned the kitchen more fastidiously than ever before. Annie prepared vegetables for an evening meal, hours before required. Gabe had been occupied for an hour with unnecessary and, I suspected, over-zealous cleaning of all the shoes and boots in the house - I even noticed a pair of Lola's shoes in the 'done' pile before he packed each pair away again.

Once at Betty's, we wordlessly watched the town go about its business from behind the window. Small talk wouldn't come as we all sheltered in our own thoughts, safely tucked away from reality for the time being.

Sometimes, if my uncle needs anything in the town, my aunt can persuade him to join her and he then provides a strong arm to carry her shopping basket. We realised that today was one of those days when we saw them, arm-in-arm in the distance, walking towards us but on the opposite side of the road.

The three of us all looked at each other at exactly the same moment that we sat a little more upright on our chairs. I covered Annie's hand with mine and Gabe smiled and nodded reassuringly, as if to say 'this is it'. He stood up and hurriedly paid for our tea while Annie and I left. We stood just outside the shop feeling as though we were in fancy dress, as different from everyone else as we could possibly get. In reality, we looked just like every passer-by, but it didn't feel that way. It felt as if Annie was a fiery beacon and should stop everyone in their tracks.

Kathleen and Bob had paused to speak with friends but were now on their way again, slowly making progress towards us. We all watched them, waiting for the moment that seemed right. My aunt, smiling, pointed something out in a shop window and my uncle laughed and raised his eyes heavenwards, in a display of 'whatever next'.

Suddenly his expression changed.

At the same moment his right arm shot up to grab his left shoulder. He didn't move forward, but folded to his knees. His face creased in the most terrible expression of pain as everything moved incredibly fast, but painfully slowly at the same time. My aunt's basket had fallen to the pavement, tipping her few purchases into the road; a tin rolled away. She was kneeling next to my uncle saying something I couldn't hear, her hands grasping his shoulders, while passers-by and a shopkeeper rushed to their aid.

So had Annie.

I didn't notice she'd gone until I saw her a few yards from them. I ran towards them with Gabe at my side.

When we reached the horrible tableau, moments and hours later, my uncle was lying on his side clutching his arm and my aunt was kneeling at his back cradling his head in one hand as Annie leaned across from the front of his prone body. I thought someone was shouting and there was lots of noise but I couldn't hear any of it properly, as though my ears had filled with water.

All I could register were the two hands holding tightly to each other; my aunt's and her daughter's.

People buzzed around the trio on the pavement. I felt Gabe's arms around me, lifting me to my feet. I hadn't been aware that I'd started slumping to my knees a few steps from them, my legs unable to hold me as though they no longer contained bones but an unstable and trembling pulp. I couldn't take my eyes from the two hands, holding tight to each other as though Uncle Bob's life depended on it. I knew there was noise; I could sense activity, excitement, but it all blurred into unrecognisable shards of colour like a turning, rattling kaleidoscope.

I don't remember getting to the hospital. I just remember sitting in the stark corridor, still watching. I watched the two women who sat side by side, faces ashen and hands tightly bound together. We must have spoken, had to have held each other, but I can't recall these details. The first recollection I have of taking my eyes away from Kathleen and Annie was feeling Gabe's hand squeeze my knee as he stood and moved to the nurses' station for news. I watched him go. Kathleen and Annie looked up but stayed where they were, letting the only man at our vigil take charge.

Gabe was wonderful. My aunt had not met him before, but she put her trust in this man who was a stranger to her because she knew that I did too. He extended the care he took of me and Annie to my aunt, reassuring her with his gentle manner and updating our waiting party. I was reminded of his love for Lola and was very proud of this strong, caring man.

I moved to take Kathleen's hand as I smiled at Annie.

'Thank you sweetheart.' My aunt smiled weakly. She turned to Annie. 'And thank you. You've been very kind... um...' and she waited for Annie to respond with her name.

'Annie. It's Annie,' my dear sweet friend replied, her voice cracking a little with each escaping emotional word.

'Thank you Annie.' My aunt smiled sadly. Annie looked at me questioning, just as Gabe returned.

'They said you can see him now.' Gabe gently smiled as he put his hand out to help Kathleen to her feet. She took his arm and he led her gently away. He smiled and nodded to us in reassurance.

I moved into Kathleen's vacant seat and put my arm around my friend, as she laid her head on my shoulder and we waited.

'She doesn't know me, Eva. She doesn't know a thing.'

All I could do was rock her gently and hold her tenderly, in place of the soothing words I could not find.

After a while she sat bolt upright.

'Poetry. It's poetry.' She grabbed my hands and her eyes sparked. 'It's writing. Poetry. The gift? I thought so hard of it and begged mum to have it, in my head the whole time we held hands in the street, while we shared a moment, while we cried for dad.' Annie loved to read, but she loved to write more. She mostly wrote poetry and had done so, with varying success, since childhood. She was very good now, though, and loved to sit and compose; always with a pencil in her hand and a distant expression on her face. She wrote humour, romance, of daily lives or fantastic events, children's rhymes and limericks. And she also wrote lists and notes to herself; she had a list for everything, she once even had a notepad she'd titled *Annie's Book of Lists*. I don't know where she got this trait; my aunt never wrote anything down, not even a shopping list - it was all stored in her head and she rarely forgot a thing. But Annie had a list for everything. 'Please say it will work. If not, I'll try again. And again.'

'Alright,' was my stilted response. Before we could talk more Gabe returned and before Gabe could speak, Annie did.

'How is he Gabe? What are they saying now?'

'Kathleen's with Bob and the doctor. Before they went in the doctor said Bob's not in any pain. I'm not really sure of anything else, it wasn't my place to ask him. But the doctor seems satisfied. I haven't seen your dad, but I'm sure Kathleen will let you know as soon as she knows more.' Annie had risen on Gabe's arrival and now returned to her seat. We all knew that Kathleen wouldn't be letting Annie know anything. Annie would either hear news from Gabe or me, or because she might be standing on the periphery while an update came; *she* wouldn't be told. She was still a stranger. And she voiced the facts that we all knew.

'No. She'll let Eva know, not me. Not a well-meaning stranger.'

All I could do was take her hand as we sat together in silence and waited. There was no point lying and telling her she was wrong.

It wasn't too long before the doctor walked towards us. Directing his words to Gabe and me, he spoke gently but firmly.

'Mr Carter's resting now; your aunt wants to sit with him until he wakes. You can go in for a few moments if you'd like to, but only for a short while please.'

'He will be alright, won't he?' I asked in Annie's place, now standing in front of the doctor as she should have been, asking the questions that she couldn't.

The doctor smiled. 'Yes, he's a lucky man, he should be fine.'He smiled again. 'I'll be back to see him when he wakes, but in the meantime the nursing staff will be in and out to check on him.'

'Thank you doctor, thank you so much.' I exhaled as I spoke, releasing my relief into the air. Gabe shook the doctor's hand in further thanks and he smiled again and left. Gabe and I both turned to Annie, whose smile was still a sad one.

'Can you go and check on them for me please Eva?' she asked without needing to, knowing that she couldn't go to her parents but that I would. I nodded and turned down the corridor.

I knocked gently on Uncle Bob's door and entered. My aunt sat at the sleeping patient's bedside holding his hand as it rested on the bedcovers. I placed my hand on her shoulder and she reached up to pat it.

'He's alright, isn't he.' I quietly asked and told her in one sentence.

'He'll be fine love. Bed rest. Lots of rest and being looked after.'

'What else did the doctor say?' My aunt turned to look at me as I set a second chair next to hers and sat down.

'The heart attack was over and his heart beating normally by the time we got to the hospital. He said your uncle would be alright, love. But he needs to take it easy for some time. He'll probably be in here for two or three weeks.'

I thought of Annie, sitting in the corridor with Gabe when she should have been sitting next to my aunt providing and receiving comfort. 'It was so frightening,' was all that came out of my mouth in response.

Kathleen patted my hand. 'I know love, I know.'I sat with my aunt and uncle for a little while, saying nothing, until my aunt spoke again.

'Go on Eva. Your friend Gabe is waiting for you, you go and see him. And that lovely girl who helped us in the town. If she's still there, please tell her I said thank you.'

My heart lurched at the empty words and it was a battle not to scream *why don't you know her*? And then to shake my aunt until she did. Instead, I kissed my uncle and my aunt and left the room, the words ebbing away inside my throat. Before I closed the door behind me, I saw my dear aunt foraging in her handbag and my beloved uncle lying asleep and unknowing. He didn't know that I was relieved and angry at the same time, or that a girl sat outside his room who was both his daughter and a stranger.

We couldn't leave the hospital and continued our vigil in the corridor. I wouldn't leave until Bob woke and I was able to see that he'd be well again, and Annie didn't want to leave at all. She seemed oblivious to how strange it would seem, the well-meaning passer-by remaining at the hospital. We broke up our wait with the occasional stroll up and down the corridor, and watched as hospital life moved along.

Eventually, our eyes and heads all snapped up to the smiling lady walking towards us. Annie sat between Gabe and me. I felt her shoulders stiffen as Kathleen approached to stand in front of the two of us. My aunt smiled and took one of each of our hands. Then she looked at Annie.

'Sweetheart, could you pop home and get some of your dad's things please? He'll be in here for a while before he's allowed home. I've made a list of what he's going to need.' And she handed a piece of paper to Annie who accepted it as though she'd been handed a new-born babe, or the keys to a castle, or the elixir of youth, or the Holy Grail.

* * *

The relief was multi-faceted. Bob was going to be fine. Kathleen was going to be strong. Annie was going home.

Kathleen hugged us all then returned to her husband. Gabe, Annie and I stood in the corridor in stunned silence until I spoke.

'You're going home Annie, you're going home,' I whispered through emotion and tears. Annie wrapped her arms around me and whispered back.

'No Eva, I *am* home.'

And Annie and I held each other again; only this time, at last, it was in utter happiness. Gabe shared in our joy and amazement and relief. But as Annie and I finally pulled apart and Gabe still smiled at us, I saw sadness.

I felt sure he was thinking of his own family.

I was numb as Gabe and I stood outside the hospital watching Annie leave, her aunt's amazing list still in her hand. We'd laughed and cried for some minutes. Our complete joy was thankfully mingled with, and disguised by, our delight in Bob's prognosis. No-one questioned or queried the trio in the corridor and their delighted and disbelieving happiness; indeed, the nurses in our vicinity just smiled at us in acknowledgment of Uncle Bob's good news. We took our delight outside and said farewell to Annie as she left for home. Home.

Gabe took my hand and we started our walk back towards the town. It seemed an age and an instant since we'd been there in terror and fled to the hospital in search of Uncle Bob's salvation. Stunned into silence, we were back among the shops before either of us spoke a word. Gabe went first.

'Wow,' was the extent of his conversation, but it summed up my feelings perfectly.

'Wow,' was my reply.

'I can't believe it's all over.' He stopped walking as we finally reached the beginning of Mill Street and then he turned to me. He took my hands and looked at me as though he was about to speak, but he said nothing and I was quick to fill the silence.

'It was so quick. So easy. Well, I don't mean easy. Actually, I do… I mean…'

'I know what you mean, don't worry.'He smiled and we continued our walk. 'What I don't understand is how… I mean there was no gift, no reminder, no jolt of memory. Don't get me wrong, Eva, Bob's heart attack was horrifying. But I don't understand what happened in the hospital. What started the memories? If the shock brought it all back I would have thought it would have been in the town, not later on at the hospital. Something must have pulled the memories back. We tried it all – all those things you said to them, the handkerchief, the cake, books, you tried everything. We didn't get as far as a gift, so what was it?'

'It *was* a gift, Gabe.' And I told Gabe what Annie had said to me; how she'd begged Kathleen to take her poetry, her writing, her list making, or her love of reading, or to take anything that would bring her home. She pleaded with her without her even knowing and somewhere, deep inside a mother's heart, Kathleen had heard.

My mind drifted to the memories I'd relived the day I'd sat on my own overlooking the town; bicycle riding, pastry making, kite flying, water fighting, Christmas waiting, Annie falling. Annie falling. I ran to Kathleen and Bob. They ran with me to the allotment, to the tree where Annie fell. Kathleen knelt down beside Annie, dropping to her knees from a run. She cradled Annie's head as she was waking, winded. Bob held Kathleen's hand and reassured her Annie would be alright. Everyone bustled around as Annie woke and was carried home.

In my life, I'd been witness to two such terrifying events – Annie's fall from the tree and Uncle Bob's collapse in the town. Both had scared me beyond words. Both had been moments where I'd known sheer, paralysing fear for the physical safety of another. I told Gabe about the similarities in the matching pair of tableaux that had been formed from the four of us. Maybe that jolt of horror had indeed, unwittingly, helped to unlock the box that contained Kathleen and Bob's memories. Maybe it was the gift alone. Maybe we'd never know.

We sat in the cottage, silent and stunned, for some time. It was an anti-climax of sorts, but a marvellous one. Life was restored to normal.

We visited Bob again later, to find that Annie had returned long before us with Kathleen's list fulfilled. Annie smiled a smile that said a million things to us, but which just said relief and happiness to her mother and father.

Uncle Bob was told that his heart attack had been minor. Never one to complain, or even to have a day unwell to my knowledge, he joked about the doctors' use of the term 'minor'. We all remembered the moment of excruciating pain that had hit him with its undeniable force. We laughed with him now, and at the same time we thanked our lucky stars.

While Kathleen and Bob were thankful for Bob's life, Gabe, Annie and I were also thankful for Annie's. It had been restored to her and she was home in every way.

I would never have wished Uncle Bob's terrible event to befall anyone, but wondered if it was true that clouds do indeed have silver linings. If the gift had been the answer, then Bob's heart attack had provided the closeness that enabled the passing on of the gift. Lola's belief in fate flashed into my mind again and I smiled. Bob and Kathleen would never know how three of us gave a second thanks after the events of that day – how we breathed a collective sigh of enormous relief at Bob's recovery, but also how we marvelled at the way that a largely unknown heartache had been repaired in an instant when another's heart was stopping. We were shocked, relieved and completely happy.

Annie had returned home and would take new delight in every part of her life and relish every tiny, normal thing. Nothing was taken for granted and she was renewed and happy.

After all the weeks of waiting, searching, tears and heartache, Annie was with her parents. I didn't really know what to say. At first I just felt numb and almost disbelieving; it was too good to be true. Then, as the moments passed, the excitement bubbled in my chest and I just wanted to laugh out loud. To let this most amazing of things just pass silently by was incongruous with how I felt. I felt that there should be some sort of celebration. Maybe there should be a party with fireworks and banners just as you might for a loved one returning home safely after a long absence, especially when you'd been unsure whether they would return at all. As it was, Gabe, Annie and I pretended that all was normal.

When the four of us finally left the hospital that evening, Gabe and I said goodbye to Kathleen and Annie and watched them walk away from us. For what seemed like the thousandth time in the last ten weeks, tears ran down my cheeks.

I felt Gabe's hand take mine and I turned to see that he, too, silently wept.

Found and Lost

Three weeks had passed since Uncle Bob's heart attack and Annie's return home. We'd tried not to show too much excitement at being with Annie and doing all the things that must have appeared completely normal to Kathleen and Bob. We busied ourselves with visiting Uncle Bob and keeping an eye on Aunt Kathleen. Gabe took on Bob's role, maintaining his allotment and doing any household chores that needed a strong hand, while he was convalescing in hospital. Aunt Kathleen's eyes sparkled with an open soft spot for the new man in the family and Bob was happy to talk 'allotment and market garden business', as he put it, with Gabe.

Each evening we were all together felt strange and I prayed that it wouldn't always be so, that I wouldn't always feel as if we were being insincere or disloyal to Aunt Kathleen and Uncle Bob.

There were two conflicting levels now; one was where life carried on as normal as though nothing had ever changed, the other where three of us knew that everything was indeed normal to the unknowing eye but, underneath, would never be the same again. We now had an awareness of another world, where people could be lost in horrible ways, but where new friendships, new lives and new loves could also be found.

Sitting at Lola's one evening, Gabe and I were listening to the wireless and chatting intermittently as he sat at the desk looking through papers and correspondence and I was sewing a button on a shirt; we were the picture of domestic bliss. I wasn't sure what Gabe was doing but assumed that the time had come to sort out more of Lola's personal effects, such as they were. I did wonder whether his task had any bearing on the cottage; he'd still offered no comment about it, or made any attempt to move out. Although, as three months had passed since Lola left us, I had to assume that such decisions had already been made and all was settled.

Dealing with Lola's papers was one thing, but unspoken between us was the task of doing something with her collections. Neither of us could. Gabe rose and switched off the wireless, coming to crouch in front of me as I sat in the armchair opposite Lola's. He took the mending from my hands and put it on the table next to me. Then he took my hands in his.

'Eva. I don't need to highlight how much has happened to us in the last few months. The situations we've found ourselves in have allowed us to act differently than we ever normally would. Our hands have been forced and we've done what we had to do.'

I was confused. 'Gabe, you're frightening me. Where are you going with this? Everything's alright now, isn't it? Please don't tell me there's more.'

'Don't be frightened. I'm just saying that things change. You moved in here when I asked you to, when I needed you to, and I thank you for everything. You've been wonderful. I don't know how I'd have managed without you when Lola died. You being here has been perfect.'He sighed, then hit me with it. 'But I think you should move back to the Burgess's now.' I opened my mouth to protest, but he pressed a finger to my lips. 'No, please don't make it any harder. Your room's still there, I checked. Please don't be angry.'

'But Gabe, why? I don't understand. Why would you ask me to go? What have I done?'

'Eva, you've done nothing wrong, I promise. You've always done everything right.'And he reassured me with gentle kisses. 'It just worries me. The more time that goes on the more likely it is that your aunt or someone will find out that you're living here, with me.'

'It doesn't matter. I don't care if they know.' He smiled at my response, indulging me.

'I know. But I want things to be done properly. No frowning or whispers. Please.' I knew Gabe so well now and I trusted that he did purely want to acquiesce to convention and not have anyone whispering about me. I could see that. I understood his thinking. Things were different now that Annie was back. We'd done what we wanted and needed to when Annie was lost. Now tradition and decorum called, having left us alone for weeks. Things were bordering on normal again, or at least as normal as they would ever be now I'd experienced the other world in which people still lived.

'Alright.'

His shoulders relaxed and the relief on his face disappointed me. I hoped he was just happy that I'd not found offence in his words, rather than being pleased I was leaving.

'Thank you. Thank you for understanding.' He leaned up to kiss me again, still holding my hands. 'Bob's coming home in two days, so everything really will be back to normal soon. Their old routines will be back and so should yours. Life will be back the way it was.' Despite the positive words, there seemed to be a dash of melancholy peppering his voice.

'Almost,' I smiled, but he didn't smile back. He unwittingly held my gaze long enough for me to see sorrow once again in his eyes. He didn't know that I could see it, but I knew it was there.

Uncle Bob returned home two days later as planned, with instructions from the hospital and two overzealous attendants to care for him in Kathleen and Annie. I returned to the Burgess's, welcomed back with open arms and a maternal bustling from the lady of the house, hiding my own guilty disappointment beneath a smile.

Now Gabe, Annie, Kathleen, Bob and I sat in Annie's family home, reunited and peaceful, cradling a secret Kathleen and Bob would never know, and wouldn't believe even if they did. To my aunt and uncle nothing had ever been any different. There'd been no tears or distress at Annie's disappearance, no fear for her or sharing in the feeling of absolute and paralysing panic that I'd felt all those weeks ago. There'd been no empty space left by her absence at their table or in their lives and no overwhelming joy and relief at her return.

I smiled at Annie and she smiled back conspiratorially. Gabe gave my hand a reassuring squeeze.

'I'm going,'Gabe whispered into my ear. 'You stay and enjoy yourself.' I took his hand to stop him. 'No, I can't,'was his response to my touch. He looked across at Annie and her parents. 'I can't stay.' His words sounded sad and final as he stood to leave.

I should have admitted to myself straight away that I'd rather go with Gabe. Annie and I knew that we'd see each other very soon; just to have her back where she belonged was enough for me for now and I also felt I should give her space to get used to being home again. But I didn't disagree with Gabe. I let his hand leave mine as he gave me a chaste kiss on the cheek, then raised his hand in a half wave to Annie across the room where she was chatting to my aunt. Annie said goodbye and came over to hug him affectionately, whispering thank you into his ear for possibly the hundredth time. The three of us could easily have been children with a secret club no-one else could ever be a part of.

'Goodbye Kathleen, Bob,'Gabe said formally and Uncle Bob stood up to shake his hand and bid him farewell. Aunt Kathleen was close behind, giving Gabe a motherly hug and kiss on the cheek. It was evident that they both liked Gabe very much and were keen to be liked by him in return. He had their rather eager approval and there were lots of instructions to 'please visit soon, you're always very welcome'. I loved them more for loving him.

I followed Gabe to the back door. There he kissed me again; a lingering sweet kiss so gentle and loving that temptation pulled at me insistently, telling me not to stay but to leave with him. He looked at me for a long moment, holding my face in his hands before heading down the path into the evening air. I leaned against the doorframe, at last truly without a care in my world. Life was perfect. Although every fibre of me would hate to ever return to those days of uncertainty when Annie was lost, there was at that moment a strange nostalgia deep inside me for the moments when it was just Lola, Gabe and me.

'See you tomorrow,' I called after him, a slight questioning inflection on the last word.

I don't know if I imagined it, but I might have caught the unexpected breath of the first 'I love you' drift towards me on the breeze. I turned and headed back into the welcoming light and warmth of the house, closing the door behind me. I returned to my darling Annie, where she completed a picture like a lost and found jigsaw piece.

Deceit of Goodbye

Aunt Kathleen and Uncle Bob asked if I'd like to stay the night, but as the minutes passed after Gabe left, the enticement of his kiss told me I couldn't wait until tomorrow to see him. I'd surprise him at Lola's and maybe stay there and make my way home in the morning. The Carters thought I was catching the last bus home to the Burgess's and they in turn knew that I sometimes stayed at the Carter's, so Gabe could be assured that there would be no shame or raised eyebrows in spending the night, innocently or not, in the home of a single man.

I smiled as I walked. Annie was home. Gabe was mine. His beautiful music filled my mind. Even before all this, before Annie was lost and was found, I'd never felt so full and so light and so whole. I knew that feeling like this went hand in hand with the knowledge of Gabe's presence.

Everything was complete, all was back the way it should be. Once again I pictured Gabe in Lola's house, sitting at his piano, just as before. I could see his hands moving over the keys like waves washing across smooth cold pebbles. Gabe. As before.

I stopped.

The world stopped.

I couldn't move.

'Everything really will be back to normal soon. Life will be back the way it was before we met.' Before we met. Gabe's words swished around in my ears. The way it was. The way it was?

Suddenly I remembered many things. How could I have been so stupid? It seemed so long ago. Lola's words like the cold cruel blade of a knife. 'When they found Edie and took her back, we were lost'.

I ran. He knew. Lola had suspected. And Miranda? Fletcher? Lola had said she prayed this time would be different.

You stupid, stupid girl.

My mind turned somersaults as my stomach did the same and I tried hard to fight the nausea that surged within me.

When Edie went home, Lola and Gabe were lost *to her*, not lost without her as I had assumed Lola's words meant. *Edie didn't know them anymore.* I hadn't listened. Bob was home and my family was now fully restored just as Edie's had been. Once restored, once safe again, once all was normal again, Edie had forgotten those she'd met whilst she was lost. Like it never happened. Everyone Annie had met while she was lost would be forgotten too. Everyone I too had met while she was lost?

Like it never happened.

Back the way it was.

I cried as I ran.

My legs wouldn't go fast enough, even though I willed them to with all the strength I had. I pushed them, forced them, almost tripping over my feet as I tried to go faster than my body could. I was willing legs of stone to grow wings and fly.

Run.

Run.

My head was spinning.

So many thoughts flew at me, hit me. It felt so long ago, when Gabe and I had first met – he'd been kind but hesitant, cautious of becoming too close. He'd visibly balked at Lola's offer to stay with them that first time. He'd wanted to keep a distance, hadn't he?

Other thoughts dropped into the right places. I'd pieced it all together wrong and only now was everything becoming truly clear. I'd only seen a superficial picture before, a reflection on a pond. I'd seen what I'd been allowed to see, just the rippling reflection on the surface and not all the life and movement that lay beneath. I didn't ask what would happen when Annie was home again. I hadn't thought I needed to. She'd be home and all would be perfect.

Lola wanted to explain to me, tell me the last thing I needed to know; the one thing, the biggest thing they'd kept from me. But she didn't get the chance. I told her to rest and she said we'd speak later.

What I'd accepted as right wasn't right at all. Miranda had wanted me to find Annie, she'd helped me and she'd been a friend. Fletcher had tried to slow us down, talk us out of it, halt the search. Gabe said Fletcher was jealous, supersti-tious, trying to limit our time together, reduce the opportunity for us to become close. I'd got it completely wrong.

Miranda wanted me to find Annie for this very reason, to facilitate what was happening now. She wanted Gabe to be lost to me. Did she want to keep him to herself? We all knew deep down that those looks weren't of surrogate sibling affection, but a different kind of love. How could I have been so naive and trusting? She wanted me to be lost to him or him to me, or both.

Fletcher had been the true friend – he'd known all along what was likely to happen when Annie was found and returned and he wanted me to stay, to be with Gabe.

Fletcher spoke the truth; this was what he'd been through – he was lost and had then been lost. He'd known it twice over. So that was how he'd managed to experience loss a second time. He'd lost his family, he and Miranda together. But then, so very sadly, he'd been drawn to and fallen in love with someone who was also lost. And he'd become a stranger to them when they'd found *their* family again. They must have gone home, leaving him behind. But he'd wanted the happy ending for us. Dear Fletcher, who I'd wronged.

Gabe had stopped Fletcher telling me the truth that day; then I'd visited him and given him the impression that I knew it all anyway. I told him I knew what I was doing. He'd said it was my choice. He pressed no further with his explanation, which would have contained the things he thought I already knew and accepted.

So now I did know.

It was Miranda who wanted Gabe, not Fletcher who wanted me.

I stumbled and righted myself just in time as I ran in the growing darkness.

But Gabe. Gabe knew all along. Obviously. He knew what might happen. He must have wanted our happy ending too, but had settled for a happy ending for Annie, to do what was the right thing. He thought she was my priority and he accepted that. He talked of making sacrifices. He'd asked Miranda, that day as I'd listened by the front door when she'd tried to force action, to *let us have a little more time.* Oh God, he'd do the right thing. Where had he gone now? I painfully recalled our conversation at Betty's after we'd seen

Randall Boyes. He said he would leave if he had to, if there was nothing to keep him.

When Annie went home he said he couldn't believe it was all over.

He'd been hinting at this very thing; not in a conscious bid to switch on the light that would show all this to me but by accident, letting some of his thoughts and fears tumble into words before he had the chance to censor them. I'd been so slow to pick up on all the clues dropped along the way. How long before I'd forget him? Would I? I hadn't forgotten Annie. Should it be instant or would it happen overnight? Had Lola thought it would all be alright because my situation was different, because I wasn't lost? Maybe Gabe too had hoped for this very thing; that this time would be different. He'd taken a chance rather than making me choose between him and Annie. He would never do that. Maybe it could be different – after all, I'd been the only one to remember Annie hadn't I?

But I was part of Annie's story, her family, and I'd been returned with her, hadn't I? Returned to how things were before. Before Gabe. Gabe couldn't be sure what would happen when she was found. No-one could. Fletcher was convinced it would all go wrong. Lola was praying that it wouldn't. No-one knew for sure.

How could my mind be turning somersaults while my legs were pumping so hard? Surely all my strength should be in my limbs, not my head? My muscles hurt with the sudden and violent exertion, but the pain was nothing compared to that inside my chest. The romantic poets might be right. It could just be possible for a heart to break. I could already feel the cracks in mine. What would it take now for it to shatter?

Run... run... come on... you can go faster than this. I knew my legs were moving, working hard, but my progress wasn't fast enough. *Run... come on...*

There was a voice, not in my head but out loud in the evening air, encouraging me. I realised it was mine as I urged myself, 'Faster. Run. Come on,' calling just like the gym master used to at school.

My legs hurt, my lungs hurt. I was afraid.

I didn't slow down when I reached the gate, still putting in such an effort towards the house that my hands hit the front door with a loud smack and my palms stung with the impact.

When I reached the house I already knew.

But that didn't stop me wrenching the front door open as soon as my shaking hands had fumbled the key into the lock and rushing breathlessly into the empty hallway like a woman possessed, tearing through the barren sitting room into the kitchen where there wasn't a sound or a soul. No odd cups on the table, no whistling kettle, no shopping basket, no cups of tea, no patchwork bag, no apron on the back of the door. There were none of the glorious, chaotic things I loved and which welcomed me and made me feel I'd come home. All were gone, except a few pieces of furniture left swathed in white dust sheets covering them like a snowy mountain range.

I became conscious of a feeling of having been here before, in the same moment, and realised that I had. The same heavy, sick feeling was there again low down in my stomach. Leaden but moveable, it was spreading up through my body and I had to swallow a few times to quell the sensation that I might be sick. It was the same as the day I'd seen Annie's empty room, only different.

Today was much, much worse. Was it all starting now, was this the beginning of me forgetting all that had happened between losing and finding Annie? Would I now think she'd never been away? Would Gabe, Fletcher, and Miranda once more be strangers to me if we met? Would I forget Lola?

Breathing slowly, trying to calm myself, I was back in the hallway. I stopped, motionless. I looked around. Here too, there were no piles of papers, no pots, no baskets, no heaps of clothes. Then my eyes dropped and I saw my fingers on the handle to Gabe's room. I hesitated, not wanting to see what I knew I would, not wanting to make it real. I closed my eyes.

Taking a deep breath in the hope of this calming me, I pushed the door and opened my eyes. In that small view, again I saw none of the things familiar to me; none of Lola's collections that had gathered in that room and remained there when Gabe had moved in, just moving aside a little to share their resting place with his few possessions. As I'd found in the other rooms, there was nothing except a few ghostly items of furniture sheathed in white. And a piano. There was

Gabe's piano. An angular white ghost, forced into silence under the snowy cover.

I leaned against the door frame for a few moments, summoning up the mental strength to move, and then walked slowly into the room towards the large white object. I pulled the corner of the piano's poor disguise. The white sheet slid fluidly and silently, creating a white cotton puddle on the floor, slowly exposing the smooth, shiny brown wood of the piano. I closed my eyes again as I lay my hand on the cool hard surface and then ran my fingers along the smooth wood. I inhaled the welcoming scent of the house, which remained constant for the time being in defiance of being closed up and deserted. I wondered how long it could hold on before it too was lost, the final part of this house's identity gone until it would be given another by new inhabitants.

I sat down. I lifted the lid. My hands were now either side of me on the rough green leather of the piano stool.

And then I heard music.

An End

Bach's 'Ave Maria'. I tried to work out where it was coming from. But I wasn't listening to the music or remembering the music. I looked down to see Gabe's hands caressing the keys, playing the familiar melody, notes lifting into the air on tiny wings.

Only they weren't Gabe's hands, they were mine. *I* was the source of the music. It flowed through my body and down my arms to the tips of my fingers, where they danced back and forth across the keys. And I wept. And I closed my eyes. And I played.

And I knew he'd given me a gift.

Epilogue

I know fear again; that heavy rock has once more found an unsteady refuge at my core. I wonder if Gabe's moved so far away that he'll be hard to find, but my real fear is that he's left to serve his country and may be lost forever. I don't have Gabe to help me in my search this time, but I do have an even greater reason to be successful.

I don't know if Gabe left me his gift because he thought he might forget me, or because he was sure I'd forget him.

I'll know when I find him.

* * *

Dear reader,

We hope you enjoyed reading *Family of Strangers*. Please take a moment to leave a review, even if it's a short one. Your opinion is important to us.

Discover more books by Barbara Willis at https://www.nextchapter.pub/authors/barbara-willis

Want to know when one of our books is free or discounted? Join the newsletter at http://eepurl.com/bqqB3H

Best regards,
Barbara Willis and the Next Chapter Team

About the Author

Barbara lives in the beautiful South West of England with her husband and three children and enjoys making the most of being in such a lovely place; with the coast or rolling hills a short car journey away and the delights of London just two hours by train, they're spoilt for choice - beautiful scenery and ice creams by the sea one day and a West End show the next. In addition to her book addiction Barbara enjoys listening to a wide range of music (Elvis being her first love), theatre, film, genealogy, history and discovering gems of the past in the occasional charity shop. Throw in being a hopeless romantic who is prone to fits of the giggles and random singing and dancing and that's Barbara.

Although writing keeps her busy in her spare time, work and family life keep Barbara busier; any writing, quite rightly, has to fit around these and Barbara says her family provide joy and inspiration every single day.

Barbara has always loved books. She loves the look of them, the smell and the feel of them and the worlds you can step into as soon as you open the cover. She could pore over the shelves of a book shop for hours and point her to a book sale or second hand book shop and she'll probably leave laden with goodies; fact or fiction, old or new.

Barbara's mum taught her and her sister to read before they started school and passed on her love of books. The bookshelf in their room as youngsters reached to the ceiling and held everything from children's encyclopaedias to natural history, adventure to poetry. It's true that you can't have too many books, although Barbara is concerned that the floor of her spare room may now be bending under the weight of them a little...

With a love of books came a love of writing and, as a child, Barbara wrote stories and plays and poems and most were tap, tap, tapped out on a little old fashioned typewriter in her bedroom. She whiled away long family car journeys with paper and pen, often recording the trip she'd been on or the scenery that passed by. She wrote plays for performance at her primary and secondary schools and the stories she thought might have inspired famous songs.

She still has lots of her old writing books and finds it funny to re-visit these; the first is from about age four and covers dogs, queens and parties. Moving on, her stories sometimes called on humour and often reflected a love of music and history.

When Barbara sat down to write Family of Strangers, it was the first story she'd written for many years; with the commitments that come with growing up (home, job and young family) she'd had time to dabble with poetry but nothing more lengthy and had certainly never attempted to write a novel.

With no plan or plot but an idea in mind, Barbara sat down to write. Now she knows that this is how it works for her; she'd like sometimes to have a writing process or a plan, but it just doesn't seem to happen that way. Apparently, her preparation for writing once an idea strikes is making a cup of tea and choosing the right mood music.

Due to this she describes her writing style as 'organic' as she doesn't map out a storyline but, most of the time, just sees what drops onto the page. She will of course note down a word or sentence as it comes to her, but the story itself appears as she writes. She writes the beginning and the end then fills in the rest as it falls out of her head, with plot twists generally happening as she goes along. Often characters pop up out of nowhere with Barbara saying 'Well, hello, what is your part in all of this?' Occasionally they answer and sometimes they just show her as the plot unfolds page by page. However, she can easily sit and stare at the page for an hour if something isn't working.

So far Barbara's books have reflected her love of history, particularly the styles and sounds of the 1930s and 1940s. Her first book, Family of Strangers, needed a historic setting in order to limit the options available to the characters; in their search for a friend they couldn't have the internet at their disposal or the ease of immediate and far-reaching communication. She loved writing in that era so much that she wanted to immerse herself again and, during a family holiday where a theme park attraction was an art deco hotel, the idea of using a beautiful and expensive old hotel was born. Couple this with her love of theatre and the shows of the West End and the foundation for book two, Sunshine Spirit, was laid.

She never planned a Family of Strangers sequel even though a number of people had asked for one, but as she was working on her third book some ideas started to grow for it. What was book three has therefore been set aside temporarily to allow the sequel some breathing space and Barbara hopes it won't be too long before it's complete and ready to read. Book three will probably now become book four. She has ideas for books five, six and seven so she reports that there's plenty to keep her busy. Still to come, Barbara hopes, are the books in her idea bank that spread from 1914 to 1960, from mystery and romance, to young adult humour. And who knows, maybe some of those stories she wrote as a child might get a makeover...

Family of Strangers
ISBN: 978-4-86751-414-6 (Large Print)

Published by
Next Chapter
1-60-20 Minami-Otsuka
170-0005 Toshima-Ku, Tokyo
+818035793528
1st July 2021

Lightning Source UK Ltd.
Milton Keynes UK
UKHW012001160721
387300UK00001B/67

9 784867 514146